Deity

MATT WESOLOWSKI

ORENDA
BOOKS

Orenda Books
16 Carson Road
West Dulwich
London SE21 8HU
www.orendabooks.co.uk

First published in the United Kingdom by Orenda Books, 2021

A catalogue record for this book is available from the British Library.

ISBN 978-1-913193-48-5
eISBN 978-1-913193-49-2

Typeset in Garamond, Neue Haas Grotesk and Courier New
by www.typesetter.org.uk

Printed and bound by CPI Group (UK) Ltd, Croydon CR0 4YY

For sales and distribution, please contact info@orendabooks.co.uk

'A disturbing insight into how one man can be transformed into an idol … I thoroughly enjoyed this. The best yet from this series!'

'Another superb addition to the Six Stories series. Matt's writing is brilliant and the podcast style of the tale is catchy and interesting'

PRAISE FOR THE SIX STORIES SERIES

'First-class plotting' *S Magazine*

'A dazzling fictional mystery' *Foreword Reviews*

'Readers of Kathleen Barber's *Are You Sleeping* and fans of Ruth Ware will enjoy this slim but compelling novel' *Booklist*

'Wesolowski brilliantly depicts a desperate and disturbed corner of north-east England in which paranoia reigns and goodness is thwarted … an exceptional storyteller' Andrew Michael Hurley

'Beautifully written, smart, compassionate – and scary as hell … One of the most exciting and original voices in crime fiction' Alex North

'Endlessly inventive… Wesolowski is boldly carving his own uniquely dark niche in fiction' Benjamin Myers

'Frighteningly wonderful … one of the best books I've read in years' Khurrum Rahman

'Disturbing, compelling and atmospheric, it will terrify and enthral you in equal measure' M. W. Craven

'Bold, clever and genuinely chilling with a terrific twist' *Sunday Mirror*

'A genuine genre-bending debut' Carla McKay

'Impeccably crafted and gripping from start to finish' *The Big Issue*

'The very epitome of a must-read' *Heat*

'Wonderfully horrifying … the suspense crackles' James Oswald

'Original, inventive and dazzlingly clever' Fiona Cummins

'A complex and subtle mystery, unfolding like dark origami to reveal the black heart inside' Michael Marshall Smith

'Haunting, horrifying, and heartrending' *Publishers Weekly*

'Just the formula to meet your self-scaring needs' *Strong Words*

'A masterly piece of storytelling' *NB Magazine*

ABOUT THE AUTHOR

Matt Wesolowski is an author from Newcastle-upon-Tyne in the UK. He is an English tutor for young people in care. Matt started his writing career in horror, and his short horror fiction has been published in numerous UK- and US-based anthologies, such as *Midnight Movie Creature, Selfies from the End of the World, Cold Iron* and many more. His novella, *The Black Land*, a horror set on the Northumberland coast, was published in 2013.

Matt was a winner of the Pitch Perfect competition at the Bloody Scotland Crime Writing Festival in 2015. His debut thriller, *Six Stories*, was an Amazon bestseller in the USA, Canada, the UK and Australia, and a WHSmith Fresh Talent pick, and film rights were sold to a major Hollywood studio. A prequel, *Hydra*, was published in 2018 and became an international bestseller. *Changeling*, book three in the series, was published in 2019 and was longlisted for the Theakston's Old Peculier Crime Novel of the Year. Book four, *Beast,* won the Amazon Publishing Readers' Independent Voice Book of the Year award, 2020.

Follow Matt on Twitter @ConcreteKraken and on his website: https://linktr.ee/MattJW.

The Six Stories Series

Six Stories

Hydra

Changeling

Beast

Deity

'Frontmen embody a kind of divine charisma, strutting across the stage and mesmerising the crowd with their god-like powers, like preachers who can open up the kingdom of heaven for you. They are the ones front and centre, their hearts on their sleeve, spreading their arms up and out and singing the lines that will lift everyone into the sky.'

—Johanna Hedva, *They're Really Close To My Body: A Hagiography of Nine Inch Nails and Their Resident Mystic, Robin Finck*

'Occasionally, something will happen that will change your opinion of someone irrevocably, that will shatter the ideal you've built up around a person and force you to see them for the fallible and human creature they really are.'

—Marilyn Manson, *The Long Hard Road out of Hell*

Where were you when Zach Crystal died?

DEPRAV

Delving into the coldest, ungodly realms of the internet

DEPRAVblog

HEALTH:
Why Gen Z are calling bullshit on gluten-free
'You're either a coeliac or an attention seeker and I don't see many coeliacs around here...' says Gemma J
Read more...

MUSIC:
How WORM made bus-rap a thing
'Freestyle at the back of the number 49 is a cornucopia of unfettered talent' – Shaun Z discovers a brand new genre and loves it.
Read more...

WTF:
Why is no one talking about the 2007 Crystal Forest video?
L0Ona wonders what terrible secrets the late Zach Crystal was really hiding from the public?
Read more...

DEPRAVblog WTF

TAGS: #WEIRD #SPOOKY #ZACHCRYSTAL #CANNIBALISM

Why is no one talking about *that* Crystal Forest video?

By L0Ona

It's dark, almost pitch-black save for a single light. That light is bouncing all over the place; being swallowed occasionally then spat back out again by the dark. It drifts in and out of focus, pixelating and leaving yellowy trails, like some kind of modern Monet or a terrible acid trip.

This goes on for the first ten seconds or so. Bouncing light, heavy breathing and darkness. There's sound too; it might be rain. There's crashing footsteps, inaudible voices, and behind it all, a buzzing cloud of interference and static. Eventually, the picture starts coming into focus, like eyes getting used to the night, greens and greys all blurring into a kaleidoscopic sludge.

About thirty seconds in, the yellow light becomes still and the rain sound quietens. All that is left is ragged breathing. Sobbing. With the phone not moving anymore, it starts to become clear where we are.

It's dark; a more consistent darkness than before. That yellow light now illuminates what looks like stone, a ragged wall; dark slate perhaps? The light is coming from a torch. The torch sits between the knees of a figure; a girl, slumped at the base of the stone wall. Sodden hair hangs over her face, her trousers are torn, blackened with mud all the way to the knees. She shifts in and out of focus like a ghost.

There's silence for a moment. As if the slumped figure and the person filming are holding their breaths.

Then the noise comes, the sound that however many times I see this video, brings me to my knees. The sound that makes me wake in the night and tell myself it's just someone outside, my mind distorting the wind that creeps through the cracks in the walls of my flat, a bottle against a pavement, someone putting out their bins, or foxes screaming out their terrible mating cries.

The noise on the video is an inhuman screech, a truncated howl that distorts then falls into sudden silence. A blast of pure, savage hate.

The girl on the floor folds into herself and the camera shakes, either with cold, or fear or both.

Then the crying starts. Both the girl and whoever is holding the phone – another girl, it sounds like – begin to sob, like children; like children waking from a nightmare to find that nobody is coming to save them.

Maybe that sound is worse than the scream?

I was initially asked by DEPRAV to write a blog post about being a former Zach Crystal fan.

Remember when Zach Crystal was your idol too? Remember when you had his posters on your wall? We all did. We all had that MySpace background too – don't pretend you didn't, because I'm big enough to admit it and so should you be. Imagine going to your friend's house after school today, going up to their bedroom and seeing posters of Zach Crystal. How would you feel about that friend?

We all know what Zach Crystal was. At least we think we do. We all know his songs; they're all still there on Spotify, aren't they? But who is listening anymore? Who would dare to say they're still a fan. Even those 'I can separate the music from the man' types are mostly silent now.

What else can you say about him? What angle are you supposed to take?

I was looking for just that angle when I fell down a Zach Crystal wormhole and found the video I've just described.

'Lulu Copeland Jessica Morton Crystal Forest video.'

I never want to see it again.

The sobbing continues for ten more agonising seconds. The camera shakes and we see a glimpse of feet. Wrecked trainers, mud. What no one wants is to hear that scream again, that terrible sound. Slowly, the girl with the phone composes herself. She takes a few shuddering breaths and begins to move – past the crying girl on the floor, towards a black maw, an opening at the end of the cave. Is it the cave where they were found, those two girls? Just fans – just fans desperate for a chance to meet their idol. Like you might have been. Like me?

Outside the cave, that blackness turns to streaks of blue and green; an endless, sodden forest.

'...It's for my mum ... it's for my mum...' the girl – Lulu or Jessica, it's not clear – keeps repeating through ragged breaths. 'Mum, this is for you ... if you're out there...'

What does she mean? Has she some hope her mother will emerge from somewhere in the five hundred acres of tangled and treacherous woodland where Zach Crystal built a hideaway, guarded by electric fences, dogs and cameras?

There's a scraping noise. A gasp. The girl with the phone turns around for a moment, a sickening lurch of perspective. For a second we see sodden clothes, lank hair and breath condensing in freezing clouds. Lulu or Jessica, hair plastered over her face, clothes torn and wet, walks towards the phone, knees at funny angles, her movements stiff, like a marionette. It's awful – like something out of one of those old, found-footage horror movies. Both girls are breathing hard and you can hear their teeth chattering.

'Is it still out there?' Lulu or Jessica says, and the light from the torch bounces all over the cave walls.

You want to tell them both to stop, to stay still. If they have a phone, why haven't they called the police?

Nevertheless, you can't stop watching as they reach the mouth of the cave and point the phone into the darkness. All you can see is that brutal Monet mess of black and brown and green. Uneven rows of trees. Through the distorted picture, you see snippets: ferns that stand almost shoulder height; a sodden, broken branch; a coil of brambles. There's no path, no light, no signposts. Just the steady hiss of rain.

There's breathing too – hard, heavy, terrified breathing, which breaks into another sob. The camera points downwards and it's unclear who is crying, but one of the girls calls out something that has troubled me ever since I saw it.

'Just leave us alone, you hear me? We just want to go home!'

The call is long and loud and scared. It dissolves into more hysterical sobbing. I found it so difficult to watch, when I viewed the video again I had to turn down the volume.

The other girl then blurts something out too. It sounds like something along the lines of 'Just leave us alone!' but I'm not altogether sure that's it, her voice is close to the phone and distorted.

They both breathe – short gasps.

'Keep filming, keep filming and then if it comes again...'

There's a noise and both girls scream. It's not that terrible, inhuman howl, but the sound of crashing, of something moving through the forest. It sounds horribly close.

The phone moves about a little, down to the floor and with a trembling hand, back up to face the forest. The girls are moaning, little involuntary noises that burn all the way to the bottom of the heart. There's something else too. At first it sounds like breathing; stabby little breaths, panting, like a dog.

'Eat,' it seems to say. 'Eat ... Eat ... Eat.'

'We're not scared of you...' one of them whispers back through chattering teeth. She sounds six years old, a terrified little girl. There's nothing convincing in those words though, and they're swallowed up by the sodden blackness up ahead.

Stillness, for a beat. Even the rain appears to hold off.

Then there's movement: a terrible shadow that could be wind, a branch, a bush, a twisted and pixelated bit of interference on an old camera phone wielded by a terrified teenage girl.

To me it looks big; to me it looks animal rather than human. Whatever it is, be it an effect of the wind, the weather, or something else, the last words of that video are spoken in a terrified whisper.

'Turn the fucking torch off ... Turn it off!'

That's where the video ends.

COMMENTS:

Mayfly776: Ew creepy

ForzaRadish: Zach Crystal fans are fuckin psychos.
TLDR: Stanning Zach Crystal = BAD DEATH
Butwhytho: Surely someone has to have looked into this? I mean rly?
BONN13: Has anyone asked Scott King yet lol?

Legendary presenter Ruby Rendall's exclusive interview with pop megastar Zach Crystal. **More >**

---

1 hr 45 • 9.00pm 20th July 2019 • Available for 28 days

RUBY RENDALL: This. Is. It. This is the moment you've all been waiting for. It's finally here. It's finally happening.

Good evening, I'm Ruby Rendall. This is live.

Tonight, my guest is an extraordinary man.

I can't quite believe it.

As you can see, we've dimmed the studio lights, given everything a bit of a spring clean in preparation for tonight's guest. His fans have been lining up around the studio all day. In fact, can we cut to have a look? There we go. Look at that. I've never seen anything like it before in my life. Can we get some audio? Yes. Listen, you can hear them chanting his name. This has been going on since six this morning…

Can we get some footage from earlier today? Yes? Let's just have a look shall we? Audio too? Wow, look at that. Look at the crowds. Can you hear the chanting too? I've not seen anything like it since The Beatles!

[Cut to footage of a vast crowd outside the BBC studios, holding banners and cheering.]

Security is tighter than it has ever been on the show. This, ladies and gentlemen, is a truly momentous occasion. You see, my next guest famously does very, very few interviews. For this to happen is incredibly rare. We have so much to discuss: his music, his disappearance, his *reappearance*, his amazing house up in the Scottish wilderness. Everything.

My guest informs me that tonight nothing is off limits. He's here to spill it all.

Yes. We are *live* and we are about to welcome onstage to

sit opposite me, the most fascinating, the most spellbinding guest we've ever had on the show. I have to say, growing up with this guy's music makes me a rather biased fan, but why on earth did I get a job on TV if not to interview the best?

Because, ladies and gentlemen, he is the best. Unequivocally. The king. The sultan of song-writing himself. His first album spent twenty weeks on the Billboard 200 in the States and went triple platinum within a few weeks of release. He was twenty-one years old.

Sold-out arena tours across the world followed. His second album sold twenty million copies worldwide in its first month … I could go on…

This man represents so much more than music though. To some he represents the dream of every child who wants to grow up and be someone. To others, his is a classic rags-to-riches story, a fairy tale – a man whose voice, whose talent, fuelled his meteoric rise to the very top.

Here he is, in all his glory, the man, the legend … Zach Crystal.

[Applause as Zach Crystal walks onto the set. He is dressed in black leather trousers and knee-high boots. His long, blond hair is coiffed and hangs over his shoulders. He wears an elaborate crown made from deer antlers, and his face is heavily made up. Medallions made from sticks and bone hang around his neck. Crystal stands before his chair and bows to the studio audience.]

RR: Welcome … welcome…

[The applause becomes screams.]

RR: Wow. *Wow.* Here he is. Zach Crystal, everyone. Thank you so much for coming. Please, sit down.

ZACH CRYSTAL: Thank *you*, Ruby. Thank *you,* everyone.

[The screams from the audience get higher, longer. Ruby winces. Crystal eventually sits down, crossing his legs.]

RR: Please … please … I know, I know, Zach Crystal … I know…

[A shot of the audience. They're mostly women in their late twenties. They are all sat still in their seats, but their eyes are wild and their mouths are open, screaming.]

RR: Are you nervous at all, right now? I certainly am, I'll level with you!

ZC: *[laughs]* No … I'm OK, Ruby. I'm OK. And you should be OK too. Please?

[Zach Crystal raises his hand to the audience and the screaming halts abruptly.]

RR: I am, thank you. I won't lie, this is a little overwhelming. I just can't believe … Is that even really you?

[Laughter]

ZC: *[laughs]* No! I'm an imposter!

RR: I mean, it's so rare for you to do interviews. This is your first full-length one is it not? On television and we're *live*. I don't think I even know what your speaking voice sounds like.

ZC: *[laughs]* I don't do things by halves, Ruby.

[Cheering]

RR: Zach, where do I start? I was watching some of your very early performances on YouTube earlier today. When you were still performing with your twin sister in bars around the UK.

ZC: When we were The Crystal Twins. They are some very happy memories. Very happy ones indeed. We were so young.

RR: Twelve years old when you began. You're now…

ZC: Forty-five, Ruby *[laughs]*. But I still feel it, you know? In my heart, I'm still that nervous little boy.

RR: The two of you looked so … It just looked like you were *born* to be on stage.

ZC: You know, I think we were. I certainly always felt at home on stage. I'm a very shy person, you see. I always have been. It was Naomi who was the extrovert, not me.

RR: We've hardly ever got to see your *face* until now, Zach. You've always worn a veil or a mask when you've spoken on camera, haven't you?

ZC: It was shyness, always shyness. I feel so exposed now, Ruby.

[Cheering]

RR: Zach, I think you look *wonderful* and so does everyone here.

[Cheering]

ZC: Thank you Ruby, thank you. That means a lot.

RR: You and Naomi grew up without much money, on the

Hopesprings Estate in Barlheath. That's up in the Midlands, isn't it?

ZC: Life on the Hopesprings Estate wasn't easy. Our parents didn't have much money and we were always scraping around. We shared everything. All the toys, books and clothes were all second-hand; all of them worn and dented, dog-eared and used, but I didn't mind. That's just how it was for a family as poor as us. The only thing I was ever bought new was my underwear.

[Laughter]

RR: Your parents both worked, didn't they?

ZC: That's where my work ethic comes from, I think. To this day, I'm always busy. I never stop working, because I remember where I'm from. I still have the attitude that was instilled in me by my parents. I had a paper round from the age of seven and I had to get up at 5.30 every morning and work until 4.30 after school, a little ghost with a giant, fluorescent-orange sack of newspapers around his neck, walking the streets of that estate. 'The devil makes hands for idle work,' my mother used to tell us, and we believed her.

RR: Your parents were quite strict, weren't they? Religious.

ZC: They were. We used to have to go to church in our best clothes every Sunday morning, and we tried to live our lives according to the teachings of Jesus. We must have looked like something else with our tatty shirts and hair slicked down with water, all waiting at the bus stop at 7.00am.

RR: I was talking with Naomi earlier, and she says you eventually found your own way, your own spiritual path.

ZC: I've been all over the world, I've talked to many people and seen a great many things. There's a lot of power out there, a lot of different ways of seeing things. I don't believe that there's any one *right* way to live your life.

RR: You and Naomi, The Crystal Twins, performed covers and your own, original material right up until ninety-four, ninety-five, when you decided to go solo. You were, what, twenty by then?

ZC: That's right. Naomi and I had performed together since we were twelve. Eight years is a long time.

RR: And that's when things really changed for Zach Crystal. You began to write solo material.

ZC: Right, right. I released my debut album *Yearn* in ninety-five. I had no idea – no idea – how huge it would become.

RR: To date, *Yearn* has sold over fifty million copies worldwide, so it didn't do badly.

ZC: *[laughs]* It's a blessing, such a blessing. I remember I was on a break from my Asia tour in ninety-nine. I'd been to Kuala Lumpur, Seoul, Taipei and I just … These were places on a map, pictures in a textbook, you know? I just lay down and cried. I cried for that little boy, that shy little boy delivering newspapers in the rain, you know? I wish I could have told him.

RR: How big was music to you when you were growing up in Barlheath?

ZC: My father was always listening to music, all the time, all these jazz records. Music was always on in our house, but I'd never really *listened* before, you know? Then, when I was about six or seven, my father, I don't know, he just sort of decided to start playing his records to me. Really *playing* them.

RS: Never would I have imagined that this was the childhood of Zach Crystal. It just sounds so beautiful.

ZC: It *was*. It was a beautiful time, really. On Sunday afternoons, when my mother was ironing the school uniforms and making sandwiches for packed lunch, my father and I would listen to music in the living room. That hour or so was what I looked forward to all week. I had no idea what was 'cool' at the time. My parents didn't approve of modern music. A lot of the themes in the pop songs upset them and we were forbidden to watch things like *Top of the Pops*. Naomi would sometimes watch them at her friend's house and tell me about them like they were this big secret.

RR: But not you?

ZC: No. I was the well-behaved twin.

[Laughter]

RR: Zach, I just … This is so surreal. You're coming off as just so *normal…*

[Laughter]

RR: I don't mean that in a bad way, I promise. I was just worried – after all your years of hiding behind a mask, of being so shy, this interview might have been sort of … difficult, but here we are, just having a conversation.

ZC: Maybe it's time for me to grow up?

RR: I have to be honest with you, Zach, I wondered if you'd even answer my questions.

ZC: Oh Ruby, of *course*. It's an honour, it really is, and now we're talking about music … I mean, it is my favourite subject after all.

[Laughter and cheering]

RR: Please, keep going, this is music to my ears.

ZC: The only music played in our house when I was a kid was my father's records. He liked jazz piano and that's what he played me on those Sunday afternoons. It was in those hours that I discovered Dave Grusin and John Lewis but perhaps my favourite of all, Mary Lou Williams. My father told me all about her, how she had taught herself to play the piano in the 1920s and became a mentor to greats like Thelonious Monk and Dizzy Gillespie. He told me about Art Tatum too; he learned to play piano by touch. 'He was blessed,' my father always said, 'with perfect pitch.' And that look on his face, that pride stirred something in me. It made me want to see that look in my father's eyes when he saw me drinking in that sound, those chords. 'Night and Day' was my favourite; the way the music danced up and down the scale, the flourish of it, gave me such a tingle in my soul.

I think my father treasured those afternoons too.

RR: You can certainly hear that in your own music, that early influence. But you and Naomi, you brought a distinct pop element to your own music, right?

ZC: That's right. You see, even though modern music was mostly forbidden in our house, my sister loved it. She had a Walkman and headphones and she listened to Wham!, Duran Duran, Frankie Goes to Hollywood, the Thompson Twins. She played them to me too and, you know, as much as I loved Dad's jazz piano music, I loved these bands too. Those pop hooks and the catchy lyrics stirred something else in me, just like the piano. I didn't know I needed it until I began to listen to them too. I listened to how the *music* was created, why it appealed to so many people.

RR: That's when you started writing songs?

ZC: It was after a month or so of listening to music on a Sunday afternoon that my father came home from a car boot sale with a battered Casio keyboard. The day my fingers first floated over those keys and I began to learn that I could dictate sound, could control the rhythm and the flow of the music, was the day that everything changed. I used to sit in that living room with these great big headphones on, plugged into that keyboard, tapping away at the keys, teaching myself how to play. I never read one single note of music. I still can't today. I learned it all by ear. I began to make little tunes, little songs, learned how harmonies and rhythms worked. I must have looked a real sight, this little kid sat there, humming and muttering away to himself, hunched over the keys. My father said I was a regular Sugar Chile Robinson.

RR: You still have that keyboard, don't you?

ZC: I do, I *do.* I write all my songs on it, still.

RR: That's amazing. Zach Crystal, with your five-hundred acre property in the Highlands, recording studio, *treehouse* – still writing songs on that thing.

ZC: *[laughs]* I don't forget my roots, Ruby.

RR: Can we talk about your house for a moment? It's truly a wonder, isn't it? Up in the Scottish wilderness, miles from anything.

ZC: It's my place of refuge, Ruby. It's where I go to learn, to create. Up in the forests, away from everything and everyone. It's where I wrote all of *Damage*, my second record, which came out in 2007.

RR: *Damage* really is close to being a perfect record, I think. I mean, every song on it, every single one is a work of art. Now you're telling me about your influences, it really starts to make sense, the place that album came from.

ZC: *Damage* was the record I always wanted to make, you know?

Just me, without the – you know – the label people telling me what to do. I was thirty-three when I wrote that album. I'd matured, as a person, as a song-writer. Writing that album reminded me of being a kid again, you see. Making other people happy with music.

RR: What are your earliest memories of entertaining?

ZC: Before I knew it, I was playing that keyboard for the whole family, putting those tinny drum tracks behind the songs. Our whole house was singing along to 'Numbers Boogie' or 'The Donkey Song'.

I never forgot that feeling. Making people happy with music. That's what brought us together back then; our family, sitting in the living room, with the smell of cooking in the air mixed with washing powder from the clothes hung up in the kitchen, everyone smiling and singing. When I'm sat there under the spotlight at a sold-out arena in Tokyo or London, Stockholm or Las Vegas, I still remember those old days in our house on the Hopesprings Estate. I think it's important never to forget where you came from, and never to forget the people who helped you on your way.

RR: We're going to play a video from *Damage* in a moment, but am I right in thinking you have some exciting music news for everyone tonight?

ZC: *Exclusive* news, Ruby. No one knows this until now, *right now.*

RR: I'm so excited and I don't even know what this news is…

ZC: I wonder what you'd say if I told you a new record was coming, Ruby, and a world tour?

RR: Oh my *God*, really?

ZC: Where do you think I was for the year I 'disappeared'? What did you think I was doing? Like I've told you, I never stop. I never stop working.

[Cheering, getting louder]

RR: Really? *Really?*

ZC: You heard it here first.

[Cheering]

RR: We're going to go to a short break, ladies and gentlemen. Enjoy the video of 'Starfall' by Zach Crystal, and we'll be right back.

Episode One: Monster-Busters

Extract from: BBC News at Ten (22/03/2018)

—Concern is growing for the pop superstar, Zach Crystal, who has now been missing from his home for more than a week. The star's twin sister, Naomi Crystal, reported her sibling missing to Police Scotland earlier this month just after she and her daughter Bonnie, thirteen, moved into the five-hundred-acre property, Crystal Forest, which is situated in the remote Colliecrith National Park, west of the Cairngorm Mountains.

Crystal, who is forty-four, and whose last album *Damage*, was released eleven years ago, has been the focus of recent controversy, after the body of his longest-serving aide and close personal friend, James Cryer, was found in the vast forest that surrounds the property by special constables working on wildlife crime in the area. Zach Crystal has not been questioned with regards to the discovery and Cryer's death appears to have been an accident. Naomi Crystal has made a brief statement, explaining that the recent media focus on the death of Cryer caused the singer significant sadness and distress. She urges him to get in touch and asks that anyone who has sighted the star contacts the police. A tearful Bonnie Crystal also urged her uncle to please get in touch with his family.'

Extract From: ITV News at Ten. (04/05/2019) 10:00pm

—Tonight: enigmatic superstar, Zach Crystal, missing for over a year, is finally home.

Zach Crystal fans around the globe have tonight been in raptures at the return of their idol. The singer, who seemingly vanished without trace in March 2018, is thought to be safe and well, and recovering at his property in Colliecrith National Park, Scotland. It is not known, as yet, where Crystal has spent the past year, but that doesn't seem to matter to the thousands of fans who have taken to the streets of Aviemore to welcome home their idol.

This news comes alongside accusations about Zach Crystal's personal life. Police Scotland have refused to comment on these claims. What is clear, however, is that the controversy that has been raging for some time now on the internet and social media has soured what should have been a day of celebration for Crystal's legions of loyal fans.

Extract from Sky News (13/09/2019) 11:44pm

—Sorry, yes, we're just getting word that … yes … a fire has broken out at Crystal Forest, the home of reclusive musician, Zach Crystal. We can confirm that fire crews from Aviemore, Kingussie, Ballater and Newtonmore are currently battling a blaze in Colliecrith National Park, west of the Cairngorms. Right now it has not been confirmed if Crystal himself is present at the property, which is said to be engulfed in a hundred-metre-high blaze.

More as we get it…

Extract from: BBC Radio Five Live – the Gordon Cantwell Show (14/09/2019) 3.30am

—One story that has opened up overnight is that the home of controversial musician, Zach Crystal, has been destroyed by fire. Crystal Forest, as it's better known, was reported ablaze a few hours ago, and due to its remote location in the middle of the Colliecrith National Park, was more or less destroyed before fire services could reach it and tackle the blaze.

Oh, my word, what a story. We'll be taking your texts and calls throughout the night on what appears to be a real tragedy. It's not confirmed, but what I'm hearing is that Zach Crystal himself has perished in the blaze. That's what's coming through right now.

Oh, my God. Oh, my word.

Zach Crystal had just announced the release of a brand new album, and tickets for his *Forever* tour were already selling out across the world.

This is a real tragedy. A tragedy for the world of music.

Extract from: TalkSport – the Boswell and Murphy Breakfast Show (14/09/2019) 7.26am

—We're taking your calls, this morning, on Zach Crystal. Yes, that's right, *the* Zach Crystal, who, I'm sad to say, was confirmed dead at 5.00am this morning. Fire-scene investigators up at Colliecrith National Park in the Scottish Highlands have confirmed the remains of the superstar were found among the ruins of his five-hundred-acre property. What a tragedy.

—Well I don't think it's a tragedy, Morris.

—Here we go, we've got Martha on the line. Not a tragedy, you say, Martha.

—Not at all, the bloke was a bloody weirdo, wasn't he? There were all sorts of rumours … those two poor girls what were found in his forest. Awful business wasn't it?

—Martha, these are unsubstantiated rumours. None of it was proved.

—Lived in a tree house, didn't he, with a load of teenage girls. That's true, innit? Good bloody riddance, I say.

—Thanks Martha. What do you think, Neil?

—I mean, the guy was a musical legend wasn't he? You can't be a legend without being a bit odd. He lived in a haunted wood, didn't he?

—True, true. He did spend a *lot* of time with teenage girls as well though, didn't he? The guy was in his forties for God's sake!

—I know, I know, but this is Zach Crystal we're talking about. Think of all the work he did for charity. It wasn't his fault that some silly teenagers got themselves lost in the Scottish Highlands, was it? They knew the dangers going in. There's wild cats and all sorts of things in there aren't there?

—We'd love to hear what you think here on Boswell and Murphy in the morning, so text or tweet us. Better still, give us a call. Zach Crystal - what legacy will his death leave behind?

Extract from: BBC News (15/09/2019)

—The crowds of mourners paying tribute to their fallen idol have not been deterred by the rain here on the Chelsea Embankment. Piles of flowers have been laid outside the gates to Chelsea Physic Garden. Yesterday, it was confirmed that pop superstar, Zach Crystal, was found dead at the age of forty-five at his home in Colliecrith National Park, Scotland.

Crystal is thought to have died of smoke inhalation during a fire that broke out at his remote, five-hundred-acre property known as Crystal Forest. The secluded mansion, which also contained guest suites and a recording studio, as well as Crystal's personal chambers in a vast, luxury tree house overlooking the property, is said to have been completely destroyed by fire.

This once little-known botanical garden in London was reportedly one of Crystal's favourite places to visit when in the capital. Huge crowds, not unlike those here now, would wait outside the garden when Crystal would spend upward of four hours here, alone.

There are tears and spontaneous outbursts of song from Zach Crystal fans the world over, who are gathering in towns and cities to mark the passing of a musical legend.

—I can't believe he's gone. I can't believe it. He was everything to me … he meant everything.

—I've been here since I heard. I've not slept. It's not sunk in. It's just … I can't believe it's happened, he can't just be gone … not like that…

Extract from: LBC – the Verity Moss Show (17/09/2019)

—It's being reported all over the world, the 'tragic' death of Zach Crystal. I'm sorry but *what?* Zach Crystal? The guy's dodgy.

—Of course he isn't dodgy. How can you even say that?

—Look, you've got this forty-year-old bloke inviting twelve-year-old girls up into his *tree house*. He had them running round the woods in the middle of the night. Those two young women, Lulu and Jessica, found dead, then his closest advisor has a fatal accident in the very same woods and now *this.*

Surely you can't come on here and defend Zach Crystal, can you?

—Verity, it's all lies. All of it. It's all a media conspiracy against Zach. It always has been. Did they ever find any evidence that any of those girls had been abused? No. Did Zach Crystal ever get arrested for murder? No. I tell you what, if this was anyone else—

—If it was anyone other than a middle-aged bloke inviting young girls to come and stay with him, he wouldn't get away with it!

—You don't get it, you lot in the media. Just because he wasn't at your beck and call.

—That's right, actually. He wasn't. The biggest pop superstar in the world decided to hide away in a remote wood, spouting rubbish about evil spirits, while young, vulnerable girls were disappearing.

—Honestly, Zach Crystal was the one helping young, vulnerable girls, he was actually the one doing some good in the world. You people will never understand. Now he's gone, now he can't defend himself, all you can do is peddle the same old lies. It's pathetic!

Welcome to Six Stories.

I'm Scott King.

Over the next six weeks, we'll be looking back at one of the most polarising scandals of recent times, one that should have opened up the floodgates, made a giant crack in the zeitgeist, made us question ourselves and each other and perhaps galvanised us into questioning how we look at things.

Yet somehow it didn't.

This was the biggest thing that never happened.

For those of you who are new to the podcast, this series is a glitch in the matrix, an anomaly; one unlike all the others. We're still doing what we always do here – listening to six different sides of the same story. Raking over old graves.

Six episodes, six interviews, six stories about one case. In this series we look back at a crime through six different pairs of eyes. We're looking six ways at one man.

Is 'man' even the right way to describe Zach Crystal?

I once said that I wasn't scared anymore, that on this podcast I'd meet monsters face to face and eye to eye. When you take the paths I take with Six Stories, *monsters are what you should expect to meet.*

The person we're going to hear from in this, our first episode of this series, has many supporters, both here in the UK and internationally. He also has his critics, his haters. 'Haters' is perhaps too mild a term.

Ian Julius is an interesting figure. He went from folk hero to figure of hate within the space of a week. Trial by media. Trial by social media. Trial by spin. Search #Freejuli on Twitter and you'll see what I mean.

Also, #killjuli if you want to see some of the darker sides of social media.

That's if you've been living in a cave and have no idea what I'm talking about.

—It's about fifty-fifty, the messages, the letters. People who support me and people who hate me. There's one – a *proper* fan, like, mental, if you know what I mean? Tattoo of *his* face, *his* signature, everything, on his chest. Wherever I go, this fucker manages to find me, doxxes me and it all starts up again.

I read all of them, you know. All the threats from the fans, telling me what they want to do to me. It's funny really. It's laughable. Then I get messages from some saying they want to shake my hand, you know? They say 'well done mate'. They know I did the right thing.

Then someone sends me a dried-up dead rat in a box. Swings and roundabouts, innit?

Ian Julius chases monsters. Or at least he did. Ian and his girlfriend used to call themselves the Monster-Busters. Their YouTube channel had more than fifty thousand subscribers. Good Morning Britain *interviewed them at the peak of their internet fame.*

I'm speaking to Ian via Zoom. I don't even know where he is and I don't ask. He appears against a plain-white background.

Monster-Busters was a simple concept – Ian, with assistance from his girlfriend, created fake profiles on social-media sites such as Boopy and Gabble, posing as twelve- or thirteen-year-old girls. That's where they waited, ensnaring much older men who would send them inappropriate messages and photographs, and try to arrange to meet them for sex. The two would turn up at the meeting point, which would be in a public area – usually a train station – and confront the predator, before informing the police. The concept is not an original one; groups like Dark Justice and Guardians of the North do similar. Monster-Busters are no more, however, and their remaining videos have been swarmed with negative comments and downvotes by Zach Crystal fans.

—We must have busted over a hundred paedophiles; most of them got convictions too. We worked *with* the police, you know? We were good at what we did. Some of the stuff we had to read, it turned your stomach. I'll never forget it. And blokes in their seventies turning up with bags of booze and condoms to meet a thirteen-year-old girl. Scum.

Ian and his girlfriend became heroes of sorts, at least online, even before they appeared on the mainstream media. Their reputation spread from their undisclosed location in the UK as far as 60 Minutes Australia, *along with countless guest appearances on LBC Radio, BBC Radio 2 and Sky News. In each interview Ian conducted himself calmly and sensibly, never raising his voice or allowing presenters to antagonise him. There was a rash of copy-cat hunter groups online in the wake of Monster-Busters – not all of whom conducted themselves as professionally as Ian.*

—We were always as professional as we could be when we did a sting. We never screamed and shouted when we caught one, or grabbed them and knocked them about, but my God, I would have liked to sometimes. We were always transparent with the police too, always handed everything over and backed off when they asked us to.

Countless police spokespersons attempted to dissuade the Monster-Busters from their activities – attempting to explain that what they were doing could potentially damage the cases against the predators they were trying to catch. This reasoning was met with derision from Ian's supporters and the general public. And the figures do not lie. Due to the Monster-Busters group, a significant amount of online predators were handed over to the police. It's an undeniable fact that the police would not have been able to convict them without the help of Ian and his team.

—Everyone knew it. Everyone knew I was in the right, that we were doing the right thing. All of them: the police, the government. I was just some bloke in his living room; I didn't have a degree or training, but I knew how to get them, I knew how to catch monsters. But then it all fell to bits didn't it?

Now, Ian's location changes every few months; every time he's doxxed online, every time his windows are broken or something unpleasant is pushed through his letterbox. Ian won't tell me the whereabouts of his girlfriend. Or even if they're still together. What we do know is that the Monster-Busters online paedophile-hunting duo has disbanded.

—It took slightly longer to catch this one than usual, that's for sure. This one was a slow burner. There's a lot of them out there who'll start with the dirty stuff almost immediately. They're the common sort and they're easy to catch. They spend all day trawling those sites for young girls, hundreds of thousands of dick-pics at the ready. Desperate, older men.

This one was in it for the long game, though, and we knew from experience that ones like *him* are the worst. They're the ones with a bit of brains. They're the charmers; they've got the chat. They're drip-drip, insidious predators – they get under the skin and burrow deeper. When we started talking to *him*, that became clear very quickly.

—*How were you able to tell that so fast?*

—So, when you're talking to these people, you have to realise something. These guys are full of lies. Everything they say is a lie.

Every single line they write is a seduction – it's telling someone what they think they want to hear. The end game is total control.

—But later, you noticed something amiss. Something else, right?

—A few things stood out. We'd been messaging with him, back and forth, for about a month. It was intense – constant, long-winded, deep conversations. It became apparent he was very isolated, very lonely. Most of them are, but the amount of messages we were getting from him was … it was odd. That was the first thing. The second was when he began to let things slip.

—Like what?

—Like where he was. That was a big one. They usually tell us where they live early on, angling for a meet-up, you know? He didn't. He was very cagey about where he was, until he said something about a … ghost … or something.

—A ghost?

—Yeah … he seemed to be alluding to something very specific. He said that where he was, was 'haunted' by some kind of spirit, some *animal*.

—That's rather niche, isn't it?

—It is – when people talk about ghosts they mean humans, don't they? Not him. He was going on about it for ages, describing it, this great rotten stag, its blackened flesh all hanging off it, its horns all tangled together on top of its head, which was a skull. Glowing red eyes. He said it was like the Mothman – it only showed up when something terrible was going to happen. I believe he was trying to scare us – trying to scare who he thought was a vulnerable young girl. Sicko. He kept asking if we were brave enough to try and find it with him, to face it. It was like a challenge. Only the 'special girls' were brave enough he said. His story rang a bell – I'd heard of it before. That's when I thought he wasn't just anyone, you know?

— There must have been more though – more clues that he was who you claimed he was.

—The thing was, we never thought it could really be Crystal. The *actual* Zach Crystal. It was him who convinced us in the end. When we accidentally said his name.

There you have it. That was their claim. There came a point in the conversation when Ian and his girlfriend claim to have been utterly convinced that they had ensnared Zach Crystal himself.

Zach Crystal, who had slipped off the face of the earth for nearly a year, and at that point – April 2019, according to Ian – was yet to reappear.

—We'd been talking to the guy for a few weeks. He was telling us about his life; he was slipping in little things – how he'd grown up, this poor, lonely boy who had to work all hours. Anyone could have done it really – impersonated him online – if they had enough knowledge. But the thing was … he was so out of touch with reality. Not in an insane way, but in a way that shows you someone who's not lived a normal life. That's when we began to turn it around, when we started to ask our own questions. We wanted to be subtle – we didn't want to scare him off. We started small, like he had started with us and as the time went by, it started to become more and more obvious.

—*What was the turning point? What was the one thing that made you realise – the moment when you were certain.*

—There were a few big pointers. He talked about how his parents were dead, how his best friend had died, how he felt anyone who got close to him, something bad happened to them. I mean these were all big things, but not quite enough. The moment we realised for sure was when we accidentally used his name, as I said before.

—*Really?*

—Yeah, it was me that did it. Just typed it in a reply. My missus looked at me, white as a sheet. My heart just sort of *sank.* I thought I'd wrecked it, spoiled the whole thing. I'd typed in what we were both thinking. But the thing was, he didn't notice. He let it go. And that's when we knew.

We'd found him.

Us, sat in our living room, catching paedophiles online. We'd caught someone who should have been put in prison a long time ago. But, you know, the weirdest thing about it all was that back in the day, I loved him too. Just like you did, just like everyone did.

Like a great deal of you listening, I first became aware of Zach Crystal after his debut solo, TV performance on The Word, *in 1995.*

It's become iconic, that performance of 'Burning Eyes'. *For many, many Zach Crystal fans, that moment was a communion of sorts.*

For anyone who is young and not English, The Word *was a controversial late-night television magazine show on Channel 4 in the mid-1990s. The show was hosted by radio presenter Terry Christian and comedian Mark Lamarr. It boasted the notorious television débuts of Nirvana in 1991 and Oasis in 1994. Ask anyone of a certain age if they saw nineteen-year-old Zach Crystal's performance following a rendition of 'Delicious' by pop duo Shampoo, and they'll tell you they did. About half of them will be telling the truth. Zach Crystal was, to be fair, a surprise guest on the show. I was aware of him, as were most of you, as a smarmy-looking, precocious Christian-pop brat. Think the early days of Justin Beiber, but nowhere near as famous. Zach Crystal was looked upon with scorn by most. He and his sister Naomi were known as The Crystal Twins and were popular with the elderly and on Christian music stations.*

So when Mark Lamarr announced Zach Crystal onstage, with a single raised eyebrow, that said it all.

Zach Crystal had no edge. He was that kid with the piano wasn't he? A Crystal twin?

But Zach Crystal had changed.

Zach Crystal had grown up.

Zach Crystal had become something beyond – he had become a force.

Zach Crystal had reinvented himself.

And what a reinvention it was.

Extract from I Loved the Nineties (Resonance Productions, 2010): Talking head – Danny Zade, presenter, BBC Radio 1

—And Zach Crystal of course … I mean, he came onstage on *The Word* and it was like, whoa! The guy had grown about ten feet and he looked like … a man. This goofy little kid we all knew and loved … well, I say loved but we tolerated him, didn't we?

But now … now he was back and he was just … I mean it was before he got weird, wasn't it? He was just amazing.

['Burning Eyes' plays in the background]

He was like … it was like he'd been abducted by aliens, who'd reinvented him and plonked him back down on earth.

[Sings] Ooh, burning eyes! Get out of my head…

I mean, it became an instant anthem. Who'd have thought it? Little Zach Crystal? The thing was *everyone* loved it. All the indie kids and the metalheads and your teeny-boppers. Man, even your nan. It was amazing. That song never left rotation, never. Not since it was released. The guy was a multi-millionaire on that song alone.

I was one of those people, blown away by that performance. So were many of you. It's hard to put a finger on exactly what it was about Zach Crystal that seemed to appeal to everyone.

There was a humility to him. I remember liking that. But also mixed with an other-worldliness. Like Danny Zade says, Zach was from another planet.

Zach Crystal was around six feet tall, 'unexpectedly tall' as many described him. He was rake thin and dressed in greens and browns – forest colours – with a crown of what looked like gold antlers atop his head.

Crystal's long, blond hair spilled over his shoulders. It should have been ridiculous, but Crystal looked elegant and mysterious at the same time. He was a stark contrast to the anoraks of the indie scene and the torn, matted clothes of the grunge musicians. Crystal wasn't like anything anyone had ever seen before.

It wasn't just the costume. It was his voice – it was the way he poured his soul, his heart into playing that piano decorated with branches and leaves. He was a lone, elfin bard from some mystical forest, his call some siren song – a style that no one had heard before. In part, the wail of Björk mixed with the melancholy of Sigur Rós, backed by an astonishingly melodic pop hook.

It shouldn't have worked, none of it. It was showmanship, it was extravagance, but it was something else too, it called to somewhere deep inside, some childhood place where magic was still real. It was an antidote to the austerity of modern music.

And we fell in love with it.

And him.

All of us.

Even Ian Julius.

—I was a bit older when he was on *The Word* that time. I was in my twenties, but I remember it, yeah. I think I was looking more at the girls he had with him. That's irony, innit? I'll admit it, though. I thought he was class. Just like everyone else.

Zach Crystal was accompanied by dancers onstage. Four of them. Female. They were all thin, pale, other-worldly. They too were donned in elegant forest-coloured attire, with glass-like tiaras and smaller antlers, plus long silk cloaks.

—They all looked like witches or something, didn't they? Like something that had climbed out of a storybook. All dancing. It was a bit weird. I think that's why it worked. It wasn't daft. It should have looked daft but it wasn't. It … I dunno, it looked good and it sounded good too.

This performance of 'Burning Eyes' began my and the world's obsession with Zach Crystal. From then on, Crystal was a superstar. More than that, he became a global megastar. His subsequent album, Yearn, *spent twenty weeks on the Billboard 200 in the States and went triple platinum. The video for 'Burning Eyes' debuted on* Top of the Pops *in the UK in April and remained number one on the singles chart until it was usurped by 'Northward Bound', Crystal's Christmas single.*

These were the early days of Zach Crystal, the ones I remember fondly. These were the days when many children's parents slaved away over a sewing machine to try and replicate those clothes, those cloaks.

Let's go back to Ian.

—*And you actually managed to arrange a meet-up?*

—That was it. That was the moment we'd been building up to all that time. I'll tell you now, we were scared, we were nervous. If it really was him then this wasn't going to be any old meet with a perv. This was … I mean, if we were right, this would be huge. It was going to be the end of the biggest superstar in the world. We were going to bring him down. Our lives would change. Which they did, I suppose, just not in the way we'd suspected.

As you heard at the beginning of this episode, Zach Crystal's disappearance in March 2018 coincided with the discovery of remains in the vast forest that surrounded the five hundred acres of what became known as Crystal Forest, Zach Crystal's remote hideaway property in the Scottish Highlands. The star had become something of a recluse since the death of his parents in 2009 and he hadn't released an album since Damage *in 2007. Bizarre rumours always surrounded Crystal, largely because he rarely spoke to the media. Zach Crystal was truly an enigma. His communication came through his music and through carefully controlled messages to his fans. There would be promotional photographs released by Crystal's publicist – shots of Crystal in his tree house, hair hanging half over his face, surrounded by twinkling fairy lights and branches, printed with Crystal's bizarre messages of affection for his fans. To many these just seemed strange and aloof – a middle-aged man pontificating about magical powers and supernatural entities.*

As the months went by and Crystal was not found, it began to seem like he really had gone for good. There were occasional sightings reported all over the world, but nothing concrete.

The official line was that Crystal had been hit hard by the death of his aide and friend, James Cryer. Cryer's body was found by Crystal's sister Naomi on Crystal's estate, deep in the thick aspen forest of Colliecrith, where it looked like he had taken a fall down a small gulley, hitting his head on an outcrop of rock.

This was not the first time that remains had been found on the property. In the same year that Damage *was released, police were alerted to the discovery of the bodies of two fifteen-year-old girls, who had been reported missing and were said to be ardent fans of the star.*

Lulu Copeland and Jessica Morton were found by Crystal's own security team in a cave close to the perimeter of his land. It's assumed that they had been trying to reach the home of the star and died of exposure in the brutal weather. However, horrific rumours abound about what actually happened to the two girls while they were in or near Crystal Forest. There are even those who say that Crystal's security team contaminated the scene and removed a mobile phone, which has never been recovered. Video footage supposedly from that very phone was subsequently leaked online. Like everything Zach Crystal, there are stories, claims and counter-claims about the deaths of these two young people, making the truth very difficult to come by. However, the case of Lulu and Jessica is never far from any mention of Crystal.

It actually wasn't uncommon for people to be caught by Crystal's security, trying to break into Crystal Forest. It's thought Crystal deliberately chose to live in the remote and dangerous Colliecrith National Park to prevent intrusion into his life by the media and fans. A dense, ancient woodland with hidden dips and gullies, great drops and no discernible paths, it's a place where it's very easy to become disoriented and lost, even for the most experienced woodsmen.

What's arguably more disturbing, though, is that there were girls who didn't have to break in – who were invited to spend time at Crystal Forest with the star. Usually in their early teens, from underprivileged or troubled backgrounds, these children were personal guests of Crystal. Of course, with no explanation ever forthcoming from the Crystal camp as to why young girls were spending their time in a luxury tree house with a middle-aged man, the tabloid press were left to speculate. This, according to Crystal, was why he rarely did interviews. In one statement released by Crystal's aide and signed by his family, he said, 'You people always think the worst, instead of trying to understand. I have nothing whatsoever to hide. The shame is on you.'

Despite protests from his fans, there were many who were uncomfortable with Crystal's behaviour. This is something I want to explore as this series goes on. I don't want to put myself in a pro or anti-Crystal camp just yet. It's important that we listen to the facts.

Back to Ian.

—When we arranged to meet him, that was a big moment. We'd told him that we'd take up his challenge – we'd go into that forest with him and find that ghost, that spectre. He told us that our imaginary twelve-year-old was a 'special girl' and that was when he openly admitted who he was, that he was Zach Crystal. He then said he needed to speak to our parents to make the arrangements.

—*I take it you two posed as your decoy's parents too?*

—Correct. When he thought he was talking to adults, he told us it would be a wonderful surprise for our daughter. We could all stay at his place in Scotland, you know, Crystal Forest. He sent us all these pictures, of the guest suites there, the views over the hills, the forests. I mean, it looked amazing, that place, it really did. He said money was no object; we'd be allowed to do whatever we liked out there. He was going to hire cars for us, send us on helicopter rides up into the mountains, that sort of thing.

Then, when he thought he was speaking to the kid again, you know, he was telling her all sorts about the things 'special girls' got to do there: watching horror movies in his tree house and all that. He sent a picture of that too. It was amazing really. He had his own place *above* the mansion – a two-storey wooden house nestled in the trees.

—*You still have these pictures?*

—Yeah but they just look like … like anyone could have taken them, you know? They don't *prove* anything. Amazing place though; little gable roofs and turrets made of wood, moss growing all over, little rickety walkways. Like something from a fairy tale, you know?

But he was also talking all this filth as well, when he thought it was the girl, really disgusting sexual stuff – telling her that he'd teach her things while they were up there. Awful. Just awful.

—*It seems such a risky thing to do, on his part, don't you think?*

—I think he got caught up in it all, just the whole delusion. He was used to getting what he wanted. Maybe what happened next was a cry for help. Maybe it was all on purpose. Who knows? What I do know was that he needed help. He really needed help. The guy was sick.

Crystal bought first-class tickets and told Ian that they and their 'daughter' would be picked up by limo from Inverness airport and driven to Crystal Forest. Everything, he said, would be taken back, however, if they told anyone, broadcast it online or the media found out.

—Did you ever ask him where he'd been for the last year? I mean, he'd been missing a while hadn't he? He was still missing, as far as anyone knew.

—Honestly, I didn't want to push it. I thought if I did that, he might get cold feet, chicken out. We just went with it. I couldn't believe it.

Ian and his girlfriend took the flight, touched down in Inverness and waited.

—He said his people were going to meet us when we arrived. There's a restaurant in the airport, he told us to meet him there. Obviously, me and the missus didn't have a kid with us, and we clocked this bloke in a suit, holding up a sign with our fake name on it. There was this big, black limo in the car park, tinted windows. That's when it all started to go wrong.

—What happened?

—We should have known something was up. We were sat in the Starbucks next to the restaurant, trying to get ourselves together. This was real. We were going to tell them that our daughter wasn't able to make it after all. We were going to film it all. We were sorting out our hidden cameras, when this massive bloke comes and sits down opposite us.

'Monster-Busters?' he says. 'You're in serious shit.'

We look round and there's all these huge blokes in suits; they're all surrounding us. Then this woman arrives. Long, black coat, sunglasses. The security all move out of the way and she sits down too. She tells us who she is.

—She was…

—His sister. It was Naomi Crystal.

Naomi Crystal, Zach's twin, had, by this point, moved into Crystal Forest on a permanent basis with her daughter from a previous relationship, Bonnie, who was thirteen at the time. There was a lot of speculation in the media about Naomi giving up on finding her brother and about how quickly she'd done so. Without Zach Crystal in the picture and the property costing a huge amount to run, Naomi eventually put the mansion up for sale. Rumours abounded about her plans to destroy the wooden tree house above it.

—She was very calm, very scary. I was totally starstruck. I couldn't speak. She sat down and told us exactly what was going to happen next.

To the horror of Ian and his girlfriend, they had been set up. Naomi Crystal explained that Ian was going to hand over everything – their devices, all the printed chat logs, everything. They were going to stay quiet about it all. She said if the media found out about it, she would 'ruin' them both.

—*What did you do?*

—Well, obviously, we agreed, didn't we? Then, when we got home, we sang like birds. Of course we did. It was the right thing to do, morally.

Then, of course, he made his miraculous comeback. And the shitstorm descended on us.

Ian and his girlfriend allegedly chatted to Zach Crystal in March and April 2019. When Crystal re-emerged in May of that year, his first act was to sue Monster-Busters for defamation, for a sum of around £30 million.

The headlines said it all: 'Return of the Zach: Zach Crystal Emerges To Sue over "Ludicrous" Claims'. 'Zach Crystal Reborn: Megastar Returns with New Album, New Tour and £30 Million Defamation Demand against Amateur "Hunting" Group'.

Crystal's second act was to do a full-length, in-depth television interview, live on Ruby, *a BBC chat show hosted by Ruby Rendall, who was a national institution. It was on this show that he announced his comeback.*

Ian Julius had to pick up the pieces.

—It's never stopped. The trolling, the abuse from his fans, you know? Honestly, it was hell. Death threats every single day. Dog shit, eggs all over our house. We had to move. I've had to declare myself bankrupt. My life is effectively over. I'm living day to day now. Still, no one really believes me.

Look at that interview, think about the absolute rubbish he was talking. All this stuff about being a teenager in the body of a middle-aged man, how you could heal people using your imagination. If you or me had said something like that, we'd be in the looney bin. But it was Zach Crystal wasn't it? So it was fine.

Ian Julius and the Monster-Busters were steamrolled by Crystal's mighty PR machine. Despite publishing the chat logs, the tickets, the photos from the airport, everything they had, online, Crystal's massive and active fanbase and the Crystal estate laughed them off as fake. Indeed, there's plenty of videos online now that will tell you exactly how *Ian faked all of it.*

Ian has become just a straw man, swept away by the might of Zach Crystal.

Or the almighty?

—We didn't give up though. We didn't give up, not once. I was being bombarded with threats, bots, trolls and Zach Crystal fans online. Everyone was saying I was just another crazy. I knew we'd had an effect though. I knew that we'd done *something*. Why else would he have come back like that? It's more than a coincidence, right? It has to be. Why else, other than to try and smooth it all over?

—I guess the pro-Crystal side of this is asking why, Ian. Why would Zach place himself in this potentially damaging position?

—You know what I think? Crystal was playing the long game. I don't know whether he knew who we were all along, from the moment we started chatting online. I mean, how could he? But he must have suspected something. I think we had him. Genuinely. I think we had him and as soon as he realised it, he used us. We were the springboard for his comeback.

And what a comeback it was. Forty-five years old now, Zach Crystal poured out his heart to Ruby Rendall and the world on the 20th July, 2019. It was his first-ever full-length television interview. For many, it was the first time anyone had heard him actually speak unguarded and without his face obscured by some bizarre mask or veil. Many were surprised at how normal Crystal seemed during the interview. It was a live broadcast, and there were some bizarre technical hitches, but the command Crystal had over a hysterical audience of fans was something to behold. For many, it was rather sinister. This episode of Ruby *outranked the Frost-Nixon interview by thirty million viewers and became the most viewed television interview in history. It was on this show that Crystal announced, among some rather bizarre claims, his upcoming new album and world tour, to the adulation of fans worldwide. News outlets around the world were screaming headlines about the* Forever *tour and album sales of Crystal's previous two releases skyrocketed. A cynic might say that all of this conveniently distracted from the circumstances of Crystal's triumphant return.*

There were those, however, who still had much to say about Crystal, about his obsession with teenage girls and their dubious rendezvous in the tree house up at Crystal Forest. Then there were the remains found in the forest and the increasingly bizarre rumours online of strange sightings just before he disappeared.

I know, we've not even touched on some of Crystal's oddest aspects, but we have five more episodes to come and believe me, these things will be discussed.

Let's stay in 2019 for now. Zach Crystal's image began to appear everywhere. He was still elfin, skinny, clothed in his elaborate forest-wear, like something from a fantasy movie, his thick blond hair tied up at the back of his head, a knowing smile on his lips, piercing blue eyes.

'Whatever they say about me,' he told Ruby Rendall in that interview, staring into the camera, 'means nothing. Their words can't touch me; they can't kill me. However hard they try.'

But two months later, Zach Crystal would be dead. Crystal Forest would be a smouldering wreck and things would only get worse for Ian Julius.

—I was naive, to be fair. I thought when he died, that it would be over. How thick am I?

The first to point the finger at Ian Julius after Crystal's death was pro-Crystal blogger, Sasha Stewart. Sasha, who has a vast following on YouTube, Instagram and her own podcast named The Crystal-Cast *is a fanatical defender of Zach Crystal and claims she spent time at Crystal Forest. Zach Crystal himself gave her a shout-out on the* Ruby *interview, further bolstering Sasha's listenership.*

Fire-scene investigators were unable to identify with certainty the cause of the blaze at Crystal Forest, but Police Scotland, in a brief statement, said they believed it had been started deliberately. Zach Crystal was the only casualty and therefore his death has been considered by most to be suicide.

Sasha's video entitled 'Who Killed Zach?' focuses on many of the apparent 'lies' spread by the 'mainstream media' concerning Crystal. She documents the heartless way the newspapers tried to capture the star's grief when his close friend and aide, James Cryer, was found dead in the forest near the property. She then moves on to Ian Julius and his 'attempted sabotage' of Zach Crystal's return. According to Sasha, it was obvious to the world that Crystal's disappearance was simply to write and prepare for the Forever *tour and the brand-new album.*

Sasha's position is that Ian's claims are completely false, that he made everything up to attract attention and make money. Crystal, Sasha claims, was in a vulnerable state after losing his best friend and having to face 'a barrage of daily attacks from the press' about his penchant for teenage girls and about the remains found on his property, which had 'all been brought up again'.

In her 'Who Killed Zach?' episode, Sasha concludes that Ian's accusations against Crystal, painting him as some kind of online predator, were the final straw, and Crystal burned down his property with only himself inside. Despite the investigation into the fire being inconclusive, Sasha, along with the majority of Zach Crystal's fan base, believes suicide is the only explanation. They argue that while Crystal Forest employed a great many staff – cleaners, cooks, drivers and the like – and Naomi Crystal and her daughter had moved in, Zach was the only casualty. Why is it that everyone else escaped alive?

Furthermore, Zach's thirteen-year-old niece survived the fire; if Crystal was a predator, surely he would have wanted to harm her too?

Unfortunately, since the death of Crystal, very little has been said by those left behind. Naomi, clad in her trademark sunglasses and dressed in black, read a brief statement from outside the blackened ruins of Crystal Forest, a few days after her brother's death:

'Today the world mourns the loss of a wonderful human being. Not only a vastly talented musician, but an advocate for worldwide charity. Today the world mourns the loss of a son, a brother and an inspiration to many the world over. Zach Crystal is still with us through the medium of what he left behind, his music and his message to help others, which will remain with us forever.'

—I was just … shocked. The whole world was shocked, but it was just … I couldn't believe it. After everything, after all of this, all the work we'd done, I just couldn't believe he'd managed to get away with it. He didn't have to answer for any of it.

I was gutted. Totally gutted. We all were.

After Sasha Stewart released her episode of The Crystal-Cast, *blaming Ian Julius for the suicide of Zach Crystal, Ian tells me his world imploded.*

—I was doxxed pretty early on by one of the Crystal nutters. Probably Spooky Sasha herself. That girl is seriously scary. There were people outside my house, stuff being chucked at the windows. I managed to get my missus away early on, let her escape somewhere else. I stayed behind, called the police, let them focus on me for a bit. But it never stopped, never went away. Wherever I went, someone would find me and it would all start up again. It's still happening now. I imagine after this goes out, someone'll find me and I'll have to move again.

—*So why talk then? What is it that you feel you need to get out?*

—Because it was true, all of what happened to us. Why would I lie? To get attention – this sort of attention? Do they think that this is what I want? To be moving house constantly, to be waking up at every little sound, wondering if some maniac's breaking in and trying to stab me? Some of them actually believe I did this for money.

—You sold your story to a few tabloid newspapers though. That's true, isn't it?

—It is. But that's the game isn't it? How else was I supposed to get the story out there? I didn't have the videos or any photos from the airport anymore – they took our phones. I had a backup of the chat-logs but that was it.

—There was no way of proving, conclusively, that it was Zach Crystal.

—Right. But it was him. I just *know* it was him.

—Why do you think Crystal was this reckless?

—OK, so this is what I reckon happened, right? Crystal had been gone for a year, hadn't he? Vanished. After his best mate, his right-hand man, had just died. That's dodgy in itself, right. His sister moves in and tries to sell the place. Why? She wants it torn down, that tree house. Again, why? What's in there that they want destroyed?

And all the years before he vanishes, he's got girls staying there, hasn't he? All those young girls from care homes and the like, that he's supposed to be 'helping'. I mean, who's letting a twelve-year-old hang out with a middle-aged bloke? If that was just some guy down the street, the postman, the guy pushing trolleys round ASDA car park, no one's letting them hang out with a kid. But it's Zach Crystal, so it's OK? That's just messed up.

Anyway. So you've got all that, his career is tanking. When was his last album? Nearly ten years earlier or something? He's not on tour. Makes you wonder how much debt he was in. Maybe he ran off to Madagascar or something, I dunno, but wherever he is, he's still looking for kids – he can't help himself. So he's online, on the apps, and that's where we catch him.

Maybe he realises it's a trap, then maybe he works out what's going to happen if it comes out that he's a nonce. Now, don't get me wrong, Zach Crystal's not stupid; anyone that rich can't be daft. So he creates this miraculous 'comeback'. PR, innit? *Good* PR. Papers over the fact that he's been chatting to kids online. So he gets his people to meet us, takes all our stuff, just because he can.

Of course his fans are going to believe him over us. We were nothing to him. Ended up as just a stepping stone to revamp his flagging career, that's all.

And it fucking well worked, didn't it? Until … well…

—*Until the fire. What's your opinion on that, may I ask? Was it, like the fans think, suicide? Or is it possible that Zach Crystal was murdered?*

—Oh yeah, it's possible alright. I imagine there was more than just me who had a problem with Zach Crystal.

Ian's right. The tide of public opinion against Crystal was at its lowest ebb in the lead-up to his disappearance. The reclusive, oddball star, hidden away in the remote Highlands of Scotland, in the constant company of teenage girls. It didn't look good. There were rumours of spiralling debts, Crystal Forest a lavish expense that Crystal could no longer afford to run.

Interestingly, when Crystal vanished; there was an upsurge in album sales. Ian and many others believe all of it was clever PR.

—Ultimately, I believe that yeah, it probably was suicide. Do I think it was my fault? Well, I mean, I wasn't the one trawling the internet for young girls; I wasn't the one paying for first-class flights to Inver-bloody-ness, was I? I think the suicide theory is probably right – I'll give Sasha Stewart that one, at least – but it's not because of me. Well, it is, sort of. But you don't kill yourself for no reason. I think he did it because he didn't want to have to face up to what he was doing. I think it all got a bit too close to home. It was all going to catch up with him at some point, wasn't it? Look what was happening.

At around the time of Zach Crystal's re-emergence, there were some rather unsavoury rumblings surrounding Crystal and alleged historical abuse claims.

From my own, brief, amateur sleuthing, I can trace the emergence of the recent claims against Crystal to a reply to actress Alyssa Milano's 15th October 2017 tweet that urged women to speak out against sexual assault:

If all the women who have ever been sexually harassed or assaulted wrote 'Me too' as a status, then we give people a sense of the magnitude of the problem.

A reply by someone called Sammy Williams joined over 63,000 others. That number in itself is damning. It says a lot about the way our society was – and still is. Here's Sammy's reply:

I was groomed online and assaulted by Zach Crystal when I was 14 yrs old #metoo

Sammy's tweet received almost no attention.

At first.

But when Crystal re-emerged in 2019, there were a great deal more of these accusations from a great deal more women, many of whom had been silenced in the past by lawsuits and NDAs. But there were also many other past accusations against Crystal that had been covered by the press at the height of his fame. Mostly the press painted the accusers as gold-diggers – wayward young girls who were out to get money from the star. The rebuttals from the Crystal camp were swift and decisive, and many of those accusers were driven underground by the vehemence of the Zach Crystal fan community.

However, in more recent years, people began using social media to speak up against Zach Crystal anonymously. Crystal actually addressed these claims on his appearance on the Ruby Show on BBC One, speaking eloquently as he forcibly denied any wrongdoing on his part.

There is a vast web of stories, claims and tangents to explore in the convoluted story of Zach Crystal. I hope to cover many of these as this series goes on. But there's one last thing I want to ask Ian, something which I haven't even begun to cover yet.

—When Zach Crystal spoke to Ruby Rendall in 2019, there was something odd that struck me and a great many others who watched it.

—Oh yeah. I mean all that weirdness from the fans it was like—

—No … actually. Not that.

—Oh yeah?

—Yeah. It was something he said. He said he saw something in his future, a vision … a dark omen of some sort. I remember he used to talk a lot about that sort of thing.

—I remember. You know what I think all that nonsense was? That was his conscience – not some forest ghost or whatever crap he used to spout. That was the embodiment of his guilt and his regret, and all the bad things he'd done in his life, coming for him. He knew. He knew it would come and bite him in the backside one day.

Then it did. And he was too much of a coward to turn around and take responsibility for what he'd done. So he took the coward's way out.

And now that's my fault.

It's a fucking joke.

—Do you have anything you want to say before we finish, a message to those who are still hounding you?

—Not really, no. Those people don't listen. They're deluded and dogmatic. They won't stop because it's easier to blame me than look critically at their hero, innit? It's up to them to come to their own realisation about Zach Crystal. I just hope that those women get some kind of justice for what he did to them. That's all I want.

And so we reach the end of our first episode.

There's a lot here to get your head around, and I've barely scratched the surface. There's a lot that we've covered and even more we haven't. With every question, with every statement regarding Zach Crystal, more and more others are spawned. Hopefully, this episode has provided an overview of the case of Zach Crystal – his rise, his disappearance, his resurgence and the spectacular fall, to his death, and the accusations that have dogged his career.

For those of you who are fans of Crystal and are still with me, I want to make something clear: at this point I am doing my best to remain neutral. It is hard, though. I have stirred a pot filled to the brim with rumours, whispers and stories. Throughout this series, we are going to look at the different sides of the Zach Crystal story. Six ways.

Our first has been from a certain viewpoint, and I am aware that there are many more. There are extremes on all sides and I realise that in doing this, I'm not going to make any side happy. Is Ian Julius to blame for Zach Crystal's death, and is he telling the truth? I don't think I'll be able to answer that question with any certainty.

The thing is, we have no way of knowing what happened behind the walls of Crystal Forest.

Because none of us were there.

Perhaps this is why I'm making this series; because if I don't, the Zach Crystal question is always going to be there. It's always going to be burrowing under my skin, a parasite eating away at me. As it is for many of you.

Next episode, to provide contrast, we're going to speak to someone whose views on Zach Crystal are the polar opposite to Ian Julius's. For every argument against Crystal, we should see the other side. Who you want to believe is up to you, but for me, I'm open to suggestion.

I've been Scott King.

Until next time…

RUBY

Episode 246: Zach Crystal

Legendary Presenter Ruby Rendall's exclusive interview with pop megastar Zach Crystal. ***More >***

---

1 hr 45 • 9pm 20th July 2019 • Available for 28 days

RR: Wow. I just … there's something about that song. I must have heard it a million times, I've danced to it a million times. *[Sings] And now, our stars, they fall,*

ZC: *[singing softly] I'll try and catch them all…*

[At this, there is a huge well of screeching from the studio audience that goes instantly quiet when Zach Crystal raises his hand.]

ZC: It's a song about trying to do so much, trying to catch all the falling stars – trying to save everyone from…

[There is a loud shriek from an audience member at this.]

RR: I know, *I know,* right? But anyway, as I was saying; seeing it here, now, with the video and with Zach Crystal sat opposite me, it just sends a tingle up my spine, like it's the first time. You're blushing.

ZC: *[giggling]* I know. I told you, I'm quite a shy guy.

RR: Welcome back everyone; just in case you didn't notice, I'm Ruby Rendall and sat opposite me is actually Zach Crystal. Zach, you've said in the past that fame comes with quite a price, would I be right?

ZC: That's true. That's so true, and people, they just don't think about that. They see the money, they see all the hotels, the tours and they don't realise how hard it is. I mean, it's so amazing, I'm so lucky, but it all comes with a price.

RR: You paid a hefty price, growing up didn't you? I mean, you were performing from the age of twelve, with your sister.

ZC: That's right, The Crystal Twins. Naomi had begun joining me downstairs on those Sunday afternoons after we'd finished our homework. We began to sing duets together, while I played the keys. Our favourites were 'You've Lost That Loving Feeling' by *The Righteous Brothers* and 'Hit the Road Jack' by Ray Leonard. At first it was really hard to play and sing at the same time, but I remember Naomi saying to me, 'Look at me instead of the keys. Trust your fingers.'

And I did. The first time we played and sang through a song with no mistakes, I looked at my father and there were tears trickling down his cheeks. He was so proud of us. More than that, *we* were proud of us.

We were only any good because of how much work we put in. We were always practising, rehearsing, getting it right, trying to be the best.

RR: Did that take away much of having a normal life growing up. Did you two go to school?

ZC: We were supposed to, but it was hard as our music career took off really quickly. We were always working, always writing songs and practising. My mother was supposed to home-school us, but to be honest, it was the music that was our focus. So, no, it wasn't totally normal. We didn't see other people, really. But that's what made us what we were. I don't regret any of it.

RR: You were both doing very well in those early days, playing in pubs and bars. You guys were so young…

ZC: That's true. Naomi is older than me, but only by an hour. She always looked after me, back then, she was always so much more confident. She's the same as a mother, now. She's so protective of that girl, so loving. I found the bars and places so scary; all those people, all that noise. Nothing fazed Naomi though. She knew what she wanted, knew what she was doing. Naomi wasn't scared to ask for things, where I was so shy. She's still that way. She's such a strong person and I admire her. We had to grow up quickly, both of us.

RR: The ramifications of that must have been tough on you both.

ZC: I think it was harder for me than it was for Naomi. I never really had many friends. I certainly never had a normal teenage-hood, you know? I never did what other teenagers did – going to parties, that sort of thing, working out who I was. It made me sad. I was sad a lot of the time. I was alone.

RR: So here were Zach and Naomi Crystal, these two stars, bringing happiness to people all over the country with their music, and inside, you were sad?

ZC: There was a part of me that just wanted to be by myself. I used to read a lot of books, sat in the back of the car, or waiting for the sound check in the dressing rooms, while Naomi was talking to people. I used to lose myself in these stories: *The Famous Five* books, *The Secret Garden*, Narnia, all of that. Places where young people escape into other worlds. I loved that idea. I still do.

RR: Was there a part of you, Zach, when you were that age, that wanted to escape from it all? Is that why those stories resonated?

ZC: I've always been a dreamer, always had my head in the clouds. Those books were an escape for me. The music business is a hard place. It's cold. It doesn't care.

RR: How hard was that then, for sixteen-year-old you?

ZC: Harder than you can imagine. I was in the spotlight the whole time. You would have thought I'd be used to it, but at that age, you just want the ground to swallow you up. However much I tried to blend into the background, I couldn't. People just wanted a piece of me all the time – the fans. But don't get me wrong, Ruby, I love them, I love all of them. All of *you*!

[Cheering from the audience; someone shouts 'Zach, I love you!']

ZC: I love you too!

[This generates a great cascade of shrieking, which eventually quietens.]

ZC: I mean it was the rehearsing, the practice, the song-writing, all of that stuff that goes on behind these scenes, you know? That was all in the way of me growing up, you see. It's like being a footballer, I guess. People want you to be a certain way; you're told you're a role model. But that's not your choice. You're still young, seventeen, and you've got little kids looking up to you. That's why I built the tree house in Crystal Forest, you see. I guess I'm trying to compensate. That kid who read all those books, always wanted to have a secret tree house, a clubhouse. It sounds silly, but it's true.

RR: And now you have. You bought five hundred acres in Colliecrith National Park, up in the wilds of Scotland. That's where you write and record your music. Also where you live, right?

ZC: Yeah. It's a wonderful place. It's an aspen forest far, far away from everything. The name comes from Gaelic – *crith* which means 'shiver' – because of the leaves of those trees. There's magic up there, those trees are magical … the leaves.

RR: Really?

ZC: Oh yeah, you put one of those leaves under your tongue and it increases your word power. I'm telling you. But most importantly, it's a place to escape to, when the work is done, you see? It's my place, my private place. I'm a very business-minded person, you see, very busy all the time; recording and in meetings. That's what I use the main house for, and when that's done, I can escape into the tree house. People, especially the press, they find it funny, they find it weird, but they don't understand, they've never tried to understand *why*.

RR: I mean, it's more than just a tree house, isn't it? It's a tree *mansion*.

ZC: Ruby. It only has two floors…

[Laughter]

RR: So what is it you do in there?

ZC: I sleep. It's beautiful up there, you know? It was built *around* the trees, you see; all that ancient wood, all those leaves are on the inside and the outside. The colours are amazing – pale yellows and greens that stretch out over the mountains forever. It's another world up there. There's other-worldly things in there.

[Zach is interrupted by screams from the audience – short, high yelping sounds, seemingly from individuals, then gradually spreading. The camera pans to the audience for a second. A few audience members are twitching in their seats, crying out with little yelps. The noises are spreading.]

RR: Um … as you were saying, Zach…

[The yelps are getting more and more frequent.]

RR: This is just *so exciting*, I think, and it's hard not to get carried away. Can we cut to…?

[One or two of the yelps are cut short and there are muffled protests as some of the crowd are ejected. But the yelping increases and a BBC One logo appears on the screen:]

Programme information – technical difficulties
We are currently experiencing some technical problems with our live broadcast. We are looking into these and hope to have the issues resolved soon.

[After a few minutes, the programme resumes.]

RR: I think, for some, having you here, is just a little overwhelming. Can you carry on about your house up there in the wilderness?

ZC: Of course, I have fairy lights everywhere and a huge TV. It's cosy – it's so comfy up there, so wonderful.

RR: Is that where you feel you can almost recapture that lost teenage-hood? You can be a kid again?

ZC: Exactly. I do all sorts of teenage things up there, too, you know – watching horror movies, singing, reading. It's a place I can escape to. I can be a teenager again, in the body of an older man.

RR: You have visitors there too, that's correct?

ZC: I have an entire visitor's suite in the main building. It's luxury, you know? Like a five-star hotel, six stars, seven stars! There's everything anyone could want – room service, a spa. Everything. I have people staying all the time. People from some of the hardest backgrounds. People who didn't grow up with anything, or have lost their families. My doors are always open to people like that.

RR: You work with a lot of disadvantaged young people. It feels to me that you can, to some degree, relate to their pain.

ZC: That's right. I want to give something back. That's what I've always tried to do. There are young people out there who have lost their childhoods, their teenage years, because they had to grow up too fast, they had to be a carer or there was addiction in their family – there was death, pain, tragedy. I want to give those young people something back. I invite them to come and stay at Crystal Forest. They have it all. They escape their hardship for a few days.

RR: There has been a lot of tabloid speculation over this, hasn't there?

[The remaining audience begin to boo loudly.]

ZC: There has. It's disgusting, the things they say about me. It's disgraceful. You try and help people, and look what you get back in return. I try and give young people who have nothing, something, and I'm the bad guy. That's why I don't talk to the media, Ruby, that's why I rarely have. Whatever you try and do, they will always want to make it into a headline, something awful. My sister's daughter – my niece – lives with us at Crystal Forest. If I was what they say I am, do you think Naomi would let that happen? I don't think so.

RR: It feels to me that you're helping them replace something that was lost, the same as you are doing for yourself? Is that fair?

ZC: Yes. It's like people don't want to hear that.

RR: I need to ask, because there's so much in the media, so much that people want to know … Is it true that you have a room dedicated to your mother in Crystal Forest?

ZC: See, that became one of those stories, another one of those cruel headlines in the papers about me. I don't understand why people read these things. Both my mother and my father died ten years ago now. It still hurts to this day, Ruby. Yes, I have many of my mother's things at Crystal Forest so I can remember her. She was a humble person who gave me everything she could. It is in her name that I want to give to others, you know?

RR: That's so beautiful. Zach, I want to break for a moment because I believe you've recorded something for us?

ZC: That's right. I know how much people wanted to see the inside of Crystal Forest. So I made a little walk-through video. A world exclusive, just for this show. My own guide to my home. It was for all the fans who want to see where I live.

[Cheering]

RR: Another world exclusive on *Ruby* tonight. So we'll take a short break while you enjoy 'At Home with Zach Crystal', ladies and gentlemen…

[More cheering, reaching fever pitch]

Episode 2: Zach Crystal Stan

—And you know what's laughable? What's *the most* amusing thing about this whole, entire bullshit debate? Let's just all stop for a moment and take a look at some of the pictures, shall we? I mean, these are pictures that she uploaded *herself*. Only a year or two before she became a *'victim'*. She *chose* to upload this one here, where she's hanging on to her mate for dear life. Look at her dress, it's almost obscene *without* being nearly halfway down her chest. Her makeup's all smeared and there's what is most probably a cigarette behind her ear.

Here's the next one – and to my absolute surprise, she's on another night out. Another skimpy little number, and this time she's too pissed to even walk in her shoes; she's got them in her hand, for fuck's sake. Oh and who's this she's clinging on to? Some random guy? You bet. You think I'm wrong?

I could go on, I really could. There's just not enough hours in the day for this sort of shite.

We will, though. We will because no one else is going on about it, are they? Number two: here she is, at some sort of bar, standing between two guys. Arms around them both. How old do you think she looks there? I mean, to me, she doesn't look old enough to even be in there.

Number three – this is the one with the video. Yeah *that* video. Which I can't show you because if I do, I'll get done for child pornography. What we can see are some of her messages though. I've blurred out a lot of it – well, for obvious reasons. I mean, she was sending these to guys on dating sites when she was fifteen. I think that's all I need to say about *her…*

Number four of the five despicable sluts, and here we have a little comparison. Here she is, standing with Mum and Dad, looking altogether respectable. You know, like a girl of thirteen should on her birthday. There's even a cake and candles. Very nice, no?

No.

Here she is on the same night, believe it or not. Maybe just a few hours later. I mean, c'mon. Really? And we're supposed to believe that she was a *victim*?

Last and in no way least – I mean that she's as bad as the others, they're all equally vile - here she is ladies and gentlemen … oh dear. Yes, ladies and gentlemen, that's vomit, and look at the colour of it – as pink as the drink that she isn't old enough to be drinking. Yes, if you look closely, that's a bit of it in her hair. How lovely. Her granny must be proud. And look everyone, she's *smiling*. Yes, she's actually pleased with herself. Isn't that wonderful?

I mean, there'll be many of you asking me why I'm putting these pictures out there; how do I have the nerve to question any of these girls? As a woman, how on earth can I give it the whole 'gaslighting' 'victim–blaming' bullshit?

I tell you why. I tell you why - because I wasn't the one who put them out there for the world to see. I wasn't the one who then tried to take them down again when the narrative didn't quite follow the way *I* wanted it to.

That wasn't me. That was *them*, ladies and gentlemen.

That was all them.

Welcome to Six Stories.

I'm Scott King.

In this, episode two of six, we are looking back at the disappearance, re-emergence and death of one of the biggest stars in the world of music and entertainment; now one of the largest and most polarising subjects on people's lips.

Superstar, maverick, genius, abuser, murderer?

Pop megastar Zach Crystal re-emerged in 2019 after making a sudden disappearance a year previously. After frantic appeals from Crystal's twin sister and alleged plans to sell off or demolish his elaborate home in the wilds of Scotland, Zach Crystal returned.

The sudden re-materialisation of the star caused headlines across the globe and was followed shortly after by the news that Crystal was suing online paedophile hunting group Monster-Busters for £30 million after they claimed they had caught him trying to arrange meetings with underage girls online.

Then he did a reveal-all interview on Britain's number one celebrity talk show, Ruby, *which was interspersed with music videos and a rather bizarre 'tour' of his lavish home in Colliecrith National Park, Crystal wielding a video camera and breathlessly showing the viewers blurred and poorly focused shots of his swimming pool, recording studio and elaborate tree house. What was confusing for many, including myself, in the interview, was the matter-of-fact way Crystal spoke, how 'normal' he seemed. Maybe it was all the years he'd spent evading scrutiny that made it seem this way. Even so, what was truly spectacular was his absolute command over his audience. Of course, a legion of dedicated Zach Crystal fans managed to get tickets to see the show, and their bizarre behaviour throughout showed how much Crystal meant to them. So maybe he didn't need to be anything more than who he was.*

During the interview Crystal announced the release of a new album, the first for more than ten years, and a tour, tickets for which sold out within minutes. Crystal – or most likely his PR – spoke out through his Twitter handle @ZachCrystalOfficial:

This rebirth – of me and of my music – was the long-term plan. In hindsight, I should have let my loyal fans know a long time ago. For that, I am sorry…

I remember the feeling that emerged in me when Zach Crystal reappeared. I remember seeing the Ruby *interview – the man many millions across the world saw as more god than human. I, like many, pulled out my old Zach Crystal records, relived what those songs had done for me, what they still do for me. For a little while I forgot about the rumbling accusations that had slowly started to become synonymous with the name Zach Crystal. I was, like everyone else, caught up in the hype. Crystal's PR campaign was relentless in its positivity and its message about the reappearance. This had always been the plan: he was back and he was going to take the world by storm. Again.*

—*Were you always confident that Zach Crystal was going to return from his exile?*

—Exactly. Absolutely correct. Anyone who's a Zach Crystal fan, a *proper* fan, will know that he was always going to return. Think about it. The number nine, yeah? It signifies the hermit in the Tarot, right? What does the hermit do? What *is* a hermit? Someone who goes off alone, to seek a sort of enlightenment, a spiritual awakening. Eight plus one, nine. 2019.

It's pretty obvious. Look at the lyrics to 'Fortune' on the *Damage* album:

Let me tell you your fortune,
Let me light your way,
Let me hold you tightly,
It's gonna be OK.

What do you call people who can read Tarot cards? Fortune-tellers. What does the hermit on the Tarot card do? He carries a staff with a lantern on it. *Lighting the way.*

So the true Zach Crystal fans knew that this was coming. We knew he'd be back.

We all knew he would be back, anew.

The voice you are hearing right now and at the start of this episode is that of Sasha Stewart. Sasha, resident of Inverness, Scotland, the closest large city to Crystal's home, is perhaps most well known for her YouTube channel and podcast The Crystal-Cast. *In fact, Sasha is something of a Zach Crystal expert and claims to have actually spent time at Crystal Forest. This is something we are sure to return to this episode.*

Sasha has agreed to speak to me via Skype on the condition that she is allowed to break down and discuss the interview on her podcast in turn. In order to speak to Sasha, I've waived many of my own rights. I imagine, if her other videos are anything to go by, she'll attempt to destroy anything negative I might have to say about Crystal. But it was this way or no way at all.

I'll admit, and it's probably to Sasha's credit, that I'm a little intimidated. Sasha is vociferous to say the least. Her tongue is diamond-edged – I've seen it carve chunks out of any Zach Crystal dissenters.

I've explained to Sasha that here at Six Stories*, there is no agenda. I'm not a police officer, a forensic analyst or any type of expert. All we do here is rake up old graves. Yet I'm still nervous.*

The case of Zach Crystal is an expansive rabbit warren, and it's easy to get sucked down into its network of vagary and nuance. What I want to try and do here is get a balanced view of the case. I want to see all sides of this convoluted and fascinating character and the things he was alleged to have done. I know that Sasha will jump on anything that I may get wrong.

I believe that talking to Sasha will allow us to see the opposite side of what was covered in episode one. Balance, therefore, should be created.

At the top of this episode, you heard an extract from one of Sasha's YouTube rants, and I promise, we'll address Sasha's opinions there. I do want to challenge her about her assessment of some of the women who've begun to speak up about their experiences with Zach Crystal, but for now, I want to give Sasha her turn to speak. Sasha tells me that it's rare these days for Zach Crystal fans to be listened to without being shouted down.

Sasha is quite an imposing woman. Twenty-four years old with a round, pale face, black hair scraped back from her forehead and vivid, blue eyes, she speaks quickly and passionately, and I feel like I'm going to need all my wits about me.

—You see, Scott, people like me, proper Zach Crystal fans, are often regarded in the way flat-earthers are – we're wacky or crazy in some way. When actually we're just devotees. We stand up for his name, when he can't.

—*I've heard you referred to as 'Zach Crystal truthers'. Does that bother you?*

—Not much, no. That's because what I say is the truth, right? What I'm saying actually *is* the truth about Zach Crystal. Crazy, right? Some people in the Crystal community do get upset though, because the term 'truther' is used as a kind of euphemism for someone who's not all there. I couldn't give a fuck, if I'm honest, but that's how a lot of people see us.

—*Why do you think that is? Surely you're just making the other side of the argument?*

—Well, yeah, we are. The truth is, we're kind of outnumbered, and anyone who isn't towing the line or is in a minority are the ones to be discriminated against, right?

—*Can I just ask, before we go on, what is it about Zach Crystal? Why him?*

—Why is anyone a fan of anyone? Because he's amazing. In every way. It's really very simple. But the thing is, you can't *be* a Zach fan anymore without being called a load of names. There are so many people for whom Zach Crystal meant everything, who he still means everything to. I've loved Zach and his music since I first met him. It's just gone from there.

—*And you'll defend him to the end, too?*

—It's why we won't let people like Ian Julius drag his name through the mud. Especially now, when Zach can't defend himself. What a surprise – people like Ian Julius and the rest of them only start piping up after Zach's death…

—*So you think Zach Crystal was innocent?*

—I think you have to ask yourself a few questions first. Innocent of *what* exactly? Ian Julius claims things but the guy has no evidence. A chat log from some app? Please. He thinks that was Zach? Tell me, what piece of evidence did Ian Julius actually have that he was going to use to take Zach down with? Oh yeah, nothing.

When Sasha talks about the opponents of Zach Crystal like this, her eyes widen, her face hardens and she moves closer and closer to the screen. It's genuinely intimidating, despite the fact Sasha and I are communicating remotely. I feel like I'm the one making the accusations. I'm going to ask Sasha about Lulu Copeland and Jessica Morton, the two young girls found dead in Crystal Forest, about the video that was released and the rumours surrounding them. I don't imagine that will go down well, so I need to find the right moment to do it.

—Can we also please just take a moment to have a look at good old Ian Julius, eh? This guy wasn't exactly an example of virtue himself, was he?

—*Wasn't he?*

Quick as a flash; Sasha pulls up a number of articles from online newspapers, dating back to the mid-2000s.

—Read this: 'Gambling Addict Fleeces Own Family To Repay Debts'. So this wee guy was hooked on poker: online poker. He had six credit cards on the go and was being chased down by about four payday-loan companies. Listen: 'Ian Wallace, twenty-nine, was caught withdrawing money from his own granny's bank account in July when a bank teller made Nora Wallace, seventy-five, aware that she'd been paying huge sums back to online loan company BareDollar.'

Wallace is his real surname. He goes by Julius, cos that's his girlfriend's name. Now, here he is again in 2018, what's he doing this time? Oh just trying to extort innocent people.

Sasha shows me an article; this one is about a certain Julian Mearns who had to settle out of court with a retired football coach after claims of historical sexual abuse were found to be completely unsubstantiated.

—This time Julius was looking for not much short of a million to pay back more debts to BareDollar by making accusations about a retired teacher from his old school. His *private* school. He thought if he did it on the sly, did it off the books rather than involving the police, he'd get away with a big out-of-court settlement.

When that didn't work, Julius had even more to pay back. So what did he do? He looked at the more ludicrous claims coming out about Zach and thought he'd piggyback on them for his own ends.

—*It is true, isn't it, that Zach Crystal paid substantial amounts of money to the families of some visitors to Crystal Forest.*

Sasha raises one eyebrow and then seems to deflate in a paroxysm of scorn.

—Aye, imagine that, eh? Imagine a rich guy, probably the richest guy on the planet, giving some of his riches to some underprivileged young women. I mean, if there's anything that shouts 'paedo', then that's it. Yes, he gave people money – more than just money – because he was doing *good.*

For a brief moment, I want to ask Sasha about her luxurious-looking flat, her high-spec equipment. But I don't dare. Instead, we turn back to the subject of Ian Julius.

—*Ian Julius claimed that he and his girlfriend were accosted at Inverness airport by Naomi Crystal and Zach's security team, and that they took their devices.*

—Right, right. It's all very action movie isn't it? It's ironic that people like Julius call *us* the fanatics, the truthers. I mean, who creates a whack-job story like that unless they want attention, or more likely in his case, money?

—*Are you saying it's all made up?*

—I'm saying there are some parts that have been, quite frankly, left out to provide a better story.

—*Can you elaborate?*

—It doesn't take much to find out about Ian Julius's character; just a bit of googling. So we've got a known con man, a guy who robbed his own granny, who accused an innocent man of abuse to try and get money. This guy goes online, pretending to be a thirteen-year-old girl. Aye, OK, that's fine though, is it? That's just fine? That's not dodgy at all. He goes online and goes *looking* for someone to extort.

—*You think?*

—So let's just say you get catfished by Ian Julius; are you going to want to go to court, or would you prefer to pay him off and not be called a nonce for the rest of your life? Also, if Ian Julius thinks he's caught Zach online, why did Ian and his girlfriend fly first class to Inverness before telling the police? Why would you do that? Did they think that Zach was just going to be there, with no security, waiting for them with a bunch of flowers? Come on.

—*To play devil's advocate Sasha, maybe they wanted to be a hundred percent sure, or they didn't want to scare off … er … whoever they were talking to.*

—I mean, that's such a flimsy argument. Let's say it *was* Zach. They'd still scare him off, wouldn't they? Because how would he know it wasn't the police on the plane? And also, if those two take child sexual abuse as seriously as they say they do – or did – why didn't they tell anyone until *after* they landed and all their devices have been conveniently stolen? When all the evidence had gone?

—*Ian says it was Naomi Crystal and Zach's security who took their devices.*

—Hmm, funny that, isn't it? I don't suppose you saw the documents that were released on CorpusDelicti.com did you?

The site Sasha is referring to is a popular gossip site where official documents pertaining to celebrities are released anonymously. Celebrity riders, police reports and the like. There is, however, no way of verifying these documents are genuine.

—The statement from the air stewardess? The one who served Julius and his girlfriend and described them as 'insufferable drunkards'? She says Julius left his phone in the toilet and that they left a GoPro on their seats. She says she had to catch them up to give it to them as they staggered into the airport.

Staunch professionals, both of them, no? That looks to me like the behaviour of someone celebrating something, not out to catch a potential paedophile.

I have to say, I've heard rumours surrounding Ian Julius's credibility too. This, however, seems damning. Sasha hasn't finished.

—OK, so let's say that, even though they were drunk, and even though they were con artists, they still thought they'd genuinely caught a paedophile. Let's say all that's true. Who did they tell first? Was it the police? No. They tried to instigate a bidding war with the tabloids, for fuck's sake!

All of this points to one thing; the one thing that Ian Julius cares about. Money. Money was what killed Zach. Greed.

—*You're blaming Ian Julius for Zach Crystal's death?*

—I truly, honestly believe that the responsibility for Zach's death lies with the mainstream media and people like Ian Julius. In fact, I'd go so far as to say that Ian Julius bears almost sole responsibility. This was not how it was supposed to end.

—*That may be so. However, Ian Julius's life has also changed quite dramatically since he made these accusations against Zach Crystal. He has his life threatened on a daily basis by fans; he's constantly on the move, terrified of being doxxed or swatted. Would it be rude of me to think you take some kind of pleasure in this?*

—I mean the guy is crazy; he's delusional. He belongs in an institution somewhere if he actually believes what he thinks about Zach. I don't take pleasure in what's happened to him, exactly, but I like to see justice being done. People call me crazy, but I'm just a fan. Ian Julius went out of his way to try and besmirch someone famous, someone vulnerable and giving. Zach was the one that caught *him.* He should have been put away for murder. He deserves all of it.

Like her idol, and like her nemesis, Sasha Stewart is herself a maligned figure. She caused huge controversy when she trawled the internet to find photographs of five women who have recently accused Zach Crystal of sexual assault in 2010 and 2011, and then showed them on her YouTube channel. Sasha also claims to be aware of the existence of a sex tape made by one of Crystal's accusers. It's a chilling and ruthless character assassination that Sasha believes is perfectly justified.

—It's OK for those bitches to try and cancel Zach after he died, but if they get called out, it's 'victim-blaming' – give me a fucking break.

Sasha has already stipulated that she's not going to tell me where and how she found these pictures, so there's no point me asking.

There's no point me arguing with Sasha either; neither one of us can know with one-hundred-percent certainty whether Zach Crystal is guilty or innocent. The only person who does is dead. That's not to say that those who have accused Crystal are lying, but there's no concrete way for us to know the truth. I wish there was. What I want to do with Sasha is find out why she's so vociferous in defence of the man, despite only knowing as much about the facts of the case as anyone else.

I want to start from the start.

—Sasha, when did Zach Crystal come into your life and change it?

—That's a great question, Scott. Actually, I was fairly late to Zach's music. I have to say, I didn't really know who he was when I first met him. I was fairly disappointed to be honest. I was expecting Leona Lewis!

Sasha Stewart was twelve years old in 2007 and was an inpatient at Raigmore Hospital in Inverness. She had been 'stepped down' from the Paediatric Intensive Care Unit (PICU) after being monitored for a head injury, and had her own room on the paediatric ward as she recovered from severe burns. Sasha still bears the scar from the head trauma; a pale, ragged line over her left eyebrow.

—Aye, so I didn't have the greatest of upbringings. My ma and da were a pair of junkies from The Ferry. One day when I was twelve, they were cooking meth in the kitchen, and stupid me goes skidding over on some shite on the floor, pulling the boiling pan over myself and smashing my head on the worktop. I don't remember much, but I imagine the pair of them were probably more concerned with how much of the stuff I'd lost them than the third-degree burns all over me or the blood pouring out of my skull.

'The Ferry' is a local term for the South Kessock area of Inverness, a deprived housing estate that is accessible to Inverness city centre via the ominous sounding 'Black Bridge'.

So I'm staying on the children's ward. It's decent; you get your own room, with a telly and a foldaway bed that your ma and da could stay on overnight. I think mine visited me once or twice, for an hour, maybe? I think I had the dressings changed on my burns more times than I saw that pair of roasters, if I'm honest.

—*That's awful, I'm so sorry it happened to you.*

—Ah, the past's the past. I'm over it now. The way I look at it now, it was a blessing in disguise, really.

—*Because it was how you met Zach Crystal?*

—Aye. You got a lot of the footballers coming into the children's ward, see? It's a closed ward with its own entrance and exit. The footballers and celebrities come there so those poor, pampered bairns don't have to see little infants full of tubes up in PICU, bless their little cotton socks.

I knew as much as I know about football then as I do now: fuck all. So when they said there was a 'very special guest' coming in to see us, I hoped it was someone decent. The nurses got all gooey and breathless, so I was thinking this couldn't be Cally Thistle's b-team goalkeeper this time. There was this mad tension in the air; everyone was scurrying round, talking too quick. I just had to lie there. Most exciting thing that was going on for me was getting my dressings changed.

Then in he comes. Through my door, with one of the nurses. Just like that. He's got his security with him and his aides. They all stand around the door as he comes towards me. He looks right in my eyes. Right, deep into my eyes, and he smiled. And … it was … The effect it had on me, just in that moment … Look, I get a lot of hate from cowardly people online when I say this but I don't give a fuck. He helped me. From that moment he helped heal me. Just by being there, just his presence. He had a magic about him. A subtle magic that not many people know about. You really had to spend time with him to feel it.

—*And you did, didn't you? You spent time with Zach Crystal?*

—It was like … we just had a connection from the first moment we met each other. There's something about him – he just understands young people. I think it was because he didn't get to be a teenager, you know? He was always on tour or practising his keyboard and singing. That's how he became the best, but he missed out on a lot of his life.

—*Tell me more about this connection the two of you had.*

—It's hard to explain it. He just … we just got on. He came, under his own steam. He didn't bring the press with him, nothing like that. He came to visit the children's ward of his own volition, just to try and help, to give something back. That's what people don't see; that's what the media don't understand. They're salty as fuck because he wouldn't tell them when he did stuff like that. He wouldn't do interviews with them, but he hung out with sick kids. If he had there would have been a circus.

Sasha's right. Zach Crystal's second and most successful album, Damage, *came out in 2007 and confirmed Crystal as one of the world's biggest pop superstars. Yet he visited children in hospitals and secure units. There was never any rhyme or reason to when he would do this, no forewarning, and he often disguised himself behind large sunglasses and hats, arriving in normal-looking cars or taxis. He did it in the various countries his tours took him to, and he often visited the local hospitals near his home in Colliecrith National Park. By the end of his visits, crowds of media and fans would fill the car parks and his security team would have to hustle Crystal out into a waiting limo.*

—Imagine, I didn't really know who he was. It took a few minutes of him talking to me until I realised. I remember a nurse stood there, staring at him like a lost puppy, like she couldn't bear that he was talking to me and I didn't know who the guy was.

Crystal told Sasha he would return later that night, when there would only be ward staff on duty. He was good to his word and returned, dressed in disguise, wearing a baseball cap, tracksuit and sunglasses. Sasha explained that she and Zach Crystal talked late into the night, him sitting on the end of her bed. He returned a few times a week after that. Sasha tells me the ward was short staffed as a stomach bug was going around, so there were only two nurses on duty. No one noticed Crystal coming in and out of Sasha's room.

—Folk don't believe it happened. Like I say, I wasn't sure who he was really at first and he found that funny. He gave me a present that first night – an iPod classic, filled with his music. He told me not to tell anyone else. I've still got it. His visits were the things I looked forward to more than anything. When he was there, I never thought about my burns. They didn't hurt as much. I swear I healed quicker – and that's what the nurses said too. They called the consultant in and he couldn't believe it.

Crystal's visits to kids like Sasha would last hours. He focused in particular on the ones with the most troubled back stories, often young girls in their pre- or early teens who were orphaned or vulnerable. Afterwards, they always said they felt better. They all reported an instant rapport; it felt to them that Crystal understood them, despite being more than twice their age.

—*What did you two talk about? How did you both connect so easily?*

—It's hard to explain really. He just knew how to talk to me. He didn't ask stupid questions about school, you know? He wasn't patronising.

—*Am I right in thinking you were actually invited to spend time in Crystal Forest?*

—As soon as I was better, yes. It was all kept quiet. It was all very low key, not like now, when people can't give to a fucking charity without taking a photo of themselves doing it.

—*What about your mother and father?*

—He helped them too, or he tried. He paid for them to go to rehab. I tried to tell him those two were a lost cause, but he didn't give up. He didn't give up on people, Zach Crystal. When social services couldn't be bothered to attend meetings – no, sorry, I mean when the fucking government didn't fund social services properly to help people like me, Zach Crystal did. But he didn't make a show out of it. If anything, he kept it to himself. That's how you know he really cared.

—*So the three of you stayed in Crystal Forest? That's amazing. There are millions across the world who would give anything to do that. I must say though, Sasha, you've been fairly tight-lipped about your experiences. I'm sure there are newspapers who would pay ridiculous money for an exclusive with you.*

—Aye, I'm sure they would. I'm sure they'd pay me and then twist my words into a condemnation of Zach. I'm not having that, I'm just not. I've talked about it a bit on *Crystal-Cast*, and I'll tell you what's already out there, but the press can go fuck themselves, basically. I'm not about money.

Sasha's position has always been consistent. Like many Zach Crystal fans, she believes the mainstream media have, and always have had, an agenda against her idol. Sasha's been even more guarded since Crystal's death, save to point out what she calls 'the truth' about Crystal's accusers. So it feels like I have a world exclusive when Sasha decides it's time to reveal a little more about her stay at her idol's home.

—Crystal Forest was amazing. It was a magical place. Everything you've heard about it was true. You had to drive for miles along winding roads, through the Highlands. When you saw the forest, it just blew you away; just this huge expanse of yellow aspen. There were little clusters of pine and fir, so it looks dappled, like sunlight or something. It was a ray of sunlight through the mountains.

—*Crystal Forest was notoriously hard to find though, wasn't it?*

—You had to drive there in a big fuck-off jeep if you wanted to find it. There was security all over, too. Cameras, fences, guards. But you could only see the fences if you know where to look. It was like an army base or something.

—*Why do you think that was?*

—The driver told us that there were motion sensors all over, because of the fans. There were guard posts every few miles, all because people were constantly trying to get in.

—*Even in such a remote place?*

—That's what he said. They were always sending folk home.

—There were two Zach Crystal fans who found their way into Crystal Forest but never came out, weren't there? Lulu Copeland and Jessica Morton, in 2007. They never made it home.

—That's right. They didn't. And whose fault was that? Zach Crystal's?

—Sasha, have you seen the video that was released online? The one supposedly from one of the girls' phones.

—Yep.

—And what do you think?

At this point, a look of sincerity seems to come over Sasha; for a few seconds, her spines are withdrawn.

—Aye, it's not nice is it? It's not great. Those two were just fans; it wasn't their fault. I don't think it's real, mind you, that video.

—Why do you say that?

—For me … well … it smacks of someone with an agenda. Like someone's made it and put it out there for a reason.

—Why now?

—Again, Zach's dead isn't he? He can't defend himself. Not that what happened to them has anything to do with him.

—What makes you think so?

—You see … up at Crystal Forest, Zach sometimes took a select few and went out into the forest with them.

—Really? Why?

—It's … it's hard to explain when you're not there and … If I go on, my words'll get twisted. It's not worth it. It really isn't.

Sasha will not go any further than this. Whatever reason it was that Zach Crystal and his teenage companions were walking in the forest, is unfortunately left to speculation. For now at least. I decide to go for a different angle.

—It looks to me in that video that there's something strange happening in Crystal Forest, something 'other' – lights, like eyes…

—Look, I didn't make it, I had nothing to do with it. So I

don't know, OK? I don't have any answers. Can we move on? Please?

—*Sure, sure. What was it like inside Crystal Forest, in the house, I mean?*

—Like I say, magical. It was true luxury. We stayed in the guest suite in the main house. It was like something out of a fairy tale, all those black beams and stuff, and loads of ivy climbing all over it, loads of flowers and trees.

—*And you stayed in the tree house?*

—Yep.

—*Just you, not your parents?*

—Yep.

—*With Zach Crystal?*

—Yep.

—*Can you help me understand your experiences in there?*

Sasha is extremely guarded around this subject. She has repeatedly mentioned on her podcast that she stayed overnight with Crystal, in the tree house overlooking the mansion. She has maintained the innocence of the whole situation and is wary of anyone trying to say otherwise.

—It was like something out of *Harry Potter* or *Lord of the Rings*. The trees grew *through* it; it was like a living house, all made of wood, with fairy lights all over. It was the most beautiful place I'd ever been. You just forgot about everything in there, all your problems, like you were somewhere magical.

—*What did you do in there? Just hang out?*

—Yeah. We hung out. We just ate crisps, watched horror movies. Chatted. It was just … normal, just nice, you know. When you were with Zach, it was like hanging out with a friend.

—*You were twelve, he was in his thirties…*

—And what? That's the thing – he didn't seem like an adult. He just seemed young, innocent. We did a lot of giggling; it was just like hanging out with another young person. He didn't see age like the mainstream press and society do – to him it didn't matter, it was about *people.*

When you were with him, he just had time for you, nothing

was a problem. You got what you wanted, food, drinks, whatever. That's all there is to say about it. That's all I'm going to tell you about it. I'm not hiding anything – that's what it was. He talked with me. It was like therapy, I suppose, just long chats – me and him. It was good for me. I felt treated, I felt *valued*. It benefitted my mental health.

—Zach Crystal did all this with you personally? Not through his people?

—He helped us. As much as he could. He tried with my ma and da, but he helped me. It helped me so much. Look where I am now. I've my own place, I'm healthy, I'm not a junkie. That 'therapy', if you want to call it that, helped me uncover so much about my past, stuff that I'd buried and repressed.

—Do you mind me asking what sort of stuff…?

—Just stuff that without having Zach, I would have just kept somewhere inside, in a box, never looked at. Never processed. Without it I'd be just like my ma and da are.

—Do you still see your parents?

—Fuck no. After Zach helped me, I uncovered a lot of shit they'd done in the past. Abuse. Neglect. All that stuff gets buried; your brain tries to cover it all up, to protect you. But Zach's therapy taught me you've got to look at these things.

—You've got to face your monsters.

At this, Sasha pauses and looks at me. Her stare is long, unblinking – it's actually rather spooky. I hastily think back, wonder if I've said something wrong. I'm about to apologise, but Sasha shakes her head and speaks.

—That's it. That's exactly it. Without what Zach did for me, I'd have never been able to do that.

—I'm really glad that it was so beneficial for you, that those … um … demons from your past were eventually purged.

—Me too, believe me. I'm doing well for myself now and it's all down to Zach.

This is certainly evidenced in Sasha's setup. From what I can see, her flat is spacious, clean, even luxurious, and her recording equipment for her podcast is top of the line. Her income, she tells me, comes from lucrative advertising she attracts for Crystal-Cast. *However, she tells me that Crystal never contacted her again after her stay at Crystal Forest, despite her reaching out to him a few times in the ensuing years.*

Sasha is reluctant to say any more about her personal experiences with Crystal. She's overwhelmingly positive and insists that Crystal was a gentleman at all times and that the allegations against him are simply people taking advantage now he's dead.

—When someone is as big as Zach Crystal, you see, there's always going to be people who smell money, like those girls. Honestly, I was there when girls like that came to Crystal Forest. They were awful.

—*Are these the same women who are speaking up?*

—I don't know – some of them, probably. But they were the same. So many of them just took the piss when they were at Crystal Forest.

—*How do you mean?*

—They caused havoc. They were hooligans, some of them. That's what the media manages to forget to report half the time. Some of these lasses from the homes or whatever, they ran amok up at Crystal Forest – demanded food, money, everything, trashed the place. You should have heard how they spoke to the staff. They used to just set the fire alarm off constantly, just to make everyone have to clear out. They thought it was funny. Zach Crystal had such a good heart, and people like them, they just wanted to take advantage and get something from him.

—*Like Ian Julius?*

—Precisely. People like him. There's others too. People who like to use Zach's name to elevate themselves, try and make themselves more relevant. There's always some maniac on YouTube popping up with some half-arsed theory or some deranged accusations about Zach. I do my best here to shut that sort of shit down. I go after these people, destroy them with facts and reason. They can never come back from that.

This is a rather tame way to describe some of the more vicious online pile-ons that happen to those who dare to speak out against Zach Crystal. I'm not in any way accusing Sasha here, but there have been a few Crystal detractors who have been doxxed, one famously even swatted for airing their views on Zach Crystal. Sasha shrugs at this, she says people get what they deserve.

—Someone has to speak up when he can't. Ian Julius deserves to be where he is. He's another one who just wants his name out there. Just like all the others, he wants to profit off Zach Crystal. It's always about money when anyone has a go at Zach. Money first, ethics later.

—Does Ian Julius deserve what's happening to him now?

—He's getting attention, isn't he? I imagine he'll be getting paid to tell his story. I thought that's what he wanted … or am I wrong? Zach Crystal isn't the bad guy here – can we just remember that? It's not just me Zach Crystal has helped along the way.

This is certainly true. Crystal did similar things, under the radar, for a great many young people. He would give huge donations to residential homes for young people with difficult backgrounds, and he always did these things on the downlow, the media always one step behind.

—You've said that Zach Crystal worked with these damaged young women as a way to help repair his own damage. Can you talk a little bit about that damage?

—I mean, it's the stuff everyone knows, really. Zach grew up in a rough place; the Hopesprings Estate in England. It was a fucking ghetto. He managed to get himself out of there because he was talented; he had a natural talent for music and that's what got him out. But it was hard for him. He could never be a normal kid, he never got to be a teenager. When he was the same age as the kids he was helping, he was practising and recording and playing gigs. That leaves you with damage.

—I've heard that Zach Crystal was rather ruthless. Didn't he drop his own sister from his act when they began to get famous?

I know how inflammatory this may be, and I prepare for Sasha's fury. However she doesn't rise to it, only shakes her head.

—It's funny how someone like, I dunno, Elon Music, Richard Branson – someone like that – gets rich, and they're applauded for it. Really, can you think of anything these people actually did that benefitted the world? Except being good at business and making money for themselves? That's all they were good at – making ruthless decisions. There's no one out there who's rich who's done it through being nice to everyone all the time. But when someone like Zach does it, someone who has gifted the world with his music, who has actually helped people, he's the bad guy? It's fucking crazy how that works. Right?

Yeah, so Zach made a tough decision, he wanted to strike out on his own. See where it got him – see where he is now because he made a tough decision. I don't see Naomi Crystal being overly concerned, do you? She and her kid lived in a mansion of her own in LA, for fuck's sake! She never had to work a job. Her daughter went to all the best schools, had every opportunity money could buy. He gave her everything. I don't see her complaining, do you? She was right there when he vanished wasn't she?

—To play devil's advocate again, Sasha, one of the big questions people ask is why it was always girls that Zach focused his efforts on. Why not the elderly or boys?

—Oh my God, I've heard that one so many times. It's like this: if I give some money to … I dunno, let's say a donkey sanctuary, you could then ask me, but what about the bird sanctuary? What about the starving-kids charity? Why didn't you give your money to something else? It's exactly the same thing with Zach. He chose to do what he did because he thought he was doing a good thing. He was doing a good thing, people! I honestly don't understand how people can sit back and criticise a man giving his own time and money to a good cause.

—Of course, two of Zach Crystal's accusers, Zofia Kowalski and Jennifer Rossi, were both in residential care when they were invited to Crystal Forest, where they allege the abuse occurred. I'm not allowed to speak too much about their particular cases but I wonder what your views are?

—I mean, yeah. They were in homes. I mean, the fact that they were in the care system wasn't good for them. They were desperate girls, weren't they? The problem is, because of their background, everyone felt sorry for them. People thought butter wouldn't melt, right? These two, like the others, were out for money, but you can't say that, can you? Because of their circumstances. You can't say that those two might have been manipulators. They might have – shock horror – actually just made things up. But, oh no, you can't possible say that, right? Thing is, I've been there. I've had it rough as fuck, but it doesn't give me a right to be an arsehole does it?

It is only recently that the voices of Zofia Kowalski and Jennifer Rossi have been widely heard. They both claim, like Sasha, to have spent time at Crystal Forest when they were between twelve and fourteen years old. They both claim that after Crystal provided them with luxury accommodation in Crystal Forest, he coerced them into 'sexual acts' with him.

—There's also something that the mainstream media tend to leave out when reporting on those girls.

—*What's that?*

—Just a trifle really. Just the fact that both of them had been moved from their care homes several times for their behaviour. I mean just little things, you know? Just assaulting staff, stealing from other residents and … oh yes, surprise, surprise – making accusations against members of staff that were subsequently proved false.

At this, Sasha's eyes seem to get even wider, her mouth turning into a thin, defiant line. These details were part of Sasha's episode about the victims on Crystal-Cast. *It's a tough watch: Sasha shares scans of internal faxes and official documents from two residential homes in the UK, with their details covered up. I don't feel comfortable with giving out the finer detail as I have no way of proving the authenticity of these documents so I'm going to allow Sasha to summarise.*

—OK, first of all, let's look at Zofia Kowalski. She was, what, thirteen in 2008, right? By the time the girl was barely a teenager, she'd had three failed adoptions. *Three*. And these weren't the fault of those parents, believe me. These were some of the nicest people, specifically trained and ready to take on some of the most challenging children. They were no match for Zofia. Put it that way.

—*What is Zofia alleged to have done while she was with these families who wanted to adopt her?*

—OK, so let's take the Williamsons for a second. They were good, Christian people who'd already adopted two children, so it wasn't as if they didn't know what they were doing, right? Within a month, Zofia had assaulted both the other children, stolen money from Mrs Williamson's purse, which she'd spent on drugs, I may add. When she was challenged, she proceeded to accuse Mr Williamson of assaulting *her*. I know, right? Remember, these were kind, loving people. All they wanted to do was provide a home for Zofia. The next couple were the McCabes. Mr McCabe was getting over cancer, for fuck's sake, when Zofia accused him of rape. Why you may ask? Oh, just because the McCabes had actually put some rules, some fucking structure, in Zofia's life.

—*How do you mean?*

—I mean like they asked her to be home at certain times, to not hang around the local park, fighting, drinking and smoking weed, that sort of thing. Pretty horrible parents, right? How on earth did Zofia cope? I'll tell you: she broke Mrs McCabe's nose and accused her husband. Not both in the same day, but I mean, c'mon.

—*From what you've shown me, the picture was similar in her residential home.*

—Homes, plural. Zofia was moved twice. Once for violence, and if you look here, this was the protocol that had to be introduced for her in her second residential home – no member of staff to ever be alone with Zofia at any time; open-door policies in communal areas; Zofia to be supervised. It goes on and on. And this is the person we're supposed to believe was 'attacked' by millionaire celebrity, Zach Crystal.

—*And Jennifer Rossi?*

—Oh this one was slightly different but only in that, where Zofia liked to fight, Jennifer liked to … well, let's have a little look at her incident reports shall we?

The reports that Sasha shows me are alleged summaries of Jennifer Rossi's behaviour in one of her residential homes. Each incident is dated and co-signed by two members of staff. There are pages and pages of these reports. Sasha flicks through them, shaking her head.

—So these behaviour logs are for the lovely Jennifer Rossi who was, let's see, twelve at the time she accused Zach Crystal of molesting her after he invited her and her key workers to come to stay at Crystal Forest, all expenses paid.

So here we go: June, 2005 is a good place to start. Jennifer absconds from her bedroom all night; police called. Found at a 'party' in a local drug dealer's house, average age of attendees at the party – mid to late twenties. All men. Lovely.

And you know, Scott, that's just the tip of the iceberg with little Jenny Rossi. Her notes also talk about her having a 'boyfriend of considerably older age', who she would sneak out and go to see pretty much every night. Here's some police-incident forms from when she had to be brought back, drunk, to the residential home. One, three, loads, too many to count. These were only the ones that the police reported. The other times are all in her behaviour logs.

The boyfriend situation was constant too. Not just that one, there were many, *many*. All of them older – significantly older.

—It seems both had their own issues to deal with. Do you know, Sasha, if either Zofia or Jennifer said anything about Zach Crystal at the time? I mean, did they raise the issue back then?

—Well, that's it isn't it? Seems weird that neither of them mention Zach Crystal at the time, but then years later, when he's dead, they accuse Zach of assaulting them.

See, that's the clever thing about those two. Back then, when they were both underage, apparently vulnerable girls, it would have been the perfect time to accuse Zach of something, right? Not now they're both fatter and older, and up to their eyeballs in debt to drug dealers, right? Now, look what happens when #metoo came along, when suddenly you're not allowed to question anyone, when whoever wants to make any spurious claim about anyone else is automatically believed. Up pop two known liars, Zofia Kowalski and Jennifer Rossi, to suddenly start accusing multi-millionaire Zach Crystal when he's been gone for the last couple of years. Pretty convenient, don't you think?

—Some may argue that the #metoo movement suddenly gave voice to those who felt like they couldn't speak up for themselves. It was a show of solidarity.

—You could think about it like that, yeah. I mean, I'm not saying all women are lying, of course I'm not. I'm saying that there were certain people who were exploiting it for their own ends.

—Jennifer and Zofia?

—Right. Making an absolute mockery of the women who were actually assaulted. But of course, you're not allowed to question them. This is the problem with the media and its reporting on Zach. They failed to mention so many things because it wouldn't have matched this great big evil portrait they were painting of Zach.

—What things?

—Everything I've just been saying. The background of those two girls, the fact that their 'assaults' only magically materialised after therapy.

—Therapy provided by Crystal?

—Um. No. From other therapists who were just after money as well. Obviously. Isn't it amazing that their allegations against Zach only came out during a movement where no one was morally allowed to question them, and that both were proven liars and troublemakers?

It's funny how they don't mention all the other girls who spent time with Zach Crystal and nothing untoward happened. It's funny that these people don't get mentioned at all. But that's the mainstream media for you.

—Have you ever been approached to give your side of the story anywhere other than your own show?

—Yes. I actually have. There was a morning television show that invited me on not long ago, just when all the accusations were springing up. I'll not say which show it was, but they gave me a research call, just to get a gist of what I was going to talk about. Imagine my shock when I get another call, not long after, telling me that they're sorry, but I'm not quite right for the angle of the show right now. What a joke. All I was doing was giving them facts about Zach Crystal, facts about the accusers. I didn't even give them my opinion, which is what they wanted. They were scared shitless. That's what it was – they couldn't bear to have the facts up in front of them like that.

—There's the other three accusers as well: Sammy Williams, Mary Wooton and Gabrielle Martinez.

—I could tell you all about them as well. They weren't all in care. They had slightly different circumstances. Yet they all had the same thing in common – the thing that the mainstream media don't like people knowing. All these women had a past, you see. All of them. There wasn't a single one who, really, you could say was an upstanding citizen. Drink, drugs, shoplifting, vandalism, assault, even soliciting for sex. It's all there, in their pasts, these black marks that, try as they might, they can't scrub clean. Just like Ian Julius, just like everyone who tries or has tried to exploit Zach Crystal for money. Isn't it weird that there's no one who's just innocent. No one who's been good in their life has accused him of anything. No one who's just a normal, law-abiding citizen has jack shit to say against Zach Crystal.

Pretty weird, don't you think?

The pasts of Zach Crystal's victims were noticed by more than Sasha Stewart. A few tabloids ran stories about the darker shades of the lives of those who accused Zach Crystal of sexual assault. These stories were not front-page news, though. Crystal's return, the announcement of a new album and tour, eclipsed them completely. Now, the voices of these people are starting to get louder once again.

—Why is it important to you to make sure these people are shut down?

—It's important to provide balance. The media simply doesn't like to do this. It's up to people like me to defend Zach now he's gone. He helped me and so I'm giving something back. That's how that works, see?

—We're coming to the end of our chat, Sasha, and I want to thank you for allowing me to speak to you about Zach.

—It's been good, Scott. To be fair, you've allowed me to speak, you've allowed me to be able to get the truth out there about Zach and about the people who are trying to cancel a dead man. Amazing, isn't it, that all these things come to light after the guy is dead?

—*To you, Zach Crystal is innocent, of everything.*

—Everything. It makes sense. It makes total sense. Look, these days, the media are frightened to dispute claims by women against high-profile individuals. What happened to innocent until proven guilty? From where I'm standing, no one has proved anything yet. All I've seen is people trying to get money from the estate of a dead man.

—*I want to talk about Zach Crystal's death, if that's OK with you? I know it's a hard subject. Especially for someone for whom he did so much good.*

—It's OK. I think it's good to discuss it, to be honest. That's what I learned from Zach, from the therapy we did together – that you need to be able to talk about these sorts of things.

—*There are many theories about the fire at Crystal Forest. Do you believe he did it? That his death was suicide?*

—It's really hard, because I think when Zach Crystal returned, he wasn't ready. Not quite. His best friend had died. I met James Cryer when I was at Crystal Forest, you know? He was always there when Zach was away at a meeting or a rehearsal or whatever. There was nothing that was too much for him. He was a fan as well, you know? He'd known Zach back in the day, back from Barlheath, where he grew up. They had a synergy, those two, and I think when James was found dead in the forest Zach found it hard to come back from that. I think that's why he'd been gone for so long.

—*Where do you think he went?*

—I think he was searching.

—*Searching for what? Something inside himself, something spiritual?*

—If you watch that interview he did on *Ruby*, when he returned, she asks him the same thing and he says he was preparing for the new album, the tour, but he also says something interesting – he says he was 'searching for answers'. He says he was 'searching for ways I could help people better'. I think that's beautiful, don't you? That's the thing about Zach – everything he did was always for others, never himself. I won't pretend I know where he went, but I know that when he came back, he was full of new life. The whole thing was ruined by Ian Julius and the rest of them. Zach's return was spoiled by the actions of a petty, jealous man and five women who wanted money. It's just so obvious to anyone who can see it. The problem is people don't want to see it. That's the issue here – people want to see Zach in a certain way. I think – and it's hard for me to say this but many of us in the Zach Crystal fans community believe it – we think Zach took his own life because he understood what he was about to face and he couldn't handle it. He wanted to help people and that lot had made sure he couldn't.

—You think the backlash would have been too much?

—I think the mainstream media were gearing up to take a side and it wasn't Zach's. That's how they work though, isn't it? If it bleeds, it leads.

—You're no fan of the media and the way you and other fans have been portrayed, right?

—It's so fucking lazy; we're cranks, we're crazy, just because we stan Zach Crystal, et cetera. But look online – look at the Zach Crystal community and see how many people saw things in the weeks leading up to the fire. So many of us saw it. I certainly did. After I'd been in Crystal Forest, my mind was more … open.

—Really? What was it you saw?

—I hadn't seen it for years, not since I was twelve. But that's not important. Let's move on, shall we?

—Can you tell me a bit more about what you mean by 'saw something'?

—Look, it's not just me, OK? It's not just me. That's another thing that talking to Zach helped me understand. He helped a lot of us understand that there are … things … out there…

I begin to open my mouth but Sasha's face fills the screen, her eyes wide and teeth bared.

—You look. You look online. On the forums, on Twitter, all over. They're all there. Fans all over the world. They saw it too. In the weeks and months leading up to the fire, we all saw it, or something like it. You think I'm crazy, but it's not just me. That's why that video that came out was just so … I dunno. It wasn't right.

I've actually looked. r/ZachCrystal on Reddit is swamped with current discussions, but if you look back into the archives, there are indeed reports of sightings of something that is called a 'Frithghast'. All of these alleged sightings, however, are mentioned after *Zach Crystal's death. Searching the word on Twitter gets a few results, mainly to do with #folklorethursday or a Pokémon character with a similar name.*

I ask Sasha what it is – what is this 'thing' that everyone saw. She shakes her head, stares off into the middle distance.

—I can't speak for any of them, but I won't forget it in a hurry. I saw it before I hit my head. I saw it before the fire. I woke up for no good reason, in the middle of the night, and looked out of my bedroom window. There it was, stood there in the street. If I see it again … well, I know my time's up.

—*Can you describe what you saw?*

—It was like an animal … a horse or a deer, something long-necked but with horns on its head. It was all rotted away, like a skeleton. Maybe it was a dream, a nightmare? I don't think so though; it felt *real*. I was scared, I turned away, didn't dare look again. All I can see in my head is that thing looking up at me with that animal skull for a head. I still shiver when I think about it. I've got goose bumps now. The worst thing about it was that it gave me this *feeling* in my bones, like a black cloud, like I knew something bad was going to happen to me cos I saw it. The next day was the day I took a tumble in the kitchen. Somewhere inside me I was almost relieved. That's fucked up, right? When I was in the hospital, Zach was the only one I felt comfortable telling about it. I dunno why. I have no idea. It just seemed right. I still wasn't quite sure who he was, remember. But I told him and I expected him to laugh or tell me it was a dream or the usual shite that adults say.

But he didn't. He looked shocked. He looked scared. He said he understood. He said he and I needed to talk, just the two of us. I remember he whispered it. Zach told me he saw it too, when he was my age. It was the same – an animal, like a shadow. It always appeared, he said, the day before something bad happened. I bet he saw it before his parents died in 2009, before his friend died a few years back, and I bet you any money, he saw it before Ian Julius ruined his life.

He called it a Frithghast.

I want to break away from Sasha's rather incredible account for a moment to address what she's just described. The Frithghast is an entity almost exclusive to the Scottish Highlands, but very little is known about it. From the limited information I can find, the Frithghast is similar, in essence, to the black dog motif, which is common in folklore around the UK. Most commonly, sighting this ghostly black creature with pale, glowing eyes is an omen of death or grave misfortune. It is sometimes thought of as a shape-shifter. More recently, the figure was appropriated by JK Rowling in the Harry Potter series, and known as a 'grim'. Scotland has its own black-dog legends: the Muckle Black Tyke is thought to be the devil himself in canine form.

This black, half-rotted deer or stag seems to be connected solely to Colliecrith National Park. The Cairngorm mountains have their own spectre, known as Am Fear Liath Mòr, who haunts the summit of Ben MacDhui, but has largely been attributed to a phenomena known as a 'broken bow', when a person's shadow is cast upon and magnified by clouds opposite the sun.

The Frithghast was reported as far back as the 1800s, mainly by game hunters, and was consequently presumed to be a deterrent manufactured by an eccentric English landowner to scare poachers from entering the vast aspen forest of Colliecrith.

'I saw a terrible thing emerging from its cursed lair,' reported Lord Percy Bikerstaffe in 1873. 'Not a sound did it make and all that I heard was the whisper of the wind through the leaves, as if in some merciless mirth at the fright that filled me.'

When pressed, Bickerstaffe, rumoured to be an occultist, among many other things, remarked, 'I fear I have awoken some ancient spirit, laid to sleep by some forest wych long in the past. For it followed me, that awful ghast, for miles, always drifting like fog between the trees, though the very light of hell that glowed through that empty skull did not leave my heart when night fell.'

Bickerstaffe is said to have vanished in the same forest, but his antics and death are widely attributed by scholars to untreated syphilis.

It appears that the legend of the Frithghast was born a long time before Bickerstaffe claims to have seen it. It was predominantly used as a cautionary tale to keep children from wandering in the treacherous ancient woodlands of Colliecrith.

There's no question, however, that Sasha believes what she saw, and who am I to dispute it? I don't feel like there's much point in arguing about these types of details. Sasha has been good enough to speak with me candidly and I want to leave the interview on a positive note.

—It's hard for people who aren't true Zach Crystal fans to really understand some of the nuances.

I think I do. I think I understand that for people like Sasha, there was more to Zach Crystal than a man who made music. I think that for Sasha, Zach Crystal was a symbol of her redemption, of her break with her past. Zach Crystal was there for Sasha when her parents were not, like he was there for a great many young people. It's definitely hard to make this measure up with some of the accusations levelled against the star.

Sasha claims to be someone who has actually spent time at Crystal Forest, and to an extent, was exposed to Crystal personally. I'm interested in what she mentioned about certain 'chosen' girls accompanying Crystal into the forest itself. Why did he do this? Did it have anything to do with this mysterious Frithghast?

I now wonder, with Zach Crystal being gone, how long Sasha will stick to her assurance that she won't eventually sell her story to the press.

I believe Sasha when she says nothing untoward happened between her and Crystal when she was twelve. That doesn't mean, however, that nothing happened with other girls.

I think speaking to Sasha has provided some balance in our investigation into the case of Zach Crystal. Fans of Crystal are dedicated to their cause and defensive of their hero in the wake of the allegations that are springing up around him like weeds. I feel a degree of sympathy for them because, as I've said before, no one but Zach Crystal is able to confirm the truth.

Unfortunately, due to legal issues concerning their case against the Crystal estate, the five women who we've discussed have all respectfully declined to speak to me. They say they don't want to do anything that could jeopardise their case against Crystal. This I understand.

I think that there will be some who are unhappy about Sasha Stewart's appearance in this series, but I believe it is important to include her. If Ian Julius gets his say, then so does Sasha. Both claim to have had personal experiences of the star and both are on the opposite ends of the spectrum of opinion about him. Where Ian Julius believes Crystal to be a predator, Sasha Stewart believes him innocent of all charges.

There is much to be explored in between.

Next, we need to try and get closer to the inner circle of Zach Crystal. I want to speak to someone who has more of an experience than an opinion. This is the way I believe we'll get closer to the facts.

In the next episode, that's exactly what we're going to do. I put out some feelers and, of course, asked the Crystal estate for comment. They have, so far, ignored my request.

The person who replied, however, comes as somewhat of a surprise. Like everyone else on Six Stories, *I've not paid anyone anything and I'm not here to push an agenda. My next interviewee told me that's why he was willing to talk.*

He's also not afraid of any negative press, social-media attention or anything else that could potentially come his way after talking about Zach Crystal.

You'll understand why in episode three.

Until next time…

RUBY

Episode 246: Zach Crystal

Legendary Presenter Ruby Rendall's exclusive interview with pop megastar Zach Crystal. ***More >***

---

1 hr 45 • 9pm 20th Jul 2019 • Available for 28 days

RR: Welcome back and I tell you what, I'm going to get my husband to get straight into the garden to build me my own tree house.

[Laughter]

RR: Oh I'm serious! I want my own.

ZC: A Ruby Forest?

RR: [*laughing]* That's right, we're both precious stones.

ZC: *[giggling]* You're worth more than me though. Rubies are pretty, crystals are…

['Gorgeous!' is shouted by an audience member.]

ZC: Thank you. You're all the best.

[Cheering]

RR: Zach, it's clear that the world is so happy you've returned … after more than a *year*, Zach. We were worried.

[Cheering]

RR: We really were. We were scared.

ZC: *[blushing, shaking his head]* I know, I know. I'm sorry, I'm so sorry.

RR: We've come to the question you knew I was going to have to ask you. It's the biggie, the one everyone wants to know.

ZC: I'm ready, Ruby.

[Laughter]

RR: You disappeared in the spring of 2018. It was after a concert, would I be right in saying that? A concert that was marred by tragedy.

ZC: That's right, yes, in Hyde Park, part of the Lazy Dayz benefit festival.

RR: You were headlining that event. It was for charity as well, and that's what made it all the more tragic.

ZC: That's right – a charity very close to my heart, helping homeless young people.

RR: Just to explain, in case there are those who are unaware: Lazy Dayz was an all-day event with many other acts performing, culminating with you as the last act of the day.

ZC: What's terrible about the whole thing is that we were going to finish the show with everyone up on stage, singing 'World in Our Hands'.

RR: You had cowritten the song with Ed Sheeran, among others. That's right, isn't it?

ZC: Ruby, it was an honour to work with those musicians. It got to number one and stayed there and did so much good.

RR: But you, tragically, never got to perform it.

ZC: That's right, Ruby. It was an awful, awful thing.

RR: Sadly, there was a terrible accident, an explosion in the lighting rig, and two of the technicians -– Peter Williamson and Gavin Jermaine – fell to their deaths.

ZC: We were all devastated. It was right that our set didn't go ahead that night. My love goes out to those two men's beautiful families. I just wish I could have done something.

RR: And Zach, this wasn't that long after the tragic accident back at Crystal Forest, involving your friend and aide. It feels like all these things happened very quickly. That must have been hard. Did this go some way to explain why you decided to disappear?

ZC: It … Yes and no. It wasn't so much the events themselves, but more about my own guilt. When I was away, I told no one where I was going, not even my own family. I was searching for answers to it all. I wanted to return better equipped, you see. I was searching for ways I could help people better.

RR: It seems to me like you were carrying a great deal of guilt. Neither of these events were your fault…

ZC: Not the events themselves, but I should have been … been more aware, been more mindful of what was going to happen. I think when you grow up very religiously, in a religious environment, you end up with a lot of guilt. I felt guilty for not doing anything to stop what happened.

RR: Are you saying you should have been able to maybe predict or prevent those tragedies?

ZC: I'm saying I should have been more open to the signs of what was to come.

RR: Signs?

[The studio lights flicker on and off.]

RR: Oh! I must apologise, a few gremlins in the—

[The shrieks in the audience begin up again. There is a scuffle as a few members of security pass behind Ruby and Zach.]

RR: I hope everyone's … OK…

[There are a few stuttering shots of the audience. A few people are involuntarily twitching in their seats and letting out little screams. Security and studio staff are trying to quell the noise.]

RR: …Anyway … er … yes, I understand how hard all this must have been for you and I imagine it's difficult for you to talk about it now.

ZC: It's good to talk about things, Ruby. That's something I've learned in my life, that it's good to talk things out, rather than keep them bottled inside. If more people talked, more people would listen and the world would be a better, more understanding place.

RR: That's beautiful. Such a beautiful thought, and I hope, after this, that people do talk more.

ZC: I hope so too, I really do. Please…

[Zach turns to the audience and raises both hands. The noise and commotion stops instantly.]

RR: There's something that is being talked about among your fan base – something I'm not quite sure I understand properly. I wonder if you'd be able to help me?

ZC: Help you understand?

RR: Please. I think it links to what you were saying before about this idea of guilt, of foresight and culpability. You see, many of your fans say that there's something they see before bad things happen to them. You're nodding, this isn't new to you?

ZC: I think a lot of my fans are opening their minds. You see, when you're a kid, a little kid, your mind is totally open. You see everything that's there, regardless of whether anyone else believes in it. Why do you think so many kids see fairies? Why do so many kids have imaginary friends? It's only when you grow up that you're conditioned into thinking otherwise; you're *told* that magic doesn't exist.

RR: Are you saying it does?

ZC: I'm saying it could.

RR: So this ghost that people say they're seeing, this Frithghast creature, you actually allude to it in one of your songs – 'Dead Eyes' from your *Damage* album – 'A shadow from the forest of your heart, the future told, in part…'

ZC: *[singing] 'The past's a dream, our paths are all foreseen…'*

[The shrieking begins again. It's much louder now and seems to be dotted all over the audience.]

ZC: Some people say that, yes. Some people think it's about something else. It can be about what you want it to be.

RR: For a lot of your fans, it's about this thing many of them claim to have seen before bad things happen.

ZC: Like I said, maybe they're finding it's a little easier to open their minds. If my music does that for them, that can only be a good thing.

RR: In the video, which we're going to watch in a moment, you're running through the forest, pursued by shadowy creatures – half skeletons. It's all rather creepy.

[Despite the increasing noise from the audience, Zach presses on, drawing his chair closer to Ruby's.]

ZC: Oh yes … that's what I wanted. I wanted it to be scary. Like I say, the song can mean a great many things on a great many levels. It can be about the darkness of the past, the hope of the future, escaping from the scary things that hold you to a place.

RR: And what about you? What is that song about to you?

ZC: My songs are very personal to me – they're like little parts of myself I give out to the fans, to the world. 'Dead Eyes' is all about escaping from the dark of the past into a better future. It's very metaphorical. But it's also about being open to things, accepting there are things we may not be able to explain out there, you know?

RR: Like this creature, this omen.

[The studio lights go off. There is a hiss from somewhere, and when the lights come back on, the camera is pointing at the audience. The majority of them are twitching and writhing in their seats.]

ZC: Right. These things – omens of ill fate – are in every culture, worldwide. You know in Korea they sell fans with timers on them.

RR: Fans as in…

ZC: Electric fans. In Korea, they say if you leave the fan on and shut the window overnight, it's certain death, so they have a timer to stop them. In Mexico, if your bed faces the door, that's sure to bring death too. These things have to come from somewhere, don't they? I talk to a great many of my fans who think they're alone in seeing strange things. I tell them they're not. I tell them they just have to speak to the right people – each other. The fans across the globe can come together and start something beautiful, a more compassionate world.

RR: Did you see something, perhaps, before these tragedies occurred in such swift succession? Is that why you felt so much guilt?

ZC: *[almost whispering]* Maybe it was … maybe it was…

[The screen goes blank for a couple of seconds before returning, and then going blank again]

Programme information – technical difficulties

We are currently experiencing some technical problems with our live broadcast. We are looking into these and hope to have the issues resolved soon.

[The screen comes back on with no sound and the image is pixelated. Some of Zach Crystal's entourage walk onto the set and touch up his makeup. Studio techs and members of the Crystal entourage speak to Ruby Rendall, who nods.]

RR: *[overly jolly, blushing]* Now, are we back? Yes, sorry. This is the issue sometimes with live TV. A few technical hitches. We're OK now though, yes. Yes. Zach Crystal, you are back. Back from another precipice, a dark place, as it were, and as we can see, your future is looking bright. The new album and, of course, the tour. *Forever*, you've called it.

ZC: That's right. 'Forever' is a defiant word, don't you think? It makes a statement. Here I am. I'm back. Forever now.

[Cheering]

RR: I'm so excited, I really am. These tickets will be gold dust when they go on sale, I'm sure. Now, as you can see, we've had a couple of hiccups, and while we get it all straightened out, we'll take a very short break, during which we'll watch the extended cut of Zach Crystal's song 'Dead Eyes'. Be sure to stay with us for more exclusive chat with Zach Crystal.

Episode 3: Secrets of The Whispering Wood

—It's an old story. Couldn't tell you how old, mind. My granny told it to me, her granny told it to her. I suppose it's stayed the same, but you know how these things go, eh? It's like any fairy tale, I suppose – told to stop me getting lost out there. All the best tales are the ones told to stop little ones getting lost. That's where the real fear is, isn't it? That's worse than any monster.

It starts off as these stories do, with a rich laird and a poor family. The laird of Colliecrith was a mean old soul, and he wouldn't part with a single rotten windfall from his forest floor without gold crossing his palm. His forest was his pride and joy; anyone who dared poach there was tortured to death in terrible ways. The laird's favourite way was to dress poachers up in deerskins and make them sport for his dogs.

The laird filled the forest with vicious wild animals – boar and wild cat – but he allowed no one to hunt them, instead letting them roam free. Those woods grew wild and dark, and folk were scared to go near.

The thing is, see, the forest of Colliecrith was a thoroughfare to Inverness from Stirling. You took it, or else you had to cross the Grampians. Let me tell you, folk were more likely to take their chances on the mountains than pass through Colliecrith, or as they knew it back then, the 'Whispering Wood'. Folk said there was something deep inside those dark woods, something ancient and evil, a living shadow that's breath was an icy wind. They said the sight of it turned the bark of the trees pale and made the leaves whisper in terror as it passed by. If you go into the Whispering Wood, folk said, that shadow would tell you things. It'd whisper its secrets to you, things about the past and the future, things you couldn't unhear. Things no human is supposed to know. The voice of the Whispering Wood, they said, could send you raving mad.

But there was a poor family who were travelling on foot from Stirling to Inverness to find work. They've got their wee girls with them, and their legs are too short to climb the mountains, but the family are too poor for horses. So they decide to take their chances in the Whispering Wood of Colliecrith. They know the story of the Whispering Wood – but they think they have no choice.

The man, so the story goes, he takes a fishing line and winds it around all their thumbs when they go to sleep so none of the family gets lost. He ties his line to the thin trunk of the first tree, and on they go, into the Whispering Wood. That way, he says, they'll not get lost.

They stuff their ears with cloth, the man, his wife and their wee girls, so as not to hear that terrible whisper that winds through those trees. They keep walking. Day after day after day they walk, and still the fishing line doesn't run out. It's alright, they think, we can't be lost, we can always find our way back out again.

The laird, though, knows that someone's in his woods. Who's to say how he knows, but he does, and he sends his hunters out to catch them and bring them to the sheriff at Cawdor to stand trial for poaching. He's had his men slay four buck and skin them, horns and all. A lust for blood, for vengeance, for punishment has possessed him.

But as the days go by, the laird's men can find no trace of the family, and the family themselves, they're lost. They can see no bird, nor beast, nor water, nor any path out of the wood ahead of them. Their supplies are running low. Not to worry, the man says, we can always follow the fishing line back out again. One more day, he says. We'll walk for one more day and if we still can't find the path, we'll go back.

What he doesn't know is that their youngest lassie has lost the little bits of cloth that plugged her ears, and she's been listening, she's had the shadow of that wood whispering in her ear all day, every day, all night every night. And what has she been doing when her da goes to sleep every night? She's been taking his knife – and that fishing line that'll save them if they get lost, that leads out of the wood, she's been cutting through it and retying it to any old tree. Why? Something's telling her to do it. Those shimmering leaves are whispering at her, that cold voice is burrowing into her mind.

On the last night, so the story goes, that wee one, the lassie, she waits till all her family is asleep and she cuts that fishing line once more and she ties it around their throats. Quiet as a cat she is, just the whisper of the wood in her ears.

The next morning, the laird's hunters find them, the poor family. They ride into a clearing where they see a sight so horrible they nearly flee there and then. The whole family, so the story goes, all dead and carved open from chin to chest. And the wee one, the lassie? She's eating them. She's eating their flesh, raw. She has this look about her, like something evil, like the very devil's looking out at them through her eyes.

The laird's hunters grab her and take the road from Colliecrith north to Cawdor Castle to see the sheriff and have her executed. The laird is furious; he wants his sport with his dogs. So he comes with them, bringing the deer skins to try and convince the sheriff to let him seek his own justice. On the way, the wee girl's like a demon, thrashing and growling. They have to tie her down to keep her quiet. The horses are terrified and the dogs won't go near her.

In front of the sheriff, though, she's like a lassie again, asking him where her ma and da have gone, where's her sister? And she's crying, just like she's normal. Then she walks over to that sheriff and she whispers in his ear. The sheriff takes pity on her, and orders the laird and his hunters to take her in. The laird and his men don't dare to tell him what's happened. They don't know what she's said in his ear but they know it's not her what's said it; they know it's the whisper of those woods in his ear, so they dare not speak up.

The laird and his men take the long road back south to Colliecrith and as soon as they get to the wood, the wee girl becomes savage again. The laird has had enough and he orders his men to hold her down and tie her into the buckskin and let her loose. That's what they do and off she runs, into the Whispering Wood, tied up in a deerskin with its head and antlers weighing her down.

The laird, in his bloodlust, sends his dogs after her and off they run into the Whispering Wood.

They wait and they wait and they wait, but there's no sound, no sight of the dogs. So the laird sends his men in to find her.

Hours go by and they don't come back either. It's just the laird left there on his own, by the Whispering Wood. Those men never come back and whether the laird hears what happens to them, or doesn't hear anything at all, he never tells. I wonder if he heard the same voice that the sheriff heard from that lassie's mouth…

The laird vowed never to set foot in there again, but it was too late. His life was forever tainted, cursed from that day on. Like a disease, the curse spread through his family too. Every death, every illness, every misfortune was preceded by a terrible sight in the Whispering Wood. A ragged shadow of a beast, a living skeleton that walks silently through those trees; a spectre known as a Frithghast.

Whatever it was in that forest, whatever that lassie became – all rotted away with horns and hooves, like an animal or something – well, it's certainly helped keep people away from there.

And it's one of the reasons I think he wanted it.

The forest I mean. It's why Mr Crystal wanted to buy it.

Welcome to Six Stories.

I'm Scott King.

Over this series we are attempting to pick apart a story unlike any other I've covered. The life and death of Zach Crystal is one that has no tangible beginning, middle or end. With every revelation about one of the world's biggest superstars comes more nuance. With every claim and counter-claim, comes a myriad of questions, conjecture and associated stories.

We have six of these stories on hand as we rake over this old grave.

We have charges about to be filed by at least five alleged victims of Crystal – five women who claim the late superstar assaulted them in the 1990s and are finally feeling brave enough to make their voices heard.

We have the disappearance and then re-emergence of the star and the claims that he was trawling the internet for underage girls.

And from the last episode, we have balance from someone who has spent time with Crystal and assured us his conduct was faultless. We've also heard about the charity work for the homeless and for vulnerable young people Crystal carried out.

Yet there's more to it than simply two opposing views, so much more. In these six episodes, we are probably only beginning to frame some of the fundamental questions we must start asking ourselves about fame and its influence.

But why here and why now?

The death of Zach Crystal has begged a plethora of questions. One of the most prominent is about what was going on behind the high fences and walls at Crystal Forest.

I think I need to mention again that in no way am I minimising the plight of those who are making allegations of abuse against Zach Crystal, nor am I an advocate for the star. But neither am I aiming to admonish Zach Crystal in some way, or decide on his guilt or innocence. I am looking for a different kind of conclusion. Or is it conclusions? I think I need to resolve how I feel about Crystal myself, and perhaps that will help many others who are conflicted about this figure.

I want answers for the side of me that, like many of you, revered Zach Crystal, for those of us who put his posters on our walls, let his lyrics seep into our awkward souls and gave them a voice. I want answers for those of us who now feel confused and betrayed.

The five victims of Crystal who have been prominent in the news recently have all given me their blessing, of sorts. I have been candid with them about my focus on this podcast and that I would deviate from my current course, should any of them have an issue with it.

So far we have talked to two people who claim to have had personal experiences with Zach Crystal himself. Ian Julius thought he'd caught Crystal in an online snare, accusing the star of trying to meet a teenage girl at Inverness airport. Julius is now regarded with scepticism by the public, and with ire by the community of Crystal fans.

Next we spoke to Sasha Stewart, a pro-Zach Crystal podcaster who has a counter-argument for any claim against her hero and believes that Ian Julius and the media are entirely responsible for Zach Crystal's death.

So where do we go next? We've heard from the two extremes of the Crystal conundrum, but, as always, there are more paths to take, crossroads to make decisions at. I think we need to get closer in, to try and push through the conjecture and find the heart of this mystery. So far, as I see it, there are three distinct paths: the fire at Crystal Forest, the claims of abuse and a mysterious entity known as a Frithghast.

Before we move on I want to add to my normal disclaimer: I'm no expert, not a forensic analyst, police or criminal profiler. I'm also not an expert on Zach Crystal. I know there's already correspondence pouring in, arguing many of the finer details that have been reported in this series. If you're looking for facts about Zach Crystal, his history and life, Sasha Stewart's podcast, the Crystal-Cast, *is the one for you.*

However, I think this particular episode of Six Stories *may be very interesting for fans of Zach Crystal and anyone interested in the man.*

—Summer and autumn, they was the busiest times. People still come to Colliecrith for sports: grouse shooting and deer stalking. That's not for me, any of that, I'm afraid. Killing things for fun? Some people say that's the behaviour of a psycho. No, I just kill when it's needed – the vermin. Sometimes control the deer. My jobs round here used to be breeding the birds for rich people to shoot, plus road maintenance, checking angler permits, that sort of thing.

Craig Kerr had been a groundskeeper in Colliecrith National Park all his working life, like his father and his father's father. A hulking, ruddy-faced man, over six feet tall with thick, blond hair and beard, hands like spades and a booming laugh, Craig looks like he was born to be outdoors. We meet in the small town of Aviemore, in a cafe on the main street. The green mountains of the Highlands rise all around us, against the backdrop of pale skies and iron-coloured clouds. Aviemore has a huge tourist population, with many Oriental, American and English voices. Craig now works at one of Aviemore's many holiday parks. It's not far from Colliecrith, and Craig tells me he couldn't imagine living in any other part of the world. The country and the forests are in his blood.

—I could never get on with the killing though. My da used to call me soft, but, hey, what can you do? That's why, when Mr

Crystal bought the property, I offered up my services immediately. I thought, he's not going to want to go round shooting things.

In the late nineties, Zach Crystal purchased five hundred acres of Colliecrith, in the midst of the aspen forest known colloquially as the Whispering Wood. The Kerr family maintained a large part of this vast forest for the Shaw family, who'd owned their land for hundreds of years. Craig tells me that, if he's being honest, he saw pound signs when the biggest pop superstar in the world came calling.

—I'm not gonna lie. There's this rich guy from England who's just bought up a load of the woods for daft money – I thought, he's gonna need me. That's basically what I told them when I wrote. It was totally selfish.

Craig actually spoke to one of Crystal's people when they came to look at the property. He handed them a CV and covering letter. Amazingly, he got a phone call the very next day from Crystal's top aide, James Cryer.

—Aye, so there you go. He gets on the phone to me and he says, will I sort it all?

—*Sort it all?*

—Well, he says, Zach Crystal knows nothing about woodland maintenance, he's a star. Can you put together a team of lads? He says the guy wants a mansion, recording studio and a tree house in the middle of the Whispering Wood. I just says, 'Aye mate, no bother.' It was mad, but I didn't say so. I just said aye. I think he liked that.

So Craig put out the word to local contractors and assisted Team Crystal with finding the best site for the Crystal Forest mansion. Money was no object.

—He wanted the forest disturbed as little as possible. I liked that. Of course, we had to do some clearance work, but it was minimal. He wanted the place right in the middle, as far away from everything as he could. Now, what a lot of folk don't know is that up there, it's not just a load of trees. It's dangerous. The woodland's ancient, the ground's mountainous, there's all sorts of gullies and pits and dips, rocks and caves. I think that's why he wanted it there, to make it hard for people to get to. I mean, the guy was a multi-millionaire megastar, so I don't blame him, do you?

Craig tells me he didn't really see himself in charge of anything; he was just helping out. But as time went on, he realised how he was seen by Zach Crystal's team.

—I'm just a guy, you know? I'm nobody really, and then suddenly all these people in suits and shades are talking to me. I'm now attending meetings with the big players. Suddenly I'm someone, you know? Someone important.

The construction of Crystal Forest was quick. Craig never spoke to Crystal himself; everything was done through James Cryer on behalf of the star.

—I said to him, I says, you know about the story of the wood? The curse, all that? He laughs. He says that Mr Crystal knows all about it and that's why he's here, and that was that. Fair enough, I thought. So long as he pays my wages, I'm not questioning it. Maybe that would be good for the place, you know? This great big project might finally bury that daft old story.

The remote location of Crystal Forest meant that a new road had to be constructed to access the site. Craig oversaw it all. He tells me that, to this day, you could place him anywhere within the five hundred acres of woodland that compromised Crystal Forest and he'd be able to navigate out of there. By the end of the construction, Craig was offered a permanent contract as Zach Crystal's head of security at Crystal Forest. He was given accommodation in the mansion, in the staff quarters, food and board all paid for, and a wage on top of that.

—About sixteen months, give or take, it took to get that place built. The recording studio a bit longer, but he was living there permanently by 1999. And I had signed the contract for my new job.

—*How much did you see Zach Crystal himself, during the construction work?*

—Oh, never. We never saw him. Everything was done through his man, Mr Cryer. People ask me all the time, they say 'Were you close to him? Were you two friends?' – but this was the biggest star on earth we're talking about. The guy was on tour and all that, wasn't he? He did come though, when the place was ready. He came to see us, and that's when I met him for the first time. I was a little bit starstruck. Who wouldn't be? He's this skinny, soft man with long hair, dressed like something out of a fantasy story. He was like a little kid, running around the place. But he was polite, he was respectful. He was actually a decent bloke, I thought. At first.

He knew my name, which was mad – knew who I was. He thanked me over and over again for the hard work and sorting it all out.

There was a party with champagne and all that, one evening. A grand opening. But actually, it ended up not so grand.

—*How do you mean?*

—Well, you would think, wouldn't you, a guy like that would have a big party, invite all his famous pals? It would all be vol-au-vents and eating sushi off naked women and that. Instead it was … strange.

—*You were invited?*

—I mean, that was strange in itself, no? That I was there. I thought so at first but – and I'm being honest here – I didn't realise just how … important I'd become…

Craig is a modest and unassuming man. He's come from a traditional, hard-working background, but he's no stranger to wealthy landowners and the like. By the time Crystal Forest was finished, though, he says he was shocked and actually slightly embarrassed at how much money he'd earned.

—I rented a suit, you know? A decent one. Got a shave and a haircut and that. I thought I was going to be hob-nobbing with the rich and famous.

Craig tells me the Crystal Forest opening party was nothing of the sort. First off, there were barely any other people there, just Zach Crystal's executives, his head of marketing, managers, drivers. It was an odd assembly of people, as if it were a work do. In fact, that's what Craig thought it was at first, a pre-party get-together for Crystal's internal people. It was only later that he realised this was it – this was the *party.*

—Like, there must have been twenty people, thirty tops. All these business guys – aides, managers, personal assistants, runners. We were all milling around this massive room, drinking fizz, eating nibbles. It was amazing, but it was also … What's the best word? Awkward. That was how it felt. It felt like one of those parties where no one shows up.

Zach Crystal was always known as rather reclusive. He was an enigma, hidden up in his mysterious forest, away from the world. But it still seems rather sad that at the opening of his new home, the only people he had invited were those that were paid to be there.

—Oh and Naomi of course, his sister, she showed up too. Alone. I remember seeing her looking about, as if she was freaked out by it all too. She was glammed up in a pretty dress, her hair done and everything. I think she was embarrassed. I think she felt a bit daft.

—*What about Zach Crystal himself – did he seem perturbed in any way by the oddness of the party?*

Craig shifts in his chair and scratches his head. Before the interview officially started, we talked at length about the fact that Craig is a former employee of Zach Crystal and about how much he feels comfortable talking about. Many, many newspapers and television documentaries have approached Craig, asking for his opinions about the star. He says, however, there's always been an agenda, and he's worried, he tells me, that what he says might be twisted to suit one. All I can do is give Craig my assurance that I'm not here to do anything of the sort. He says he'll talk to me as I'm the first person not to offer him money – 'As if after working for him, I'd need any more.'

Craig tells me that, yes, there were things that he found strange about Zach Crystal, and now, in the aftermath of what happened and in view of the ongoing investigation and with the survivors of Crystal's voices finally being heard, he's starting to question what he saw. Ultimately, Craig has not formulated an opinion about his former employer. The money he received working for Zach Crystal has homed and clothed Craig and his family for the rest of their lives, and this means there's a degree of loyalty to Zach Crystal still in Craig's heart.

That said, he's not here to speak out in defence of Crystal, either.

—He showed up about an hour after Naomi arrived. He'd been up in the tree house part, you know? He was all dressed up, as usual, a face full of makeup and wearing this mad cloak, like he was a king. He was quite a … He was quite something, quite a sight. And yeah, he was acting a bit off, a bit strange. I thought he might be on something, you know? He was like a kid, really hyperactive; laughing really loudly, fluttering around the groups of people, a social butterfly sort of thing. I tell you what he reminded me of – a wean; a little girl on her birthday party, all full of cake and overexcited, you know?

—*So he thought it a success?*

—Aye, and I think something else too: I think he thought all these folk that worked for him were his friends, his mates. All these guys in suits, all the managers and strategists and marketing bods. I might be wrong, but that's the impression I got.

—*Did he interact with you much?*

—He came and said hello, shook my hand. He had this nervous energy coming off him. I was still pretty starstruck by him, to be fair. I couldn't help myself. It felt like he'd graced us with his presence. There was something else I noticed too – how the other guys acted round him, like he was … They were all falling over themselves to laugh at his shite jokes and listen to his daft wee stories. They couldn't get enough of it.

—They were all on the payroll though, right? It was in their interests, no?

—Aye but it was *more* than that. It was weird, like I say. Maybe it was cos you never saw him, maybe it was cos of his get-up, all that makeup and costume perhaps. But it was like they were all desperate, really desperate, to impress him, for him to speak to them.

There was something else too – something else that happened that night and, I mean, I don't want to speak ill of the dead or nothing…

—It's OK – I believe many people have already spoken ill of him.

Craig looks up at me, lines of confusion crumpling his brow, then he shakes his head.

—No, not him, not Mr Crystal. It was Mr Cryer. It felt like he was Mr Crystal's only actual, genuine mate, like, his only real friend. But I dunno, after what's been coming out, I wish maybe I'd said something earlier.

—What happened?

—So I go for a piss, right? Toilets are down a long corridor, and as I'm just about to turn the corner, I hear someone kicking off, really going for it, you know, but in a whisper. Someone's getting told off. Now the carpets are brand new, thick, and they don't hear me coming, so I go sneaking along, wondering who's getting it, you know? Cos I recognise the voice, the one doing all the sort of whisper-shouting. It's Mr Cryer. He's going off his head but as quiet as he can. He's having a go at someone about a message, a text message or something. All I heard was, 'Get it sent, get a fucking *chopper* over there.' I dunno what he's on about.

—Who was he telling off?

—So I just start whistling away, walking round the corner like I'm just away for a piss, you know? I come round the corner, and Mr Cryer's got this fella up against the wall by his neck. It was one of the kitchen staff, one of the cooks – the Spanish one. Geraldo Bravo, he was called.

As soon as Cryer sees me, they jump apart, stand up straight. Cryer's still got his hand on the guy, but it's like in school, you know, when you and your pal are having a bit of a rammy and the teacher comes along and you give it 'Och, he's ma best mate sir'. And you pretend you've got your arm round him. It was like that. I just nod and walk past – none of my business, you know?

Anyways, about an hour later, this load of young lassies turn up, these teenagers, out of nowhere. It was mad. At first I thought that something bad was going on – all these guys in suits, you know? But it turns out it's Geraldo's teenage niece and a load of her daft mates.

—*Why do you think they were there?*

—Honestly. I don't know. Maybe they were fans? Maybe they were there to make it more like a party? I didn't like it though. It made things even more uncomfortable, all these blokes and these teenage girls all dressed up and giggling and that. It was just weird.

—*What did the girls do?*

—Oh, they got taken up to see the tree house with Mr Crystal. They couldn't believe it.

—*Did that seem odd to you?*

—Not at all. I'm telling you now, it didn't seem dodgy or wrong or anything. It was like those lasses were being taken to meet their hero. Mr Cryer was there too. It was all above board.

—*And how do you feel about it now?*

—After what's coming out about Mr Crystal? Yeah, maybe it does seem wrong. Maybe it *was* wrong. But … it's hard to explain. It was like, everyone was there, all his people, all Mr Crystal's top staff and even his sister. It just felt … I mean he wouldn't do anything bad would he? That would be crazy with everyone there.

Craig says this was the first time that he ever felt uncomfortable at Crystal Forest, but at the time he thought this sort of thing was perhaps normal and it was just him who felt odd.

—That night, at that party, I really started thinking about whether I wanted this job after all. I nearly quit there and then. I thought, this isn't me, this isn't for me. But I never said nothing, you know? I thought, here's me, green behind the ears, sweating through a rented suit. I don't know about famous people, about these sorts of showbiz parties.

In the end, Craig stayed; the money and the freedom to work in his beloved forest was just too much to turn down. As Crystal's star ascended higher and higher, Craig began seeing, from an insider's perspective, how things worked in the Crystal camp.

—Mr Cryer, he was just … I mean, Mr Crystal was the star, but Mr Cryer was the driving force behind him; he sorted out everything, he was on everything. Like a plate-spinner, you know? When you're as big as Mr Crystal was then – and that was his heyday wasn't it, ninety-nine onward? – when you're that big, you have to fend off a lot of shite. Mr Cryer was the one who made it his business to do just that. He was like an attack dog. Any journalist, anyone had anything bad to say against Mr Crystal, and James Cryer was all over it. I saw the guy just get scarier and scarier. You didn't fuck with him. No one fucked with him; no one dared. He and Naomi Crystal, they were the ones not to be messed with.

By 2004, James Cryer had amassed a team of private investigators and lawyers known internally to Crystal Forest staff as the 'Bastard Squad'. James Cryer, Craig tells me, actually read an internal email from a member of staff, referring to them by that name.

—It was written by the head housekeeper. She was a mess – she thought she was going to get sacked, sued, kicked out on her arse. Mr Cryer just thought it was funny. I think he liked it.

—They enjoyed their fearsome reputation? Encouraged it?

—It just happened gradually, you know? I think that party was the first time I saw it. Yeah, everyone knew you didn't mess with Mr Cryer and Ms Crystal. You did what they said, no questions. They knew everyone's business, all the staff – where we were supposed to be and when. You didn't mess about at Crystal Forest. It was regimented, like the army up there.

—Sort of like a dictatorship?

—Aye, but it was all about keeping everything right for Mr Crystal, you know? The guy didn't do interviews, didn't talk to journalists or telly, so they had to manage his image. They had to keep the money coming in, keep the tours going, the albums selling. We all had to sign stuff saying we wouldn't talk to the press. We all knew if we did that they would ruin us.

As Craig says, the Bastard Squad spent a great deal of time attacking any voices critical of Zach Crystal with threats of huge lawsuits, all of which they won. They had enough money behind them to hire the best legal team, and publications would back down or else settle out of court. Because Crystal would rarely do interviews with the press and because he was such a huge star, there were many, often ludicrous stories coming from the media about him, about drugs problems, debts, failed relationships, the usual headlines that seem to dog the world of pop.

It was around 2004 that Zach Crystal's work with young people in the care system began to be leaked to the press. Craig tells me that this was all the doing of chief aide James Cryer. As we heard in the last episode, Crystal would often visit residential homes and hospitals to brighten the days of the children staying there. Crystal would also make huge donations to these homes and institutions and buy much-needed equipment and resources. Before 2004, all of these donations went unmentioned, he would never announce them, but after Jessica and Lulu, photographs of Crystal visiting these places were taken by Crystal's own PR team and given to the press. In each photo, Crystal is surrounded by balloons, toys and smiling faces. It's interesting to note that all of the children he's pictured with happened to be female and around the ages of twelve to fifteen.

—Mr Crystal was so big it was hard for anyone to get close to him. He even had a decoy. Not many people know that, but he employed a guy who looked exactly like him to go out the backs of places into cars, sometimes, try and draw the crowds away.

No one was close to Mr Crystal. Well, no one except Mr Cryer, that is, until he died, of course.

The body of James Cryer was found by Naomi Crystal early in 2018. It's thought Cryer took a fall from a steep ridge in a dense part of Crystal Forest, not far from the house. An inquest ruled Cryer's death as accidental.

Before we come to the last few years of Craig Kerr's involvement with Zach Crystal, there are a few more significant events in the singer's life I want to discuss. The first was his accident in 2004.

—Oh aye, I remember that well; took a tumble didn't he? Leaped off a box in rehearsal and slipped. Broke his leg. He was up in Raigmore for a few days. I remember that cos we had to turn that dance studio into a physio room while he was away.

Zach Crystal had to undergo surgery for a displaced fracture on his right tibia after slipping in one of Crystal Forest's studios. It was a significant injury, which required a good deal of physical therapy. The South American leg of Crystal's tour ended up being cancelled. Crystal himself caused pandemonium at Raigmore hospital in Inverness, with many fans and the media camping out in the car park to get a glimpse of the star. Crystal himself would often sit at the window, wearing a surgical mask and sunglasses, waving to the fans, and was regaled with cheers of adulation as he was discharged, James Cryer and his personal bodyguard helping him into a black limo, one leg in a cast.

I have heard from cynics that there was nothing more wrong with Zach Crystal than a twisted ankle and that this was yet another bizarre PR stunt to show the star in a sympathetic light. Whether this was Crystal's choice or a decision by his people, Craig doesn't know. He does know, however, that for a long time, when he saw him at Crystal Forest, Crystal's leg was in a splint.

—He spent most of his time in that tree house of his. You had to be specially invited to go up there. Only the cleaners and Mr Cryer could enter that treehouse without a specific invite from Mr Crystal. Anyone else – instant dismissal. None of us dared go anywhere near. But he did have a lot of visitors up there, a lot of well-wishers.

—*That strikes me as odd, considering the lack of people at the party.*

—Ah, it wasn't friends he had up there with him, it was fans. Lots of those unfortunate girls; the ones from the homes and that. When he broke his leg, he let lots of them come to visit him in there. Mr Cryer organised it all.

According to Craig, during Zach Crystal's rehabilitation for his broken leg, there were so many visitors to his tree house, the staff at Crystal Forest were working flat out. The visitors quarters at Crystal Forest were full and when one set of visitors left, another would arrive.

In the years that followed, unless Crystal was on tour, Crystal Forest always seemed busy with fans. Only a select few were allowed to spend time in the treehouse. At the same time, though, security was upped – there were more patrols in the forest, and there was state of the art CCTV, inside as well as out.

—Oh it was madness. Loads of teenage girls all over the place and their parents or their carers. It was bedlam sometimes. All those cameras too. You had the kitchens working twenty-four-seven, the housekeepers never stopped cleaning. I stayed out of the way, me. They were up till all hours, in the tree house, watching horror movies apparently.

—*Did you ever go inside the tree house, any time you worked there?*

—Like I say, instant dismissal without an invite. But I came close though.

—*Really?*

—Oh, aye. It was a funny one. It was a year or so later – 2005 maybe? I was up on the top floor. We called it the Crystal Museum. It was where he kept all his stuff – his costumes and his outfits and awards. It was all in glass cases, all dark with those motion-sensor lights inside them, so when you went in there, the cases lit your way. I thought it was spooky, but he liked it. All his tour posters, all his merchandise. He had one of everything – every poster, every keyring, everything, mounted in these cases. I also knew that whenever anyone was in the Crystal Museum, those sensors would set off lights up in the tree house. He could watch you on his own CCTV up there.

—*Really? Why?*

—The entrance to the tree house was behind one of the cases. There was a secret lift, you know? There was a keypad at the very end of the museum. If you were Mr Crystal or Mr Cryer, you knew the code and it would make one of the cases slide open. There was a lift that went up there that housekeeping had a key for and after that another two security doors. Mr Cryer kept that key in his office and housekeeping had to ask him for permission to clean. He was very security-conscious was Mr Crystal. He needed to know if someone was coming. There was a secret exit from the tree house as well. A ladder that led into the forest and a lift that went into the garages. I know all this because I saw it all being built. It was crazy – proper Indiana Jones stuff.

—Why though? Why was it so cloak and dagger?

—Listen, I couldn't tell you how many times I got emails or letters asking for access to Mr Crystal. We all did, everyone who worked there. Because he was so elusive, everyone wanted a piece of him – journalists, fans. I've been offered ridiculous money to take photos up there. I've been offered all sorts to take people's kids there, to ask for autographs, everything. Even now. Even now he's dead, people still want to know if I can get them to look around the ruins of the place. You're the first one that hasn't.

—But you never had the code back then?

—Not me. Nope. Only Mr Cryer and Mr Crystal, and Mr Cryer himself let the cleaners in.

—You say you came close to going up there.

—Well, like I say, I was up in the museum. They wanted a new security system installed and I was just having a look, you know? Anyhow, the case door slides open and it's one of the housekeepers.

—OK.

—So we says hello and that, and she's away, but I notice the door isn't closing – the glass case is jammed. Must be a fault, so I go to have a look and I see something's dropped off her basket. At first I thought it was a washcloth, so I go to pick it up, but it's stuck in the door somehow. I get into the lift and pull it out. But then the doors close on me and it starts going up.

—To the tree house?

—Aye. I'm shitting it. By then he'll be able to see me on the camera. I'm not supposed to be up there, but I figure I've got a good excuse, no? Problem is that once I'm up, I don't know how to get back down again.

—So what did you do?

—Well, that was it. I was stood there like a lemon for a wee while, in front of the security door, the lift open behind me. It was quiet there, dead quiet. Even if the wind was raging outside, you could have heard a pin drop. I was a bit … uncomfortable, you know? Then I hear something – I mean, it was probably just wind in the lift shaft or a sound from the speakers or the intercom or whatever, but it gave me … this *feeling*.

—*What sort of feeling?*

—Let me tell you something: the forest, that forest, has never scared me. I feel like I know it and it knows me too. That sounds daft, I know, but it's true. One morning though, when I was wee, I was out at dawn with my da and we were watching a herd of deer graze. It's a beautiful sight. They're like ghosts: they make no sound, they come and they go like they were never there. Any movement though and off they go. So I'm stood, stock still, watching, drinking in the sight of these delicate animals when … I dunno, there's this *feeling* in the air. It's not wind, it's like a cloud passes over your heart. I feel all the hairs on my body standing up, and I'm scared. I'm so scared I slip my hand into my dad's and we say nothing. We watch. Those deer, they feel it too, I swear, because they all stand up from their grazing, in one movement, look one way and dash off, vanishing, quick as a breeze.

—*What was it that spooked them?*

—I've no idea. Not even now. The feeling was gone a moment later. I asked my da and he just says that sometimes there's things that the forests still hold secret. I never forgot that fear though. Never. And that's what I felt when I was stood there outside the lift while this *sound*, this soft wail of wind, calls out and disappears again.

Eventually I had no choice, did I? I thought I had to call Mr Cryer. I just hoped Mr Crystal wouldn't go off his nut. I was about to call Cryer when I looked down at what I'd pulled out of the lift door. I thought it was a duster or a cleaning rag or whatever, but it's not. It's some pyjamas. Bottoms. Girls' pyjama bottoms. Little frilly things, with bows, like what young lassies wear. Not little kids' ones, but … small, you know, young adult size. The cleaner must have dropped them from the washing basket, I thought.

—*What on earth did you do?*

—I didn't know. I didn't think, I just stuffed them in my pocket. Prayed he hadn't seen it through the camera. Then I called Mr Cryer on my phone. I was terrified because all the time I was explaining what happened – the door had stuck and I'd gone up – I had these pyjamas in my back pocket. I could feel them in there.

—*What were you scared of?*

—Someone finding them. Mr Crystal or Mr Cryer finding out I had them. Then I'd have to explain and I'd drop the housekeeper in the shit too. It was all such a mess, you know? I can't really say much more. That was how I felt. I'm not implying anything.

Such an incident can be seen in a number of ways. I'm sure there are those out there who will regard what Craig found at Crystal Forest as very dubious. There are also those who won't. There are several potential explanations – both innocent and nefarious. We can read what we want into the discovery but we cannot know exactly why they were there. It's entirely possible, Craig tells me, that they came from the guest quarters on the lower floor – they could have been brought up by one of the young women. Or else they belonged to Zach Crystal himself. That would beg even more sinister questions. What interests me here is Craig's fear upon finding the garments; that cannot be disputed. Certainly around this time there was increasing media scrutiny around the young women who were allowed into the sanctity of Crystal Forest. The mentality among the staff, Craig says, was that the media reports were bitter grapes. Zach Crystal did not allow the press anywhere near him, so they reacted by spinning unpleasant rumours.

Craig tells me that not long after these unsavoury whispers began to spread online, Crystal released the Damage *album and started a sudden and very public relationship with actress Zadie Farrow. At this point, Zach Crystal was thirty-three years old. It was rare, Craig says, at this point, that Crystal spent much time at Crystal Forest.* Damage *sent Crystal stratospheric and his image was everywhere, even if he himself was not, save for carefully orchestrated events and carefully choreographed and pre-scripted appearances.*

—I don't know when he started dating Ms Farrow. One day there was nervous energy at Crystal Forest, lots of cleaning and that going on, stuff being chucked out.

—*Stuff?*

—From the tree house. Junk, I imagine. Mr Crystal kept a lot of junk up there apparently. There was always loads of rubbish. He was like a teenager; the cleaners were always bringing down bags and bags of pizza boxes and fizzy-drink bottles. I think he wanted the place spruced up. It wasn't every day you brought home a movie star, right?

Zadie Farrow was slightly older than Zach Crystal, aged forty in 2007. The pair met at the premiere of Dark Tide, *a horror movie directed by Tony Almiron in which Farrow starred and was eventually Oscar-nominated for. Crystal, well known for his love of horror movies, was said to be absolutely infatuated with Farrow.*

By this time, Zach Crystal was possibly the world's biggest music star. His appearance grew ever more flamboyant: tailor-made clothes, all of which were themed around woodland. He wore tiara-style headdresses with short antlers fixed to them and either veils or elaborate masks that covered most of his face. Tall, with his mane of thick, blond hair, only his piercing green eyes peering out at the world, he was quite a sight. He was graceful and soft in his speech and movement, always standing tall and regal. Personally, I think he looked like some kind of pagan deity, summoned to our world.

—*How were they together, Zach and Zadie?*

—In all honesty, you never really saw them together. They were both busy people, you know? The only time I ever saw them together was when they were doing photo shoots in their crazy costumes for publicity. They never seemed *unhappy*, just … different people, I guess. That's how it seemed to me; they were never really *together*.

Craig tells me, in these ensuing years, Crystal's elusiveness began to become detrimental to his image.

—There were even more folk trying to get to him at Crystal Forest. Not just young lasses but photographers, journalists too. It became a real problem.

With the increased incidents of people becoming lost or injured in Colliecrith National Park as they were trying to reach Crystal Forest, the park service and Police Scotland eventually clamped down hard. Anyone caught on the Crystal property or that of the neighbouring Shaw estate would face arrest and a hefty fine.

But unfortunately, there was to be a terrible tragedy in Crystal Forest that same year. At the time, Zach Crystal fans were trying to find their way through the forest at Colliecrith to their idol's home in larger numbers. The great majority were caught at the perimeter and ejected by Craig and his security team, but some, unfortunately, weren't so lucky.

—It was insane. It was more than you'd ever think. Two or three a week, easily. More in the summer. Most of them would get the coach or the train to Aviemore or Newtonmore, sometimes Dalwhinnie. We're talking a day and a night's walk to Colliecrith from there. But they tried it. Some of them drove. Taxis round here had to have signs in Japanese as well as English, telling folk they wouldn't take a fare to Colliecrith. You think that being head of security is all glitz and glamour? No way. Most of your time you spent being called all sorts by crazy girls who've camped out in the Cairngorms all night.

Crystal Forest's state-of-the-art security meant that there was no way any of the fans were able to access the property, but that didn't stop them trying.

The deaths we've mentioned before, of two fifteen-year-old fans – Lulu Copeland and Jessica Morton – is an incident that Craig remembers well.

—Poor wee things. That was the worst day of my whole life. Finding them two lassies. Horrible. I can't forget that day, even though I want to.

Jessica Morton and Lulu Copeland were reported missing by staff from their residential home in Truro in July 2007. CCTV caught the girls at Truro Bus Station late one night, boarding a bus to Bristol. After that, nothing was known of their whereabouts. The story was floated briefly on the UK news, but quickly vanished again and the girls were forgotten. Many have argued since that this disappearance was woefully under-reported and the investigation distinctly lacking. From the outside it seems that a lack of communication among police forces across the UK hampered the investigation, which eventually petered out entirely. There are many questions still being asked about how the two girls managed to get all the way from the south coast to the Scottish Highlands, undetected. A cynic may argue that had Jessica and Lulu been middle class and from a stable background, there would have been significantly more effort put into the search.

It was a month later that the pair were found, by Craig, in Colliecrith. His face darkens as he recounts the discovery.

—I was on my rounds, just outside the perimeter. There were some trees needed felling, but they weren't part of Crystal Forest. So it was a load of admin, basically. That's why I was out there … and … I mean…

Craig falters and dissolves into a coughing fit. A few heads turn our way as he splutters, and when he raises his head again, his face is red and his eyes are bloodshot and watering. I give him a few moments to compose himself.

—Sorry.

—*It's OK – we can skip over the details if you'd rather not talk about it? No problem.*

—It's not that. It's not that, mate. It's just … all the stories of the Whispering Wood. That's what I thought they were at first, you know? Just stories, the daft things your granny tells you to keep you from hurting yourself, eh?

But there was something. Something I found during the build. I mean at the time, I just thought it was nothing, you know? Just a little bit of weirdness.

—*Yeah?*

—It was probably nothing and I didn't want to cause a fuss, so I never said anything.

—*What was it?*

—Well, you see maybe I imagined it, but I swear down when I was scouting out the land, I found a cave. That wasn't so weird, cos the forest was full of dips and ridges and rocks. There were lots of little divots like that in the land. But this was more than that. It was almost hidden by ferns, and it was … I dunno, there was some funny marks on the rocks round the entrance.

—*Was there anything inside?*

—I'm pretty embarrassed to say, but it gave me a bad vibe. For some reason it reminded me of seeing those deer when I was wee. You remember? One of those secrets the forest keeps. I just wanted to get away. So I did. I just went away. Thought I'd come back but – and this was the weird thing – I could never find it again. None of the workmen mentioned it either so I just kept my trap shut. It was too weird.

—*What do you think it was?*

—Just … I dunno. I dunno what it was. Just a cave, right? Just a cave in the woods. Maybe an animal lived in there. I dunno. I just know I didn't want to see it again. Ever again.

I ask Craig about the video that's emerged recently: what looks, from the blurry mobile phone footage, like the inside of a cave, and the two girls.

—I haven't seen it and I've no intention of seeing it either. Maybe it's real, maybe not…

—*Could you ever bring yourself to watch it?*

—No. Never. Just in case … just in case it *is* real.

—*What would that do to you if it was?*

—If it was real, it would stay in my head forever; it would haunt me, day and night. It would consume me. Those poor lassies. I'd never be able to unsee it, you know? I'll never watch it. Never.

—*Is the similarity to the story of the Whispering Wood part of what makes you so uncomfortable?*

—We all knew that story, the one about the little girl and the laird – our grannies had all told us it. But, it's the laird's family that's cursed, not Mr Crystal. It's the Shaws, who own the other half of the forest.

—*And do that family still own part of Colliecrith today?*

—Aye, the bit that wasn't Crystal Forest goes a long way all around.

The Shaw family owns a great swathe of Colliecrith National Park. Interestingly, around 70% of the park is privately owned, and used for rough grazing and managed moorland. The parts of the aspen forest neighbouring Crystal Forest have been in the Shaw family for over three hundred years. As Craig says, the curse and the Frithghast are said to centre only around that family.

—When the Kerrs were working for them, the Shaws had us do very little in the way of maintenance – the bare minimum, you know? They liked it dense, wild. It was there, right there on the edge of Crystal Forest where we found those girls.

So, over the years I was working for Mr Crystal, we'd had a bit of back and forth with the Shaws, you know. They were happy to let us get on with the maintenance of Mr Crystal's property. What we couldn't get them to do is come and take a look for themselves. That day in 2007, the weather had been awful – winds and storms. Trees on the borders between the properties had snapped off and fallen. It was a mess. A dangerous mess. I got in touch with the Shaws and they asked me to take photographs, so that's what I was doing that day, taking photos of the trees that needed clearing. There were a good few, all tangled and broken, matted together like hair. It was going to be a bit of a job, I could see that. There was one of those little ridges, a wee bank hidden by undergrowth. It was a mess. I went down the hill, picking my steps carefully. It was slippery, dark and muddy. And real quiet – colder and darker once you got down there. There was these little gusts of wind, making the leaves on the trees rattle. In and out, in and out. Like the forest was breathing. I'm right down, almost under the bank, when I finally find it again – that cave: a load of rocks, great big slabs, all covered in moss with these markings all over them. There's a nasty smell too … And I had that feeling again, from all those years back, all the hairs on my body standing up, and I remembered seeing those deer, how they'd looked up then vanished. I remembered my father's hand tightening around mine.

And that's when I saw it. It was down there, right under the hill, when I thought I saw … I mean, it was just cos of all the chat, you know? Everyone at Crystal Forest talking about it … It must have been a dream or something, a hallucination.

—*What did you see?*

—It was there, in the distance behind me, way back in the densest part of the trees. It was a trick of the light of course. Or it was my mind playing tricks that made it look like that.

—*Look like what?*

—A shadow, black against the green of the ferns. I thought it was a deer at first. It *was* a deer I suppose. But … not … It was more like a shadow; like a deer that had rotted away. I only saw it for a second … white bone. A skull. Looking at me with those empty eye sockets. Gave me the shivers, it really did. That old story, that old childhood fear. It all just got to me in that darkness, in those woods.

—*Did you take a photo?*

—I wish I had. I wish I'd thought. But in that moment it was like … it was like all rational thought had just gone out of my head. It was like that shadow had got inside me, like there was a black cloud over my brain. It was horrible. It stank and the leaves were hissing and shimmering, and I just … I needed to give my head a shake.

So I ducked under some broken boughs, to hide, you know, to get my head together. But under there was where the cave was.

Frightened and shaken, Craig moved back into the cave, its rim thick with trailing roots, and there he saw two shapes in the semi-darkness.

—I'd seen that print so many times, you know? It was the black-

and-white image of him, half his face covered by his hair – the 'ZC' logo above. It was that print, on a kiddie's rucksack. Just sat there in the entrance to the cave. This horrible feeling went through me, and I knew. I knew it was going to be bad. I just knew.

Craig crept forward along the muddy floor and into the back of the cave. He was met with a grisly sight. Two cadavers.

—I thought it was only one at first. She was lying flat on her back and … she was a mess, a *mess.*

Lulu Copeland was only recognisable as human by the remnants of the Zach Crystal T-shirt she was wearing and her trainers.

—I threw up, and it wouldn't stop. I was dry heaving, coughing up bile. I never saw the other one, I never even saw her. I couldn't look anymore.

Jessica Morton was at the back of the cave, curled up in a foetal position, also dead.

Exposure was the official cause of death for both girls.

Zach Crystal and his team stayed tight-lipped about the whole thing. It was a tense time and Craig tells me all of Crystal's other employees were silent too, terrified of speaking up and getting it wrong. In hindsight, he thinks it wasn't the right strategy for the star and his people to take.

—He should have come out then and said something, been sympathetic, you know? Shown some compassion. I think his PR team feared these deaths would ruin his image completely. This was when *Damage* had just come out – Mr Crystal was probably the biggest star in the whole world at the time. I think, honestly, he just left it to his people to sort out and they made the wrong call.

Indeed, the wall of silence from Crystal concerning Lulu and Jessica only led to speculation about the case. I'm not entirely sure where and when they started, but there are rumours of some truly gruesome details about the bodies that have never really been explained.

Reading the ghoulish threads on Reddit and the archives of forums speculating about what actually happened to the two young girls is a horrendous experience, but I'll try to summarise the principal theories. These are that the body of Lulu Copeland had effectively been butchered, and that her head was missing and a good deal of the flesh from her thighs and arms had been hacked off.

These rumours also suggest that some of Lulu's flesh was found during the autopsy.

In the stomach of Jessica Morton.

Craig doesn't doubt that the bodies were in a mess. He says that's probably what started the rumours. Or else there was a leak from someone inside Crystal Forest. He has no idea who might do this and why they'd suggest such horrors.

—There's plenty of scavengers out there. Badgers, pine martens, wild cats. That's what they think did most of the damage. That's what must have been living in that cave, see? I think something like that ripped her open. Some scavenger. For whatever reason, it left the other girl, Jessica, alone. I think that's what caused these terrible stories, these rumours. This terrible accident mixed with the story of the Whispering Wood, then the radio silence from Mr Crystal's people. It all made it sound so much worse than it probably was.

But I still can't explain it – why one of those girls was eaten and the other left alone. I don't want to think about it really. What I do know is that I'll never go back there, to that forest, to that place. Whatever it was I felt when I was a kid, it was a warning. That forest secret I saw was a warning, and I didn't heed it.

—What did you do when you found the two girls; what was your first action?

—You know who I phoned first? It wasn't the police. It was him. It was Mr Cryer. I phoned him first to tell him what I'd found. Says it all, doesn't it? About the power in Crystal Forest at the time.

I have sympathy for Craig where he has little for himself. He tells me Zach Crystal's team weren't trying to cover anything up, they were just concerned with limiting any potential damage to Crystal's image. I wonder, though, if Zach Crystal himself knew about what had happened, or knew of the rumours that abounded later about Jessica Morton eating her friend's flesh. We also cannot ignore the horrific parallels between this and the old story of the Frithghast.

—Aye, he knew what people had started saying in the aftermath of the whole thing. There was a meeting about whether he should put out a statement or something, but the team was dead against it. They knew the papers and the TV would twist it all up. So that's when Mr Crystal really stepped up his charity work, you know? The work he did for young lassies like those two. I think he thought that would make it go away.

—*Did you ever tell anyone outside Crystal Forest about what you'd seen?*

—No. No way.

—*Why was that, do you think?*

—You didn't mention it. You just kept your mouth shut about things like that. Everyone knew that. It was better to say nothing. I'm not daft. Even talking to you about it now, after the fact … you know it still scares me.

—*Craig, I've heard that there were times when Zach Crystal led his fans out into the forest at night, is that true and if so … why do you think he did this?*

—I … I don't know where you heard that. In fact I don't want to know. I can only say that I never understood it, but sometimes, yes, that's what he'd do. I used to ask if he wanted us to come with him – you know, keep them all safe. But he wouldn't have it. The forest was his, Mr Crystal said, and he'd walk in it alone if he wanted to. I don't want to remember those times. It was just awful, it just felt like something bad was going to happen.

—*Why was he doing it, though?*

—I never knew. None of us ever did. When you're dealing with someone like that, he does what he wants, when he wants. You just get used to it. You just have to keep your mouth shut and let him get on with it. Sometimes I think I kept my mouth shut for far too long.

The deaths of Jessica Morton and Lulu Copeland should have made much bigger headlines than they actually did. Their vulnerable status, the fact both of them had criminal records, combined, possibly, with the weight of Zach Crystal's own PR, meant the story seemed to disappear very quickly. The grisly rumours that came out after the fact, however, have never gone away. I'm shocked that what could have been such rich tabloid fodder … simply wasn't. Craig, however isn't. He tells me that you never underestimated the power wielded by Zach Crystal and his team.

—Do you think this was one of the reasons that Zach Crystal was so rarely interviewed, because he controlled the narrative so much?
—Oh for sure. And I think those deaths only made him withdraw more, if that was possible. He handed the media just a few scraps.

Zach Crystal's presence seemed to make his rare interviewers nervous. They would often trip over their words or else seem completely enamoured by him. He, in turn, was very reluctant to speak at all, and if a journalist managed to catch him he'd often walk away with a coy wave of his hand.

—Believe me, he worked a lot on his presence. His answers were pre-scripted and what sometimes look like spontaneous interviews were all strictly and carefully choreographed by Crystal's team. He read a lot of books about power – you know those self-help ones: about how to be in command the whole time. He was a master at it. We were all in awe of him at Crystal Forest. Even more so as he got bigger. When he was there, it was a different atmosphere, you could feel it.
But the next year, it just all fell apart.

2009 was another significant year for Zach Crystal. His relationship with Zadie Farrow ended abruptly, and, tragically, both his parents passed away. Maureen and Frank Crystal died, one shortly after the other, of 'natural causes' at the luxurious home their son had bought for them on England's south coast. Zach and Naomi both attended the funeral with three-year-old Bonnie. They were photographed, rather tastelessly, by tabloid newspapers and gossip magazines, crying together. Naomi wears her trademark sunglasses but is dressed modestly. Zach, however, wears a full Victorian-style veil over his face along with a black cape. He stands hand in hand at the graveside with his niece and his sister.

Craig tells me that after the funeral Crystal became an almost permanent resident at Crystal Forest, up in the tree house. He was rarely seen, but his presence was everywhere.

—We were scared then. Scared of him, scared of Mr Cryer.

—*What was so scary about him?*

—He was just … unpredictable. In the lead-up to his parents passing, his behaviour was just … peculiar. More than usual.

—*How so?*

—So … sometimes Mr Cryer would get me on the phone. 11.00pm, 3.00am, whenever, and I'd have to go out – out into the forest and do a sweep of the property. Now. That minute, that second.

—*Really?*

—Aye – he would always tell me to 'report *anything,* anything you see or hear'.

—*Was he looking for something in particular?*

—If he was, he didn't tell me. Everyone had their theories. Once one of the housekeepers told me that Mr Crystal had seen something out of his window. He was terrified up there, blocking up all the windows and doors. Screaming, chucking stuff about.

—*The Frithghast?*

—Maybe. I don't know for sure. No one would say anything. They were all too scared in case something got out. There were cameras everywhere, a brand-new security system throughout the property. Everything was transmitted up into the tree house. He knew exactly who was where at all times. Remember as well, we were pretty much under siege too; there were journalists and fans all over the place, trying to get in. I think it was all too much for Ms Farrow, she couldn't take it anymore. There were also groups of young girls coming for visits every other week. The security was stepped up; they were all signing confidentiality agreements, NDAs. It was a tough time. Then, after his parents passed … it felt like he wanted to be everywhere at all times, in control of everything.

—*Omnipotent, perhaps?*

—Aye. That's a good way to describe it. Omnipotent. He made sure he was. You could hear him screaming at staff. The cleaners were forever cleaning up after he'd trashed rooms. Then you wouldn't see or hear him for weeks. He'd be up in the tree house.

—*What caused these outbursts?*

—It was the media coverage. He was obsessed. He read everything, and anything negative sent him into a fury. The Bastard Squad got bigger, more ruthless, they would go after anyone who said anything, bring them down.

Zach Crystal reached an out-of-court defamation settlement with the Daily Mail *in 2010 – rumoured to be for around £60,000 – for their coverage of the star in hospital in 2004, in which they accused him of faking his broken leg.*

—Basically, the *Mail* had sent journalists and photographers dressed as orderlies into Raigmore to get photos of him in bed. He wanted all of them tracked down and charged. The irony being that Mr Crystal had his own photographers doing exactly the same thing.

Bloggers, YouTubers and columnists who suggested anything untoward about his liaisons with troubled teenage girls were either threatened or sued, or both.

For Craig, though, even more troubling was Crystal's need to control others' behaviour.

—He wanted people tracked, he wanted people followed. He was paying PIs all over the place. It was like he wanted full control over what anyone thought and said about him. It was crazy. As the years went on, it became a way of life. Everyone was in a high state of alert a hundred percent of the time. He asked to join us on our patrols, eventually. Nearly every night, trudging through the forest, stopping at very noise, every movement. It was exhausting.

—*What do you think was wrong with him?*

—Hard to say. I don't want to defame the guy, even now he's dead. I'm too … still too scared I suppose. But he was utterly consumed by this idea of something in the Whispering Wood – it was like he was *desperate* to see it. Maybe he thought that, if he did, he'd be able to predict the future – have control over that too.

He still had the lasses coming to visit too – all of them up in the tree house. I think they were all saying they saw things too. It was getting out of control – feeding his paranoia.

—*Did any of that ever trouble you? Did you find or see anything else that made you wonder what was going on in the tree house?*

—Thing is, see, Mr Cryer was always up there too – he always organised the visits. That's why I just kept my head down, got on with my work. I thought, if Mr Cryer's up there, then it's OK. Mr Crystal organised gifts and money and all sorts for those girls. He spared no expense. He was defiant about it, right to the end. That's what he wanted to do, so he did it. No one could tell him 'no'. Not even Mr Cryer.

A few people, including Sasha Stewart, have speculated that Zach Crystal saw the Frithghast twice more. Once before his friend and aide James Cryer had his accident in Crystal Forest and then before the fire. I put this to Craig. He shrugs.

—Maybe he did. I don't know. He never saw it with me. But, believe me, he was looking for it, all day every day. So who knows?

—*Are you OK to talk about those two events?*

—Aye. I mean, I felt like I'd been pretty much pushed away by that time. I only ever really ate and slept in my room, you know, I spent most of my time in the woods. It was Naomi who found Mr Cryer, the poor sod.

Naomi Crystal – concerned about her brother's state and the increasingly loud voices from the #metoo movement that were supporting his alleged victims – moved to Crystal Forest permanently in 2017 from her home in LA. She brought her daughter with her – Zach's niece Bonnie, who was then thirteen years old. Craig tells me Naomi's presence brought a sense of much-needed calm to the place.

—Aye, she was sound, she had her head screwed on. She was forceful. Firm but fair, like a teacher. But she didn't let up. She was very protective of him as well. She took over – took full control of the place. She was her very own Bastard Squad. She stopped the lasses visiting, which was a relief. She kept him away from any limelight. Honestly, I think it was her idea for him to just vanish for a bit, get away from it all. Especially after Mr Cryer died.

—*It was Naomi's idea for Zach to vanish? If that's true, she must have known where he went.*

—Maybe. If she did, we didn't know about it. It makes sense though, especially after Mr Cryer died. I think without him, Mr Crystal was a bit lost.

—*Did Naomi Crystal and James Cryer ever butt heads? It seems like there was a bit of a power struggle at Crystal Forest?*

—No. Not that I saw, because it was all for him, all for Mr Crystal. They were dedicated to him. Both of them. Then Mr Cryer sadly passed and Mr Crystal disappeared.

Just a quick reminder: the body of James Cryer was found in the early hours of a cold, January morning by Naomi Crystal. Cryer had been deep in the middle of Crystal Forest and had slipped, falling from the edge of a hidden ridge, hitting his head on a large boulder. The circumstances are odd but not entirely suspicious. I ask Craig what he thinks Cryer was doing out there in the first place.

—I mean … he could have been doing anything. What I and everyone else think was that Mr Crystal saw something and sent him to investigate. I don't think it was much more complicated than that.

—*I'm interested in the place where he was found. You knew Crystal Forest like the back of your hand – was there anything odd, anything that stood out about where he fell?*

—It was just another one of those caves, like the one I found those poor lassies in. There were lots of them, where trees had fallen or where there were rocks.

—How was Naomi when you came upon her with Cryer's body?

—Bless her. She'd try to revive him, tried to drag his body up the hill. She was covered in mud. Poor woman. I felt for her too. She'd just walked into a nightmare.

—A few months later, Zach Crystal vanished. What about the staff at Crystal Forest? Was there a lot of speculation about the disappearance?

—Ach, we all had our theories. Some said he'd gone into rehab, probably. Or to some kind of retreat. It was only when Naomi wanted to sell up and get rid of the place that we thought he must be gone for good. She was in full control of it all by then. She stayed in a guest suite and sent Bonnie away. Away from the bad atmosphere, I suppose. Loads of folk were let go, great sections of the place was shut down, boarded up. The swimming pools, the gym, all that. Naomi wanted the tree house taken down too. She wouldn't even go up there.

—Why was that, do you think?

—I'm not really sure. I know one place that Naomi didn't like, and that was the 'memorial room'.

—Memorial room?

—Aye. It's gonna sound odd but I think I understood it. Mr Crystal had kept a lot of his ma's things up there, when she passed. Her clothes and her trinkets and all that. The thing about Mr Crystal was that he never threw anything away; he'd put all the clothes on mannequins and that, you know, to keep them. He'd got his ma's old dresser and put all her stuff on it, her jewellery and all that, you know?

—Did you ever see the memorial room?

—No, but the housekeepers used to talk about it. They said he would never let them clean in there. He would take their trolleys and do it himself.

—Did that strike you as odd?

—Aye, maybe, but the guy *was* a bit odd. I mean that in the most respectful way, of course. He was … eccentric.

—*When Zach Crystal disappeared, did anyone think that maybe he'd actually died?*

—Some of us thought that maybe he was dead. But more likely he'd fled overseas, vanished, you know? The guy had enough money to do it and it would be very like him. Leave a mystery like that. I think his parents dying, then his best mate, it fucked him up bad. So that's why we were so shocked when he came back.

Craig says that the Crystal Forest staff that remained in service were as shocked as the rest of the world when Zach Crystal returned. But while he was there, in the house again, it was like he was not, Craigs says. He was rarely seen by anyone. It was like he was a ghost, flitting briefly into sight, and only ever accompanied by his sister. Zach never explained where he'd been, but it seemed not to matter. A new album and a tour was on the cards and it felt like the world had fallen in love with Zach Crystal again.

Unfortunately, we have come to the part of the interview I've been dreading. So far Craig has been affable, good-humoured and willing to engage. He's told me there are things he is still conflicted about, but it's clear he still has a great deal of respect for Zach Crystal, and that he was genuinely sad when Crystal passed in 2019.

—Aye … the fire. It was such a … such a sad thing to happen. I'd been there since the place was built. Yeah, it was a fucked-up place sometimes, but this was the biggest star in the world. Things were never going to be normal, you know? I was sad, aye, when it burned. I was very sad. It, and him, had been a big part of my life, a huge part of it. I have a lot to thank him for, I'm not going to lie.

—*Was there a degree of relief at all? For him, if you see what I mean?*

—Aye, aye, I see what you mean. Finally he found peace. I know there's a lot of folk out there who hate him, who don't have any sympathy for him. I get it. But when you're there, right there, at the time, it's different. When he came back – it just felt like things were back on track at Crystal Forest, if you know what I mean? Then that Ian Julius popped up and started claiming he'd caught Mr Crystal online. Catfishing wasn't it?

—A lot of fans blame that for Zach Crystal's death.

—I see that side too. I think if it had been a few years ago, then the Bastard Squad would have been able to control it a bit better, but in 2019, people were more switched on and everything was online, Twitter and whatnot. Ian Julius chose the right time to do it, if he *was* lying that is.

— What do you think?

—I don't know. I'm sorry, but I've seen a lot of crazy things. I've been along for most of the ride, and one thing I've learned is that you have to deal in facts. You have to be sure. I never saw Mr Crystal do anything to anyone. Certainly nothing they're accusing him of. But I wasn't there all the time. Could he have done it? Maybe. Like I say, I only know what I saw.

—One last thing, Craig. Every single person who lived or worked at Crystal Forest was out when it burned down, all except for Zach Crystal. That seems amazingly coincidental.

There's a long silence. Craig sighs.

—I know. I know. It *was* though – just a coincidence. Bear in mind, even though Mr Crystal was back, there was still only a skeleton staff at Crystal Forest. And none of us really saw Mr Crystal anymore, anyway, not to talk to. I guess we just … we all had somewhere to be. I can't speak for anyone else but I was out on perimeter that night, with some of security. I guess it was just another one of those weird things.

It's nigh on impossible to track down any other members of Crystal Forest staff who were working that night. Craig tells me they all had confidentiality and non-disclosure agreements in their contracts. They all knew the power of those agreements and what could happen to them if they spoke out.

They still do, he says.

—So why have you been so gracious, so generous with your time?

Craig smiles and shrugs. He tells me he's not worried.

—I guess a part of me wants to find out what happened as much as you do.

Something occurs to me, and I'm suddenly paranoid. I look warily around the busy café. There are two men in suits sitting a few tables away. Is that too obvious? I look at the woman with her baby on the table beside us.

—Can I ask – did you seek permission from Naomi Crystal before speaking to me? Are we being watched? Recorded?

Craig laughs, long and loud. This certainly turns a few heads. He hunches his shoulders and speaks to me in a stage whisper.

—Maybe we are. But put it this way: if we were, there's not a lot we can do about it now, is there?

With that, Craig Kerr, trusted employee of Zach Crystal for nearly twenty years, is gone. His hulking shape disappears through the café doors and out into the street, the luscious mountains rising all around.

It's hard to know what to make of this interview. We've learned a lot about the goings-on behind the walls of Crystal Forest, but little about Zach Crystal himself. I think, sadly, the star proved as elusive to Craig as he did to the rest of us.

There are some troubling aspects from this episode: the discovery of a child's clothing, for example. Was that a simple, isolated incident? It seems Zach Crystal had a whole team around him, led by James Cryer, then his sister, dedicated to picking up after him. The gradual breakdown of Crystal's psyche is the most troubling of all – his desperate need for power and the ease with which he was able to wield it.

I didn't expect too much in the way of revelations from Craig. I am left feeling slightly unfulfilled, though. Craig was very good at not elaborating on certain aspects of his time at Crystal Forest. As much as the folklore surrounding the place is interesting, there is much about Crystal himself and the strange circumstances surrounding his death that remains elusive. I'm lucky that at least someone from the Crystal camp has spoken to me, I suppose. Of course, there are legal restrictions around what Craig can and cannot say, and ramifications if he breaks these. I do still suspect that someone, or someones, in the employ of the Crystal estate, was either present in that café or else Craig was recording our interview somehow. I think the need for control that Zach Crystal displayed during his life has most likely continued since his passing. His sister Naomi, who now runs the Crystal estate, has been a fierce defender of her late brother's honour. Bonnie Crystal has never spoken about her uncle. She has, in fact, successfully avoided the gaze of the public eye completely. I'd certainly admire anyone who would attempt to get through Naomi Crystal to speak to her.

This episode has given us some rare insights, though, and I would not be surprised if Craig Kerr becomes more in demand after this episode has aired. Maybe that's why I was permitted to talk to him.

I pack up all my equipment, get to my feet, shrug on my jacket and walk into the car park. That paranoid feeling still clings to me, and I watch every passer-by, but the looks I get back only make the feeling worse. Just as I try to force my mind to take a more logical approach, I spot that a note has been pushed under my windscreen wiper. I left the cafe not long after Craig; if he put it there, I didn't see him do it.

Or was it someone else?

I think about the video that's recently gone online – the inside of the cave and Craig's staunch refusal to even look at it – in case it's real.

I stand for a while, looking around me. Aviemore is a small but bustling tourist town; the roads are constantly busy with people crawling up into the Cairngorms. Aviemore is also not so far from Crystal Forest, and I wonder if, among the waiters, cooks, dishwashers or even patrons in the cafés and restaurants here, there's someone who maybe once worked at Crystal Forest? Clearly the power of Zach Crystal has a long reach.

The paper is a printed copy of a small article from the Inverness Courier, *undated. The article contains a blurry photograph of a teenage girl and the headline 'Please Come Home – Mother's Plea'.*

Beneath is only a few lines:

`Inverness mother Marie Owen (42) has reached out again to beg her daughter Kirsty, who turned nineteen` *this month, to come home. Kirsty Owen has been missing from the luxurious family home in Upper Myrtlefield, Inverness, for the last three years and is thought to be living in Edinburgh or northern England with a community of fanatical Zach Crystal fans.*

'I just want Kirsty to know that I've forgiven her. She's in no trouble, and I'm sorry.'

Anyone with links to Kirsty Owen is asked to contact Inverness police.

Below the article is a phone number, handwritten on the paper in felt tip.

As has happened before, someone is trying to control the narrative here. For what end, it is hard to see. So I guess, like we've done before, we'll go with it.

This has been our third.

And I have been Scott King.

Until next time…

Legendary Presenter Ruby Rendall's exclusive interview with pop megastar Zach Crystal. **More >**

---

1 hr 45 • 9pm 20th Jul 2019 • Available for 28 days

RR: 'Dead Eyes', everyone. What a song. It's just … stunning. Welcome back to a very special edition of *Ruby*. We're live with the enigma that is Zach Crystal. We do apologise for a few earlier technical hitches. I assure you that we seem to be back in business. Also, I need to say that, unfortunately, the presence of my guest has proved too much for some of our studio audience, and I just want to assure viewers that everyone's OK; those who need assistance are being attended to.

[The camera pans around to the audience, who are cheering. There are a number of empty seats and many more members of security standing among the crowd.]

ZC: Thank you … oh Ruby, you're making me blush again.

RR: You've just announced your tour; tickets will go on sale very soon. I hear there's a new album coming too. I can't wait. Zach. The *world* can't wait!

[Cheering getting louder]

ZC: You're very kind – you're all so kind. Thank you so much. It's been a long time coming. Finally, I've felt ready to come back out and face the world.

[More applause]

RR: Zach, you're so humble. I really admire that in someone of your stature. You've helped so many young people, and I just wonder, maybe it's now time to help yourself.

ZC: [*nodding and tearful*] Maybe it is, Ruby … maybe that's something I haven't done yet.

RR: You've had great heartache recently, great tragedy in your life.

ZC: That's true, Ruby, the last few years have been very, very hard. People look at the money and the fame, and they have their own opinions. They think that when you're famous, maybe you shouldn't, or you can't, feel things as much. It's not true, it's just not true. All the money in the world cannot stop the grief of losing your parents. Losing your best friend.

RR: Your parents passed in 2009, didn't they?

ZC: That's right. Both of heart failure. Very close together. It was a terrible, terrible thing. It was sudden, very sudden.

RR: I can't imagine how hard that must have been.

ZC: The media, the tabloids, were swarming like flies, trying to get pictures of me and my sister's grief; it was awful.

RR: You have to be a certain way in front of the cameras, don't you?

ZC: You're so right. You have to make sure you're upset in the 'correct' way. My sister, Naomi, she has a beautiful soul, but she doesn't show a lot on the outside. She maintains a strong … a strong mask if you know what I mean?

RR: Sure … sure. Of course.

ZC: The press said she was 'stone-faced', that she didn't care. I felt like I had to cry for both of us. I had to cry for her, to show them. It's why I spent so much time hidden from them, so much time away.

RR: We've touched a little on the tragedy in your life. To come back from all that, well, it's just mind-blowing.

ZC: I made a resolution to myself, Ruby, after my parents passed away. Whatever I felt, whatever pain and guilt that I felt, I would plough back into helping others.

RR: And that's what you continue to do. For so many.

ZC: But I know there's more. Much more I can do.

RR: You've given so much of your money…

ZC: No, *no.* I don't mean money. Money is all well and good, but there's something better. Something far better I can do. It's something I'm working on. Something that will change the world for good.

RR: You're full of surprises Zach. Can you share with us what it is?

ZC: It's all about opening your mind, all about belief. I believe very much in the ability to turn bad things into good things – I feel I can do that. I feel like I am on my way to be able to do that.

RR: Wow, that's quite something. Can you elaborate? Can you tell us more?

ZC: Since the passing of my parents, since the passing of my best friend, I've realised there are signs in the world that tell us when bad things are going to happen, but most of us have closed our minds to them.

RR: You mentioned this earlier didn't you? About how we're conditioned into not believing in magic. It struck me as quite sad. Would I be right in thinking that Crystal Forest is some way of fighting back against that?

ZC: It's true, Ruby. It's true and it works. What I'm discovering is that I can change things. I am trying to harness the power – that magic – to heal people, to help people. The young people who I work with, they're helping me understand how to do that.

RR: I think I follow you…

ZC: I built the tree house in Crystal Forest to be a place where you don't have to see things normally – it's a place of magic, where you are able to use your imagination. I have thousands of clothes to dress up in, jewellery, makeup. You can be what you want to be up there; you can be ageless, timeless. The young people I help, they've often had to grow up too fast. They've had that time taken away from them, that time when they could read, and they could dream. I give it back to them. I show them the place my music comes from, and I see their minds starting to open up again.

RR: Almost like regression?

ZC: For me, maybe, but for them it's beautiful. There's magic up there, real magic. Magic heals wounds. I heal them with it and their magic heals me.

RR: In this state … in this opening of the mind, you talk about being able to see things.

ZC: That's right. There is so much to see with an open mind.

Often, very often, some of the young people open up in the therapy sessions I provide for them. They realise that they've seen things too, but they've let their minds dismiss them. They've let themselves be conditioned not to believe. When they're with me, that world is open again. Sometimes we see things that frighten us.

RR: There's an old story attached to that piece of forest, isn't there?

ZC: There is and that's another example of magic. That story is centuries old, passed down – it has so much magic, so much power. It is that which I'm trying to harness. Turning a bad thing into something good.

RR: Are you saying it's true?

ZC: It's just what I've been saying: we're conditioned not to believe in spirits, visions; we've trained our minds to be closed to them. Not me. I have seen things up there. I saw things before my parents died; I saw them before my best friend died. I *know* there is magic there, and I know that one day I can use it for good.

RR: Zach, you've faced a great deal of criticism for spending so much time with young girls.

ZC: I know. It's amazing isn't it? You offer help, therapy, companionship, support, and what do the media want? They want a bad guy. They want Zach the ripper. I take these girls into the magical places and I help them. They open their minds, they shake off their shackles, they allow themselves to remember, to feel. Then we talk about it. It's very beautiful, very cleansing.

RR: There have been people – women – saying that there were incidents between you and them in Crystal Forest.

ZC: Incidents. Right. *Incidents*. It's funny they should talk to the media about it, isn't it? You would think, wouldn't you, Ruby, that if something bad happened to you, you would go to the police, right? You wouldn't sell your story to a tabloid or a TV station. You wouldn't want *money* from it, right?

RR: I—

ZC: You know who *does* talk about these things, who tells the truth? Sasha Stewart. She is a very special person. She's someone who was there, someone who has spent time at Crystal Forest. She's talking about it for free on her podcast.

RR: That's very true. Obviously I can't promote her podcast on the BBC, but it's true, she has been there. Up to Crystal Forest. Nothing bad happened, am I right?

ZC: She's been all over Crystal Forest, she's been in the tree house, and the only things that happened up there for her were good things. You can see how it helped her. She's doing so well now, doing so much better with her life. Up at Crystal Forest, you see, she was finally allowed to dream. Dreams and imagination are powerful things. Soon they're going to be even more powerful.

RR: So what is it you actually do up there, in Crystal Forest, in that tree house?

ZC: There's a lot of just having fun – dressing up, dreaming, imagining. It's also very therapeutic. We talk to each other up there. Talking helps those troubled young people – it helps them heal. We look out at the forest, nature all around us. It's very beautiful, serene. In the evenings we watch horror movies, just like teenagers do.

RR: But you're not a teenager, Zach, you're a forty-five-year-old man.

ZC: Maybe so, but age is just a number. My heart is something else. That's the other thing with these girls: they never had a proper teenage-hood either. They all had to grow up so fast, it's sad. Up at Crystal Forest it's like something from a *Famous Five* story – a clubhouse, a magical palace in the forest.

RR: Your image, Zach, it seems like what you wear and how you are, it's like something out of a story. Like out of an old book.

ZC: Maybe I am … maybe I am a figment of imagination – someone's imagination. Maybe that's why I'm here. Maybe I'm a dream … I think if we all dreamed a bit more, allowed our imagination more space, the world would be better, don't you think?

RR: So what would you say to those who doubt you?

ZC: Whatever they say about me means nothing. Their words can't touch me, they can't kill me. However hard they try.

[Applause, getting louder. Crystal stares straight and resolute into the camera.]

RR: When you put it like that, Zach, it all just sounds reasonable. It sounds constructive – it sounds genuinely helpful. We're going to go to something else now, another exclusive that we've been keeping up our sleeves. We've managed not to leak it and … Well, would you like to introduce it?

ZC: Aw Ruby, I'm shy, you know that.

RR: Ladies and gentlemen and everyone else – it is my absolute *pleasure* to share for the first time *ever*. The premiere of brand-new music from Zach Crystal.

[Applause and cheering]

RR: Yes, yes. Recorded back up at Crystal Forest, this is rare footage. A pre-recorded performance, by Zach Crystal, from a studio session in 2007. A track that was cut from the *Damage* album. This has never been heard before now. This is called 'From the Start'.

[Wild applause]

Episode 4: The Special Girls

Hi love, just me again. I don't know if you're sick of my voice yet ... Well, I guess you have the choice to turn it off if it gets boring. I'm sorry for the tears. I'm sorry if hearing this makes you sad. You'll be twenty-three tomorrow. Well ... when I'm recording this, you will. It's on the calendar, even though I know the date. Why would I need to remind myself of the day I gave birth to you, love? Silly, I know. Silly of me to write your name on the calendar like that. Silly of me to bake you a cake as well. But I do it. Every year. Just in case ... just in case...

[...]

Sorry. I'm back. Composed myself and had a cup of tea. Tilly's in here now with me. Well, not *with* me as such, but with me as much as cats allow. She's never liked being stroked much, though, has she? Not by me, anyway. I feel that she just tolerates me. She's tolerated me more in the last few years. Sometimes she even comes and sits on my knee in the evenings. Bless her. She came running into the house with her tail like a bottle brush just now. I don't know what she's been doing out there in the dark. I guess that's what prompted me to record this for you my love. Tilly always used to run up to your room when she was scared, didn't she? Maybe there's foxes or something in the garden tonight.

There was a shadow out there earlier that scared me silly too...

Poor old Tilly. Maybe we need each other more than we know.

It was you who was always her favourite, though. She never minded you picking her up. She would climb into bed with you, wouldn't she? Leave your bedroom covered in cat hair. She used to sit around your neck too, didn't she, love? When you were doing your homework. What a sight it was. Bless. It was you she ran to when we went to the shelter, do you remember? We looked at her through the cage door, those sad little concrete paddocks that you said looked like death row. She ran straight to you, didn't she? Rubbing that fur of hers against the cage and purring. They'd never seen her do anything of the sort before. That's what they said, wasn't it? You said she'd chosen us.

Poor old Tilly. I hear her in the night you know, scratching at your door, even when it's open. I go up and she looks at me as if to say 'Where's she gone? What have you done with my Kirsty?' Poor old soul. She's not getting any younger. Remember when we first moved here? We were all a bit like Tilly. We'd never seen so much space before. And a garden! A real garden that was *ours.* I've had to start getting someone in to help me with it lately. My arthritis just won't let me get on like I used to.

Tilly spends a lot of time sat at the windowsill in the living room, staring out at the drive, and I wonder if she's waiting for you to come home. Or maybe she's looking at that ...

No, it's nothing. Just silly old Tilly.

I'm sorry. I know I said I'd try not to, but I can't help it. I can't help it Kirsty, love. I miss you, and every year it gets harder. I just want you to know that I've kept your room just how you like it. I've not been prying into your things. All I've done in there is change the bed sheets, open the window to let the air in. That's all. I've left the posters up. It's hard for me to do that, love. You know it is, but I've left them. I haven't messed with them. I remember you making that collage for school, from all your magazines, sat at the table.

I've said all this before. I'm sorry, love.

What else? What else has been going on? There's a new café opened down the high street. All vegan. Me and Mary from number nineteen went down and had a try of their cakes. They're so fancy and you'd never think there was no butter in them. It's done up nice inside, too, you know. They do all sorts – pizzas and breakfast and everything. I said to Mary, I said, we'll have to come back, won't we?

What else? Mary keeps telling me I need to sell up and move somewhere smaller. She says she doesn't like me rattling around the place all on my own. She says it's too much, but I always tell her that you might have gone to university and it would be the same. I'd have still kept your room ready if you ever needed to come home, love.

If you ever do want to come home, love, I'll be waiting for you. I'll have the heating on and we can sit in the dining room and play a game of Monopoly, just like we used to.

Well ... that's it for now, love. That's all I've got for you. I'm sorry if it's a bit sad, and that I don't have much to say. I'm trying to get out, trying to do more than just rattle round the house like some old ghost.

I'd better get back downstairs and get your cake iced, hadn't I? Or else Tilly will have her face in the buttercream. You know what she's like...

Speak to you tomorrow, my love.

I miss you.

I love you.

So, so much.

Welcome to Six Stories.

I'm Scott King.

Over these strange six weeks, we're delving into something that at its heart, I guess, is a cold case.

A fire. Four tragic deaths.

Allegations. Rumours, whispers.

Like always, we're raking up old graves.

This grave is very different though – we're trying this time to find the door to an elaborate mausoleum. We're perambulating the winding paths of a graveyard, searching for the most direct way into a heavily fortified and guarded plot. Unfortunately, it seems most of the ways in are barred.

The case of Zach Crystal, unlike many of the cases I've covered, is well known. Globally `so. The enigmatic musician, whose disappearance, return and subsequent death will live long in the history books, is the subject of this series. Will we ever be able to fully explain the man? I doubt it. Will we be able to prove or disprove the allegations of, among others, five women – Sammy Williams, Mary Wooton, Gabrielle Martinez , Zofia Kowalski and Jennifer Rossi – who have claimed they were assaulted as teenagers by Crystal.

No. At least, that's not what I'm here to try to do.

Will we be able to find out exactly what happened at Crystal Forest and the circumstances of the fire that rendered it a ruin? Will we be able to say for sure whether Zach Crystal took his own life in light of the allegations that surrounded him?

I doubt that also.

So what are we doing here – in the Highlands of Scotland, in the shadow of a dead man? We've spoken so far to three people who sit in varying places on the vast and complicated Zach Crystal spectrum. What have we learned and where will we go next?

I've spoken to people who believe he's guilty, those who believe he's innocent, and last time someone who I believe is, to some extent, towing a party line when it comes to his old boss. Why, I am still not sure. Perhaps it is simple loyalty to a former employer, who set Craig Kerr and his family up for life.

Crystal was a bizarre and secretive figure. When he gave interviews, they were heavily scripted, choreographed affairs, especially after the claims against him began to surface. The only one that didn't seem to be a power play to control the narrative was the Ruby Rendall interview on BBC One. Crystal, on the surface, was philanthropic, generous and charity-minded. Zach Crystal did seem to be making it his life's work to help troubled young women. A number of these woman, however, are now claiming that they were sexually assaulted by Crystal, up in that mysterious tree house in the depths of the Whispering Wood.

In this episode, thanks to a note placed on my car by persons unknown, we'll hear how Zach Crystal was able to spend so much time with these young women.

We know that Crystal had created a cabal of power up in Crystal Forest. His increasing paranoia and his need to control everything that went on in his residence went hand in hand with his rise to pop superstardom. We've also heard that one thing Zach Crystal desperately wanted control over was whatever it was he believed lived in the Whispering Wood. Was there something deeply wrong with the man, or was there really something there all along?

In this series, I've discovered that there's only so far you can go in investigating Zach Crystal before you hit a brick wall. It's an elegant and well-presented wall, though, with a neat Zach Crystal logo painted on its surface. Because, you see, with fame, comes power. If someone has a certain amount of power, it allows them access to things others are denied. As we saw in a previous season of this podcast, fame allows someone to be whatever they want to be. It gives them the time and capacity to create a persona. A veneer.

However, we're not talking about mere fame here – a flash-in-the-pan YouTube star or last month's bestseller. This is a man who was so famous, so powerful, he had his own decoy on the payroll. When we talk about Zach Crystal, we're talking about a musical legend, we're talking fame and power beyond the imagining of us mere humans.

We're talking about something akin to a god.

Is this too strong a word to use? Perhaps. But you see, for those who worshipped at the temple of Zach Crystal, that was precisely how he was seen.

And it is this status we shall examine in this, episode four of our series.

I have realised that to knock on the door of an ivory tower when you're wearing cheap shoes is useless. When you're dealing with this sort of power, you have to rifle through the rubbish instead. Although I wouldn't call our fourth interviewee rubbish herself. Certainly not.

Many of you will have heard of Marie Owen. You may have seen her name in the press. Many of you will be looking at me askance for even giving Marie a voice on this podcast.

Marie Owen is a remnant, a by-product – someone chewed up and spat out by the Zach Crystal machine. Until now, Marie has never found anyone who really wants to hear her story as she tells it. There are plenty who've told it for her, of course. And there are many who will say her story's irrelevant, that she does not matter.

Yet she mattered enough to someone for them to pass her number on to me. I still don't know who that someone was. Craig Kerr? It's certainly possible.

But that's precisely why I want to talk to her. I'm not going to get anything tangible from the Zach Crystal side of things, so why not look somewhere else instead?

—There are people who hate me. I know that. I still get letters. There are people out there who believe I should be burning in hell for what I did. I want to let those people know that I am burning there. I have been burning in hell for most of my life.

I am in hell now.

Marie Owen lives in the Myrtlefield area of Inverness, perched on the outskirts of the city. There are locked gates and security cameras, and a long, paved driveway lined with tall hedges. My little car looks very much out of place here, the automatic gate closing silently behind me. All around is quiet, with a stunning view over the Moray Firth.

I have to say I'm not surprised by the air of humility in Marie Owen. The sixty-one-year-old smiles at me with her mouth, but her eyes – and she will share this view entirely – hold a fathomless sadness. She carries it in her walk, in her manner. The house, vast as it is inside, is dusty, the ornaments and photographs tired, the furniture sun-bleached. The houseplants are clinging on to life. For such a huge house, there is very little in the way of things. The modern, minimalist decor looks barren. The carpet is worn in three distinct tracks, from the kitchen to an easy chair in the living room and up the stairs. An ancient cat sits on the windowsill – scraggy and skinny, it stares out into the empty driveway. It doesn't even look up when I enter. This house is the saddest place I've ever been.

—*Can we start at the start? You've not always lived here, have you?*

—Johnny, Kirsty's father, left us when she was only a baby, thank God. That's when we lived in that awful tower block in East Kilbride. I had some problems. Not going to lie here. I'm not going to try and tell you that I was perfect. I was far from it.

—*Did Kirsty's father ever have anything to do with his daughter?*

—Aside from nearly killing her, and me, numerous times, no.

—*I'm so sorry that you had to endure that, Marie.*

—The harshest thing about it was that I blamed myself. Every time he came home drunk, every time he spent all our benefit money on cocaine and gambling, it was my fault. I couldn't keep a house, I couldn't get a job, I couldn't even keep the baby quiet. No wonder I was fat and useless to him. I always felt I deserved it, his fists, that it was always my fault.

The only time he ever got in touch was when he'd seen Kirsty on television with *that man*, I'm sorry, Mr King, I can't say his name. He phoned and asked me if she'd managed to get any money, and if she had, that he was entitled to some of it. That was Kirsty's father.

—*After he left, things didn't get much better, did they?*

—No. No they didn't. In some ways he was right. I wasn't a fit mother. I didn't know what I was doing with a little baby. I had no friends, no family, and I couldn't cope. Pathetic, I was.

It's heart-breaking to hear Marie speak like this. I'm sure there are many who feel that she got what she deserved, but for me, right here and now, I don't believe that is true. Marie, at least, sought out help. She was upfront about the fact she was struggling, both financially and mentally.

—I feel that Kirsty never forgave me for giving her away like I did, but it was for her – it was so that she didn't have to be raised by someone like me.

Marie put one-year-old Kirsty into foster care with South Lanarkshire's children's services. It was a decision that broke more than just her heart, but she tells me she never doubted it was the right one to make. She simply could not cope and wanted Kirsty to have a better life.

—People have their opinions about me for sending her away when she was a baby. But really, what did I have to offer a little girl? A disgusting little flat in a tower block, where all the furniture was broken and the lift didn't even work. Worst of all, me. What did I have? No job, no hope. I couldn't cook. I had no idea how on earth to be a mum. I wanted better for my child. That's all I wanted.

Marie was not in a good place. She could barely look after herself, and while some see giving her daughter away as throwing in the towel, there is an argument that it was a selfless act. I am not here to judge Marie on her decision.

Baby Kirsty was eventually adopted.

—They were a lovely couple. A bit older. Always wanted a little one but couldn't. I never met them, but the social worker gave me a letter that they'd written to me. I still read it occasionally and still cry every time, all these years later. They told me I could write to Kirsty. Social services would put them in the 'life book' that she would get when she was old enough. Eighteen. It seemed a long, long time away. They said that I could visit. When she was old enough to understand. They said they would sort it out. You know, it was that that kept me going. It was that that stopped me ending it all. It drove me forward. Small steps, but forward steps. I started looking out for myself a bit more. I just kept thinking about what Kirsty would think when she was older.

Marie was as good as her word. She wrote to her daughter weekly, saving up the letters and delivering them to social services.

—I was getting myself back together, but it was a slow process. It wasn't easy. I was a wreck. A broken person. The good days were outweighed by the bad ones, when I'd just lie on the sofa staring at the wall. I wouldn't wash, wouldn't eat, wouldn't clean up. He'd taken everything from me. He'd ruined me. It was years and years later when I went into therapy, when *that man* paid for me to speak to a professional. That's when I began to heal. That was when I began to learn real things about myself. I knew then I never should have had a kid. My own parents had no idea how to parent, so what hope did I have?

Anyway, I'm not the victim in all this. Not by a long way. I was taking it a day at a time, every day would be one closer to that eighteen-year sentence. Every day was one day closer to seeing her again, to making it up.

Nine years I did it. Nine years, a day at a time, then everything fell apart.

When things began to unravel for Kirsty, it wasn't anything to do with Marie. It's not possible for me to find out a great deal about what happened. I can only go on what Marie tells me. She said she didn't hear anything about it until Kirsty was suddenly transferred from her adoptive family to a children's home.

—I was going out of my mind. I still wasn't allowed to see her. All I knew was that she was now in a home. I was terrified. I'd been in and out of those places when I was a kid, when my parents wanted rid of me. I know things are different now, the facilities are better, but the feeling never goes away. That feeling that you're not wanted. That shame is like acid – it burns and burns, right down into your bones, right through into your heart, through your heart and into your very being. It becomes you. I couldn't have that happen to my Kirsty. But what could I do?

I eventually found out it was because of her behaviour. After all that time her adoptive parents decided they couldn't cope with her anymore and gave her up. Just like that. It was disgusting. I was raging. I wanted to find those people and … well…

Kirsty and Marie were eventually reunited. Marie took this perceived slight against her daughter as motivation to get herself together. Eventually, after some supervised visits and gradual contact, Kirsty was released into Marie's full custody. She was eleven years old.

—It wasn't easy for either of us. I'd moved to Perth, the fair city, to try and start again, you know? I had a job. This would have been, what ninety-five, ninety-six? It was ninety-six, cos that was the Euros wasn't it? I was working in a bar on the football days and it was manic. I would get home, shattered. Then I'd have to cook and clean and be a mum. Don't get me wrong, I loved it. I loved every second of it. This was a privilege. We didn't have much, but I gave her everything I could. I still would.

It was only after living together for a few, idyllic months, that Marie started to notice some of Kirsty's more challenging behaviours.

—Things would go missing, turn up again in funny places. It wasn't stealing. I think it was an attention thing. Nothing valuable – it wasn't money or anything, but, for example, my spatula might disappear, just *gone* from the kitchen drawer, then reappear under my pillow. That sort of thing. It was all about challenging me. I'd already given her away, and her adoption hadn't worked out. She was testing me, challenging me. I don't blame her. I never have.

—*What was she like, day to day?*

—She was quiet … sat in her bedroom listening to music … *his* music. She had posters of him all over the walls. She'd cut out every article in every magazine about him and made a collage with them. She was utterly obsessed.

—*Did that trouble you?*

—Maybe, in hindsight, but at the time – you tell me who wasn't obsessed with *him* back then. Of course, Kirsty was growing up, becoming a young woman, and things began to get a little bit … Well, show me a parent who doesn't have a bit of a rough time with their kids and I'll show you a liar. We had our ups and downs, sure. There were arguments.

—*Were they just normal young-girl-parent arguments?*

—I've always felt so guilty – there's always been that thing between us: the fact that I gave her away. It's always been there, no matter how many times I explained it to her. I've always wondered if she secretly hates me for it. Maybe she does. I don't know. Kirsty acted like most girls would – sulking, staying in her bedroom, playing *his* music really loudly. The thing was, with all the guilt I felt, I never really knew what to do. I would just end up beating myself up about it, you know? It always felt like it was my fault in the end.

I think I let her get away with too much, but it was never bad stuff, drink and drugs.

—*What was it?*

—We didn't have a computer at home so Kirsty spent a lot of time at the library. I know she was there because I would go with her, do the shopping in the precinct nearby, you know? The bar was near too, so she could go to the library sometimes when I worked in the day. But it wasn't books she was interested in, it was the internet. She was on the fan sites and the forums, talking about *him* with all the other fans all over the world. I didn't mind. In fact, I was kind of glad she'd found her tribe, her people. So I saved up and we got a computer at home. We got the internet. That was a mistake.

This was 2004 when Kirsty was twelve. Marie says her phone line was constantly in use by Kirsty. MySpace was ascending rapidly as a social network and Kirsty was amassing thousands of friends, talking to them on forums and chat rooms long into the night. Marie says she never monitored Kirsty, never poked her nose into what she was doing.

—I wanted her to know I trusted her. That was so important for us. It would have been different if she'd been out, causing trouble, but she wasn't. She didn't really have friends in school – all her life was online. On the … on the forums talking about *him*. She wasn't interested in anything else. She barely spoke to me.

—*That must have been so tough.*

—She never wanted to *do* anything else except talk to other fans. It was hard. I was beaten down by all of it, by everything. I wasn't coping. I just wanted to find something, some common ground that we could share. That's why I made such a stupid decision – a whole load of stupid decisions, really.

Marie sighs and sits back in her chair. The cat on the windowsill stretches itself out and glances around before hunkering down and resuming its observation of the front drive. I'm still getting over the juxtaposition between Marie and her beautiful house. I excuse myself to go to the bathroom – all modern fixtures, a bath sunken into the floor. I look through the door of her bedroom. It has a gigantic bed, a view out of the window over the Moray Firth. But everything is shabby, the bed isn't made, and the bathroom could do with a scrub. I know money doesn't buy happiness, but here, it looks like these lavish surroundings have fallen into disrepair. One door remains closed, upstairs. Kirsty's bedroom I presume. I don't look inside.

—I was clearing up her bedroom. It was a tip – full of mouldy cups and plates, you know? She was only twelve. Twelve going on sixteen. There was one of her magazines lying on the bed, open, and I don't know what it was that caught my eye. I just … I don't know why I did it.

There was a full-page spread in Whoop! *magazine documenting Zach Crystal's accident at Crystal Forest and how he was currently an inpatient at Raigmore Hospital, Inverness, with a broken leg. Next to it, half finished, was a get-well-soon card that Kirsty had made herself.*

—It sounds soft, but it brought me to tears. It was beautiful – decorated with glitter and stickers. She'd clearly spent a lot of time on it, you know? That's what gave me stupid idea number one.

Marie waited for Kirsty to return home and nonchalantly explained she'd heard on the news about Crystal's accident. Kirsty told her mother she was making a card for the star and asked if Marie would put it in the post.

—So I says 'why don't we go up there together and you can give it to him yourself?' The way her face lit up … What an idiot I was. It was a couple of hours on the train to get to Inverness and we'd go through the Cairngorms. I would pack up some food, we'd make a day of it. Kirsty was over the moon. She was so happy, she hugged me. Finally, I thought, finally, I'm getting through to her. Finally, I'm being a good mother.

Zach Crystal spent a few days at Raigmore hospital with his leg in a cast after falling while rehearsing for his South American tour. After that, there was a long convalescence at Crystal Forest and physical therapy. Marie remembers that the train journey from Perth to Inverness was stunning. The Highland main line winds through the Cairngorms National Park and the weather was clear enough to show off the park's stunning natural beauty. Kirsty happily chatted to her mother the whole way, about Zach Crystal, of course.

—I didn't mind. It was what she was passionate about. She told me all about him, his hard life growing up and playing in bars with his sister in England, how he'd bought this huge piece of forest up in Colliecrith. I didn't know he was so close. She played me some of his music on her Discman … Aye it was OK. I told her all about

The Beatles in the sixties and the Bay City Rollers. I told her how the girls went wild over them too.

'He's different, Mum,' she kept saying, 'he's different to all them.'

I have to say – and it sounds so daft – but that journey, that train ride, was the best time of my life. When we got there … not so much.

On arrival in Inverness, it was clear what a huge deal Zach Crystal was. The route to Raigmore hospital was being controlled by police to ensure ambulances could get in and out. No taxis or cars were allowed anywhere near. The city was more or less in gridlock. Marie tells me she had not anticipated the sheer scale of this.

—There were police all over. We got the number two bus, which was full of girls Kirsty's age and older. They were all carrying flowers and teddies and all sorts. There were people with speakers, playing his music. It was a carnival atmosphere. It really was something else. We got as close as we could and I just thought, now what?

Marie pushed forward with the crowd, closer and closer to the side of the hospital where Zach Crystal's window was visible. The thronging crowd got larger and larger and as the hours went by, they got closer and closer to the front.

—The closer we got, it was crazy – there were girls screaming and fainting. At one point there was a movement at his window, and I thought we were going to be crushed to death. We were due to get the train back at four, but there was no way, no way in hell, that I was going to tell her we had to leave.

The police had erected a cordon with crowd-control barriers. Marie says the atmosphere had gone from jovial to hysterical, and she began to get a little worried.

—There were lassies passing out, people thirsty and hungry. They'd been there all day. There were some real … I don't want to say *nutters*, you know? But real super-fans.

—*What was their behaviour like?*

—It troubled me; it was odd. They were all screaming, as you'd expect, but the screams were … I dunno. They weren't the screams of wild fans – they were short, sharp blasts, like a chant. They did them all together as well. I thought it was something to do with him, that I was just old, I just didn't understand. But then, remember that interview he did with Ruby Rendall, when the crowd were all twitching and screeching? That brought it all back. That's what it was like.

—*How was Kirsty through all this? Did she join in?*

—She was … I'd never seen her like it. She never took her eyes off that window. When he opened the blind and waved, there was just this *roar* from everyone, girls screaming, crying. It was bedlam.

Marie and Kirsty found themselves close to the front of the cordon, where a few policemen had been joined by Zach Crystal's own security. That's when, Marie says, she had stupid idea number two.

—I remembered Take That back in the nineties, how much they meant to me. How much they meant to so many young women and girls. There was a helpline set up when they broke up, you remember?

—*I do.*

—And I just … I wanted this to be a memory for Kirsty. I knew that at some point, probably sooner than later, I would lose her. I just wanted her to have something in the bank, some happy memories with me, you know? That's where stupid idea number two came from.

Marie held Kirsty up as they reached the front of the barricade, and Kirsty handed her card to one of Zach Crystal's security team, who smiled back and pocketed the envelope.

—Kirsty was made up. I thought the guy was just being kind, you know? Just pretending. The card would end up in the bin. I never thought *he'd* even hear about it…

As darkness fell, Kirsty finally conceded it was time to leave. The pair picked up a pizza, which they shared on the train home, and as night fell across the rolling forests of the Cairngorms, Marie felt that finally, her life was changing. She was right. Although not in the way she had hoped.

—It was the next day, early in the morning, when the phone goes. I nearly didn't make it – I was washing my hair. I pick it up and there's this soft voice on the other end asking if he could speak to Kirsty. I asked who it was and he says it's *him*. Crystal.

—*Did you believe it?*

—I thought actually it was Kirsty, you know, playing a prank, so I says I'll go get her, trying to catch her out. She was asleep. I said to her, all nonchalant, like, 'Morning love, Zach Crystal on the phone for you.'

Well, she jumps out of bed, and I still think this is all some prank, some joke. But she's shaking. Actually shaking. She says she can't believe it. She gets on the phone and the poor girl can barely speak. Then she hands it over to me and says he wants to talk. I'm laughing away, but when I get on the line … I dunno, there's something in his voice. I just … Suddenly it's not funny anymore.

—*What did he say?*

—The guy was polite. He was soft, like I said. He told me how beautiful Kirsty's card was, what a beautiful and talented young girl she is and he hopes things are OK at home. I'm all over the place. I don't know what he's on about. I said they were, thank you very much, and next thing he asks if we want to come and visit when he's back on his feet. It was surreal. I thought I was dreaming. I look at Kirsty, who's like a little puppy, her eyes all wide. I say OK, I say sure. It was all very strange.

—*How did he get your number? Zach Crystal must have received thousands of similar cards. Why Kirsty?*

—I asked Kirsty the very same question. Her answer … Oh my God, I still feel it. I still feel that chill that went through me. Kirsty told me she'd put other things in the card, after I'd seen it. Our house phone number, our *address*. Her email, her MySpace page, everything.

I'm not daft. I know what it's like to worship a pop star, to want nothing more than them to notice you. I get it. It wasn't even that that upset me, you know?

—*Was there something else?*

—Two things. A photograph of herself and a little note. The note was all about how unhappy she was at home. That was the deepest cut of all. I knew I wasn't perfect. I knew we had our problems, but it was so bad for her, she'd had to tell *him* about it. That broke my heart.

Tears trickle silently down Marie's face.

—I just wish she'd asked my advice. The photograph. I've not seen it and I don't know if I want to. I don't think it was explicit but … I don't know…

The next day, Zach Crystal called the house again.

—It wasn't him, not at first. It was his manager or whatever, his PA. James Cryer. He was very nice, very polite. He wanted to speak to me, wanted to check if it was OK, Zach Crystal speaking to Kirsty. He said that Zach is very good at talking with young people, they made him happy and he thought while he was in hospital that he would call as many fans as he could, make them happy back, you know?

—*Were you OK with it?*

—I was … because it just seemed amazing. That someone like him would call *us*, our wee flat in Perth. I also knew what it would do for Kirsty; how this had brought us together like this. I couldn't turn round and say no could I?

So Marie passed the phone to Kirsty. She says that first time, Kirsty and Crystal talked for about half an hour. Afterward, Kirsty was on cloud nine. She was agreeable, she was happy. She sang with Marie – Zach Crystal songs, of course – while they cooked dinner.

—It was like we were a proper family. And it was all thanks to *him*.

The phone calls became daily, then nightly, Kirsty often talking to Zach Crystal for hours at a time. Marie says she didn't sit and monitor the calls. Kirsty would often take the phone into her bedroom.

—Did you ever ask what a thirty-year-old global superstar had in common with a twelve-year-old girl in Perth?

—Not like *that*, I didn't, no. Maybe I should have. That's what a shitty mother I am. I just knew he made her happy. According to Kirsty, they had a lot in common. He'd had a tough time growing up, being a star so young, and I honestly thought he was doing her a favour, that he was helping her, and me as well. I hate to say it, but that month or so, it was beautiful. It was the best month of our lives.

Zach Crystal was released from hospital and with his South American tour cancelled, travelled back to Crystal Forest to rehabilitate.

—His aide, James Cryer, would often speak to me. He would tell me how much the calls with Kirsty were helping *him*, you know? Helping him get better. James used to say he knew it was weird, but the two had hit it off and were becoming friends. I told him how hard Kirsty found it, making friends in real life and, you know what? I thought this might even help; that she had a story no one else had. She was friends with *him*.

I watched her thrive, and things only seemed to get better.

Packages began to arrive. Makeup, flowers, gadgets, and even televisions and games consoles. Suddenly all their bills and rent were being paid. There was fresh food in the fridge and the freezer was full to bursting. Marie and Kirsty had never been closer. But things were about to go downhill, very quickly.

—She had a camera. A little digital one I didn't know about. And she was still talking online to people too. I'm sorry to say, I did snoop. I looked at her computer when she was at school. She'd left herself logged in and I just … I was protective. I was curious.

—Was Kirsty telling the others about her friendship with Zach Crystal?

—That was the thing. She wasn't. They were talking about other things. Strange things. A few of them had said they had seen something – a ghost of some sort, but it was an animal. Kirsty was saying she'd seen it too. Apparently, it always meant something bad was going to happen. Well, I was determined that was not going to happen. Looking back I wonder – maybe she'd *meant* me to see all that.

A week before Kirsty's thirteenth birthday, she dropped a bombshell. Marie now realises that this was when things really got out of control.

—Kirsty came downstairs one morning and asked me if she could go and stay with *him* for a while. In that place of his in Colliecrith. I was about to tell her no, but she told me I was allowed to come too. She said we would stay in a guest suite. Better than any five-star hotel. I mean, you've seen what Crystal Forest looked like. It was paradise. He told her the both of us could go, stay as long as we liked.

—What were your initial thoughts?

—Any mother, any parent would have been dubious. At first. But the thing was, he'd done so much for us. The money kept arriving in my bank account. More money that I'd ever seen before … And I felt like I owed it to him. That's how he had me, that's how he had her. Money. I put money over my own daughter.

It's a chilling sentence, one that has been levelled at Marie Owen since the death of Zach Crystal and the subsequent allegations that came out in the wake of it. It makes sense to me that Marie does not want her name out there. As many of you will know, Marie has been through her own trial by media. Like many who have publicly condemned Crystal.

'I Sold My Daughter to Zach Crystal' was a recent story in Coffee Break! *magazine. 'Call Yourself a Mother?' was a headline in the* Daily Mail. *Delving into the comments sections is to be drenched in a furore of bile and hate toward the parents of those who share similar stories*

to Marie's. Then there are the lawsuits. Many people have found themselves being sued for defamation or slander by the Crystal estate. Many of these people signed NDAs when they first met Crystal, but neglected to read the small print.

I ask Marie if she and Kirsty had to sign anything before their visit.

—Oh all sorts. We did it all on the train – on that same route through the Cairngorms. But this time it was in first class, with a load of *his* people in the same carriage. Honestly, I didn't even read what I was signing. It was too much of a dream. Kirsty told me it was all to do with images – so they were allowed to take photos of us at Crystal Forest for publicity, that sort of thing. She was happy, so I just went along with it. They'd earmarked everywhere I had to sign, and I just thought they were sorting it all out for us. I thought they were being kind … How stupid I was – how foolish. I blame myself, entirely. It was all my fault.

Marie, a little like Ian Julius, is a much maligned figure. It feels like now, however, with Kirsty gone for so long, that she no longer cares about the consequences of talking to me. She says the Crystal estate can sue her, they can take her house.

—They took my daughter. Nothing else important is left.

On arrival at Crystal Forest, Marie was surprised and reassured that there were several other young girls and their families.

—It was like a holiday resort or something. Honestly, it was beautiful, like something out of a dream. I remember Kirsty was a bit put out. I think she thought she'd be the only one, but it reassured me. I felt better about the whole thing. This must be what he did – he helped families like us, girls like Kirsty.

Talking to the other families, Marie soon realised that all of them had their problems. Some were foster carers, some were adoptive parents, some had suffered addiction and domestic violence. Crystal Forest quickly became their place of salvation.

—It was beautiful. Stunning. It's truly an amazing place. The guest suites in the main house are just as magical. There's fairy lights on everything; wooden walkways, little iron gates. It's like being in a kind of make-believe fairy-tale palace. I can only imagine what the tree house was like. But it's also very – how would you describe it ... controlled, is the word, maybe. Everything has rounded edges. There's little lights showing you where the paths are, there's clear signs and locked doors. You feel when you're there that there's a lot going on behind the scenes, as it were. The staff are very quiet, very discreet. They don't talk to you. But that's why it's so good – everything is so clear. You have this sense of freedom, that everything has been taken care of.

—*Were there any real restrictions on you when you stayed there?*

—The only rule was that you couldn't go into the forest, into those woods, unsupervised. We were told, in no uncertain terms, that if we were caught in the woods without permission, we'd be sent home.

—*Did that not strike you as a little odd?*

—Not really. We were told they were dangerous. Lots of gullies and steep banks. It was untamed ancient woodland; there were no paths, no guides, nothing. Just the forest. I thought it was all about insurance, image, that sort of thing. He couldn't take any risks.

Marie and Kirsty were fed well, their rooms were luxurious, with all mod cons, and they had use of Zach Crystal's spa and sauna whenever they wanted. Marie tells me she got used to being waited on hand and foot. She spent most of her days in the spa, or eating and watching television in her room, while Kirsty spent her time with the other girls.

And Zach Crystal.

—I just thought she'd be OK. We saw quite a lot of each other, to be honest. We ate together, and she would tell me all about the fun they were having. He was like a teenage girl, himself. He had them all dressing up, trying on clothes, watching movies. That's what she told me. She would bring me things to sign – consent forms – and I just ... I just did it, I just signed them without really even looking, I'm afraid.

Marie says this in a monotone. She knows that what she did wasn't right, but all the while, she said, she saw Kirsty changing.

—It was like she was turning into someone else … in a good way, I thought. Someone new. She seemed so much more confident, and I just thought that everything was going well for her, that this was a blessing, you know? There, in the middle of nowhere, I didn't have to think about anything anymore. I didn't have to think about how I'd failed her. She was getting something exclusive. It was once in a lifetime. She would remember it forever.

—*What was it that Kirsty was getting, aside from a magical experience?*

—Kirsty told me that all of them were getting 'help'. She was always so vague – you know what kids are like. But when I managed to wheedle it out of her, it seemed that they all sat with *him* and just sort of … talked.

—*Kind of like group therapy, perhaps?*

—Maybe. They shared their problems. That was all she told me, and at the time, I thought it was a good thing. I thought it would help her, having others there who'd been through what she'd been through. Now I see it for what it was. Kirsty would come back with new little sayings, little ways of speaking that just weren't her. It's hard to explain.

—*Can you remember any of the things she said?*

—It was all – and I thought it was good at the time – all this stuff about opening your mind, allowing yourself to have new experiences. She talked a lot about 'opening', how she was now open, how I needed to be more open, to not follow the herd, that sort of thing. Now I see it for what it was.

—*Which was?*

—I think it was manipulation, brainwashing. And it seems to me now like some sort of competition. They were all competing to see who could be the most messed up. Then they would 'open' themselves to … to *him*. For him. All for *him*.

—*How did that manifest itself?*

—Apparently he would always home in on one – a different one every night. When Kirsty would come back to her room, she would be miserable, lamenting that one of the others had been chosen as his 'special girl'.

—*What did that mean?*

—Kirsty said that the special girls would get to walk in the woods with him at night.

—*Why? I mean, what was the purpose?*

—It was all about 'opening your mind'. Being 'truly open with yourself'. Apparently he said he could only take those who were most open to see certain things. It was never Kirsty. I was gutted for her. That's what she wanted, the whole time we were there. It felt like she was building and building up to being taken out with him into those woods.

I wish there was some way I could find out for sure what these nightly excursions were about. It feels like we're so close, yet there's something crucial missing.

—*Do you know if Kirsty ever talked to the girls who went out into the woods with Crystal? His 'special girls'?*

—Like I say, while we were there, she was much more open with me, but only to a point. It was like that forest thing was a big secret.

—*I have to ask another question: although Kirsty wasn't a 'special girl' – did she spend time with Crystal in the tree house, alone. At night?*

Marie sighs, deep and long. She can't meet my eye. The pain emanating from her is palpable. But I had to ask. Eventually she looks up, eyes wet with tears.

—I … don't know … for sure. She never told me if she'd been chosen. She had her own room next to mine, but I know she would stay up in the tree house late at night. They would watch horror movies … but they all did, they all did it. All the girls. I don't know…

A week into their stay at Crystal Forest, things went very wrong.

—Maybe it was something like that which bothered me. I don't know. One night, though, I just couldn't sleep. I was tossing and turning, adjusting the air-con, going to the bathroom every five minutes. I just felt that something was wrong. Maybe it was mother's intuition? Doubt that somehow.

So I thought I'd get up, go and give Kirsty a knock. It was about midnight, and I figured she'd probably still be up. If not, I'd just pop my head round the door. She was in the room next to mine. At Crystal Forest, it was like a luxury hotel – the rooms were *huge*. Kirsty's bed was on a mezzanine next to a window that looked out into the forest. Everything lit with flickering lights that looked like candles. It was stunning. I notice her door is ajar, so I pop my head in. The fairy lights are on – green and yellow stars and that project across the ceiling. I can see her bed but can't tell if she's in it or not. The carpet's thick and I climb up the little steps to her bed. The curtains are open and the forest is out there, in the dark. Beautiful. But Kirsty's not in bed. In fact the bed is made. They have the housekeepers make your bed every day. It's smooth; like she's not touched it. That's when I got a bit worried. Midnight. Maybe it's OK, I think. She'll be up in the tree house with all the others. She's thirteen.

—Did you ever think about going up there and checking on her?

—It's embarrassing to say but I didn't know how to get up there. I'd never been. His staff would come and collect Kirsty, and I'd go to the spa, the swimming pool. But then … I dunno. I just had this bad feeling. I thought I'd phone Mr Cryer – I had his number. I just thought I'd check Kirsty was OK. All the rooms had a phone next to the bed, so I go to pick it up when I hear something from outside.

—In the forest?

—Raised voices – someone having a row. That seemed odd; it was late. But it was still, there was hardly any wind. I looked out and couldn't see anything. I was worried. What if he'd finally taken her out there and something had gone wrong?

—What did you hear?

—I couldn't make out the words. It was … it was unusual. It felt like I shouldn't have been able to hear anything. The windows were all reinforced glass and the rooms were high up, looking over the woods. But then there's this … there's this gust of wind. I can hear it making all the leaves in the forest tremble, they all shiver. They all moved together too, like a wave. It was a strange sight. Maybe that wind caught the voices, brought them to me.

In what she describes as a 'strange state', Marie decided to investigate. It sounded like an argument, the rise and fall of the voices. One of them, she says, was distinctly female.

—I was worried. I don't know, it all seemed to hit me then, how little attention I'd paid to what Kirsty was doing. I thought I'd go out there, just in case, you know?

—*You said earlier that no one was allowed out into the forest, unless they were with Crystal.*

—That's right. We were told we could go anywhere in the house, but if we wanted to visit the museum on the top level, we had to be accompanied. That made sense; it was full of priceless stuff – all his stage costumes, his capes and stuff. And we knew we couldn't go outside into the forest. Or we'd be sent home. But I thought they'd understand, I really did. I wasn't going to go far.

Marie put on some clothes and left her room. Walking out onto one of the walkways, she climbed down a wooden staircase and through a gate that said 'Strictly No Unauthorised Entry' on it.

—It did feel dangerous. It felt forbidden. I knew I was doing wrong but I could hear the voices much louder out there. It sounded really bad, a really vicious argument. I was praying it wasn't her – it wasn't my Kirsty out there.

—*You walked into the forest?*

—It's right there, right on the doorstep, just past a perimeter fence and you're there, in that wood. No paths, nothing. It's wild but it's also beautiful.

—*No one saw you?*

—I wasn't really thinking about that to be honest. I just wanted to find Kirsty. There was a lot of security out there. We were told it was because of crazy fans trying to get in. There were thermal-imaging cameras, night vision stuff, guard patrols, fences. I felt almost like someone was going to catch me at any moment. Tell me to leave. But I just didn't care.

Marie walked into the Whispering Wood alone. She tells me it wasn't all that dark. There were bright lights at the perimeter fences and the fairy-lights wound artfully around the trees at the mansion itself.

—I thought I'd pretty much be able to see, but once I got into the trees, it was almost jet black in there.

—How did you know where to go?

—I could hear that arguing, those voices on the wind. That breeze was making all the leaves hiss as well, all chattering together all around me. It was a strange sensation … it was like … Well, it felt like it was laughing at me.

Marie pressed on, following the sounds of the voices until she reached a small ridge of rocks jutting up through a gap in the trees.

—They hadn't heard me coming. I'm sure of it. The wind was getting up and the whole wood was … it was whispering, I suppose. I thought it was going to be some of the girls, but it wasn't. It was two adults. They were nearly nose to nose, going for each other.

—Who was it?

—It was Naomi Crystal and James Cryer, *his* aide. They were stood there, in the middle of that wood, going at each other. But it was funny cos it sounded like they were also trying to keep it down, trying to keep their voices low.

—Did you catch what it was all about?

—No. The whispering from the leaves was so loud, it covered up their voices. I saw their faces though – they were both angry.

Then I saw something else – some movement in the trees beyond them. The ferns grow right up to your shoulders there, and it was moving away through them. It was like an animal or something. But it didn't look right. It was black, dark against the ferns. And … rotted-looking. I mean it must have had some disease, mange or something. It was horrible. I remember it made me feel horrible. I didn't want to look at it. I turned away and when I dared to look back, it had gone.

Marie says she never found out what it was she saw, or indeed what it was that Naomi Crystal and James Cryer were arguing about that night. She says one of them must have heard her, because they stopped suddenly.

—It was Naomi who called me over. I was terrified. I'd never spoken to her before. She'd only arrived at Crystal Forest the day before. I'd only ever seen her in the papers and that, you know? In the magazines. She'd just been dating that musician, the scary one, the Satanist – what was his name … He did that song, 'Embrace your Emptiness', I think it was called? I don't know. I'd seen her with him in the gossip mags. She was much scarier in real life. Always wore these huge sunglasses, whatever the weather.

Naomi Crystal has remained somewhat of an enigma in the story of her brother. Zach Crystal broke away from their act The Crystal Twins when he was twenty, in 1994. Around the same time, he hired James Cryer to become his chief aide. It's hard not to see a link between the two. By all accounts, however, the twins' relationship had remained cordial.

Six Stories *fans will remember the person with whom Naomi Crystal had a brief relationship in 2005, shock-rock musician Skexxixx, who was at the peak of his infamy at that time. Coincidences are funny things.*

I ask Marie if she'd noticed any tension after Naomi arrived at the mansion.

—Now that's an interesting one. Not tension as such, but I do remember, when she was there, he wasn't around as much.

—*James?*

—No, Zach. Ugh, saying his name makes me feel sick. But he wasn't. He would stay up in the tree house a bit more, perhaps.

—*What about the rest of the staff?*

—It was hard to say, really. I wasn't paying as much attention as I probably could have been. I know that after Naomi arrived, everything was a bit more … um … how would you describe it? It was a bit like when you're at work and the boss is there, everyone just pretends to be a bit more busy that usual. She commanded a lot of respect. She had her daughter with her too – she was around Kirsty's age. I thought, if *she* was there too, then…

—*What happened when they saw you in the woods.*

—I was scared. Naomi scared me more than James. James said 'hi', and Naomi asked me what on earth I was doing. She was like a schoolteacher. I felt like a kid again in front of her. She told me that the forest was restricted, that I shouldn't be there. She asked James to escort me back to the mansion. He didn't say much. It was like he was scared of her too – he kept giving me these guilty little looks, like we were kids getting caught doing something naughty, you know? It was all very strange.

—*And you had no idea what they were arguing about?*

—None at all, and I didn't dare ask.

—*What about the creature you saw; did you tell anyone about that?*

—No. I was supposed to as well. We were supposed to report 'anything' we saw in the woods, from the windows. I was just too confused and scared to say anything.

The next day, there was a very different atmosphere at Crystal Forest. Marie says when she went down to get her breakfast the following morning, a couple of Zach Crystal's staff approached her and asked her, in an aggressive manner, to sign another non-disclosure agreement. It was clear that she was no longer welcome in the house.

—The atmosphere was totally different. The staff, who'd been quiet and polite before, were suddenly all around me all the time, in my way, or else telling me where to be.

—*Did Kirsty notice?*

—Not at first. She was still up in the tree house. I went to my room and found all my stuff had been shoved into my suitcases and placed out in the hall. The door was locked and when I asked the housekeeper, she said they were 'preparing for the next guest'. It was horrible; I had just been frozen out.

I remember wandering about looking for James Cryer, to find out what was going on. I had to before Kirsty came back. Then he found me, and his whole demeanour was different. When we arrived, he had been so kind, so welcoming. Now he was so cold, so … aloof. He wouldn't even look me in the face. He told me it was time up, that we had to leave. I asked him what I should say to Kirsty, and he told me that was up to me, that it was my problem, not his, and then he just walked away.

I called his name, I said, 'Mr Cryer, what can I do to make things right?'

He just looked at me like I was a piece of dirt on his shoe and told me we had until the end of the day to leave.

—What did you do next?

—What could I do? Our stuff was packed. Our time was up. I was so scared about what Kirsty would say. This was my fault. I'd ruined all of it for her. Just like I knew I would. If I'd just minded my own business maybe … maybe she'd still be here…

It's hard to watch Marie, sat there in this vast room with its views and thick carpet, giant TV on the wall, silent as a black eye.

—I turned out to be the bad guy. Kirsty and my relationship wasn't easy, but I felt that we'd been getting better, I really did. I'd never felt like she hated me, not really. Until then. When she actually said it – 'God I hate you' – it cut me to the bone, to the very bone. I've never felt pain like it.

The two returned to their home in Perth, and were greeted by a huge surprise.

—When we got back, all our things were gone from the flat. We didn't have much to begin with but I remember sinking to my knees. The place was bare and there was a 'For Rent' sign in the front. I thought we'd been evicted. Then I get a phone call from

James Cryer. He says we've got a new house. This place. *He'd* bought it for us. Zach – 'to say thank you'.

But I knew what he'd bought from us. I knew what he'd bought from me. And I willingly sold it to him.

My silence.

Kirsty wanted to have as little to do with her mother as possible. Marie never dared ask what happened between her and Zach Crystal at Crystal Forest.

He would occasionally call. Just to speak to Kirsty.

—Kirsty used to laugh a lot when she spoke to him. It always cut deep, because whatever I said to her, I got rolled eyes, or a sigh … or just nothing. A part of me felt maybe he was like a father figure to her, the father that she never had. That's why I let it go, that's why I let it carry on.

For her. It was always for her.

My heart cannot help breaking for Marie at this point. Think of her what you will, but this tired old woman in a too-big armchair in this too-big house seems utterly broken.

—After we got back, Kirsty went off the rails completely.

Kirsty started going missing from home regularly, and when she was at home, there were rows. Marie tells me they were savage – endless screaming. The neighbours even called the police a few times, she says. Not like back in the flat. Kirsty began hanging around with a group of local troublemakers and some nights she wouldn't return home. Marie's overriding guilt, she says, always prevented her from properly clamping down on Kirsty's behaviour. She was always terrified that social services would take Kirsty away again. So she let her get on with it, hoping it would stop. It never did.

—She always said she'd seen this end coming. This break-up, this wedge between us. She always said *he'd* helped her see things – that bad things that were coming, and now they were here.

—Zach Crystal has often mentioned this idea of foresight.

—Like seeing into the future? After we got back from there, when she did talk to me, she would mention old memories she'd been able to 'unlock' at Crystal Forest and they were … they were strange, unnerving. Horrible really.

—Would you be OK trying to explain them?

Marie steels herself and speaks. With each word, it's difficult not to react in an emotional way to the horrible familiarity of what I'm hearing.

—She … It scared me. It kept me awake at night. I used to have to force myself not to go into her bedroom and look out of the window. In case … just in case.

—She saw something?

—She told me she'd been seeing … it … since she was a little girl. Whatever *it* was. Some kind of ghost, some kind of spirit. She said that being there and talking with the other girls, she'd found out they'd all seen it too, before bad things happened. And … and *he* had told them that it … that it made them special somehow, that to see it was to truly understand. I said it didn't make sense, and that made her angry. All the rows, the fighting, the running away. It was all my fault, all of it.

—Did you ever mention to her what you saw in the woods at Crystal Forest?

—I wish I had … I wish I had, but I felt too guilty. I felt that Kirsty would blame me even more for us getting kicked out of there.

Kirsty and her mother were never able to patch things up. Kirsty told Marie that Zach Crystal was the only one who could help her and that she was working on returning to Crystal Forest by herself when she was old enough. Certainly, Kirsty felt she had found solace and camaraderie there, and always strove to return. Marie tells me Kirsty told her, in the heat of a row, it was the only place she felt she ever really belonged.

—I started hearing of all the accusations from folk – the lawsuits. He was taking people down for saying anything about him. He was ruthless. I kept my mouth shut. The rent was paid and the fridge was full. I didn't have to work.

And I had my daughter.

—Where is Kirsty, today, if you don't mind me asking?

Marie slumps further into her chair.

—She lost all reason, I think, when *he* started dating that woman, that film star, Zadie Farrow. Kirsty was inconsolable. That was the last time I held her. That was the last time I held my little girl, when she heard that news. Kirsty left for good after that happened. She was sixteen. I was always so scared that I'd hear about her on the news, that she'd end up like one of those poor lassies that got lost in the wood, trying to get to his place, you know?

This house is what I have to show for it all. That's why I'm still here. To remind myself of what I lost.

Kirsty was couch surfing, living with other Zach Crystal fans, following the tours, thronging outside the venues to try and meet their idol. Kirsty, having had first-hand experience of Crystal Forest, was revered among the fan community. Marie believes she was never invited back though.

—And that was my fault. But why? I didn't even hear anything. It makes me think that they were just looking for an excuse to get her out of there. Maybe it was Kirsty who'd seen too much. After all this time, that's what I think.

—You think something happened to Kirsty at Crystal Forest?

—I'm sorry. It's been all these years and I still can't bring myself to think that he … that he did something to her. But I don't know. I've got no evidence, anyway.

—Have you ever been able to talk to the parents of any of the other girls who went to Crystal Forest?

—Never. I imagine they're the same – that they've all been bought. They're all like me now.

—And have you heard from Kirsty since Zach Crystal died?

—I know she went down to London for the vigil with all the other Zach Crystal fans after the fire. She lives with friends somewhere now. I think they're fans as well. There was a whole community of them, you see. She'd met them all online, back when it all started. That's how I know she's OK.

—How do you know?

—I'm there too, online. That old computer of hers. I joined the forums too. She doesn't know it's me, but I'm there. A 'lurker'. It's all moved onto Reddit and stuff now, but I'm there. I follow it all, just so I know she's OK. Cos somewhere, inside it all, between all the shite, I'm still trying to be a mum.

Who can blame her, really? Who can blame Kirsty for wanting to be away from me. What a failure I am. I've always been. I'm no mother, I never was. All I can do is send her these recordings – I send them to her phone. Who knows if she gets them, and if she does, if she even listens? But what else can I do?

Marie plays me the message you heard at the top of the episode and she weeps, silently. One day, she tells me, she thinks that Kirsty might come back. The swelling of negative press around Zach Crystal recently has given her some hope, she says.

Enough not to do, as she says 'anything stupid'.

—It's the only thing that's keeping me going. I thought that when he died, something might … I don't know, something might change.

My big question – and I imagine it's many of yours too – is why hasn't Marie spoken out against Zach Crystal until now.

She tells me it's the fear, not of having her house taken, or the money stopping. Marie cannot jeopardise the hope she has that Kirsty will come home one day.

So why now? Why here, why talk to me?

I tell Marie about the newspaper article under my windscreen wiper. She nods.

—I've been there, to that place, I've met *him*. I know what kind of power he has … or had. No, 'has' is right. That power hasn't gone, just because he's dead. But it feels now like those powers … they're starting to fade.

All of us – all of us shite mothers, who've been crucified in the press; all of those girls, like Kirsty, who've been called worse than shite, who're told they're leading folk on, that they deserved it; all of us – each one of us is a snowflake, that's what they say isn't it? You're a snowflake.

Enough snowflakes together, well, they make an avalanche. Isn't that right?

And when the avalanche is over, I'll be searching through it for my daughter. I think he made her believe that there was something terrible on the horizon that only she and a select few could see. But he never saw all this, did he?

You know that video? The one that came out, the one with those poor girls in the forest? Maybe it's fake? I don't know.

—*Yes I know. So you've seen it too? What did it make you think?*

—I thought I wouldn't be able to watch it – I thought it would be too much. But actually it made me wonder something. While everyone else is arguing about whether it's real or not, I was thinking something else.

What if those two weren't trying to get *into* Crystal Forest at all? What if they were trying to get *out*?

I'm sad that Marie Owen has not felt able to tell her story until now. I believe as she does, that this is the beginning of a whole lot of attention for her. She tells me that it's been so many years since her daughter left, and simply waiting for her to come back has not worked. It's time to try a new approach. Maybe Kirsty will hear this, see the other things Marie will most likely take part in – documentaries perhaps – and change her mind. And maybe she won't.

As for what Marie says about the video, I can't speculate. So far I've heard no evidence that either Lulu Copeland or Jessica Morton were among Zach Crystal's 'special girls'. But after talking to Craig Kerr last episode, the aggressive silence and secrecy that surrounded Crystal could have covered up anything. Perhaps this was why the story of Lulu and

Jessica never made the headlines that it should. The official cause of death was exposure, but that has been roundly disparaged, and there are also rumours that the claims of cannibalism came from Crystal's own team. I wonder if this strange repetition of the story of the Whispering Wood was yet another cautionary tale; a warning from Crystal to leave well alone?

What Marie has now, which is different from before, is support. As the days since Crystal's death turn to weeks and months, it seems like the tide against him is finally starting to turn. More and more people who did not grow up with his music, who had no emotional connection to the star, are now seeing a different side of the enigma that was Zach Crystal. With the accusations of the five women starting to gain attention, more and more are starting to feel that they too can share their experiences of Crystal. The support for Zach Crystal still exists, but its power is dwindling. Zach Crystal defenders are starting to look more and more delusional. And as a generation comes of age without Zach Crystal in their lives, they begin to see him for what he is. A man. Nothing more.

After hearing Marie's account, I still have many questions that need answering. Some of these answers may never come. Instead they sit, tantalisingly close, hidden by power and adulation, by fame and money.

Could the 'therapy' that Kirsty and, it seems, many other girls received from Zach Crystal have been a sinister way of coercing them figuratively and perhaps literally into the star's arms? I now think of his work with the vulnerable young people in the care homes and psychiatric units. This was something we all applauded at the time, something I, until not even that long ago, held tight to in the wake of allegations and rumblings about the man.

This journey still feels like it's just begun – pulling apart a myth bit by bit to see what lies within. But right now, it's hard to know where to turn. How can I find the answers I'm looking for?

I have reached out many, many times to Naomi Crystal via the Crystal estate and received no reply. I doubt I will. Naomi Crystal is a mother. She does not appear in magazines anymore and as far as I know, is trying to live a normal life. After speaking to Marie, I feel a little guilty about my attempts to get in contact with her. I imagine Naomi wants to raise her daughter in peace.

James Cryer is no longer with us and his family will not speak to me.

It feels like I've hit a dead end.

But I've been doing these series for a while now, and I've often found that when it feels like you're out of options, the way forward presents itself to you. And I think an opportunity has presented itself from within Six Stories *itself. I feel like I have one more way of getting some insight, however brief, into Naomi Crystal and what exactly was going on at Crystal Forest.*

Because sometimes, like Zach Crystal often said, 'you just have to want it hard enough'.

This has been episode four

And I have been Scott King.

Until next time…

RUBY
Episode 246: Zach Crystal

Legendary Presenter Ruby Rendall's exclusive interview with pop megastar Zach Crystal. ***More >***

---

1 hr 45 • 9pm 20th Jul 2019 • Available for 28 days

RR: There it is everyone.

[Cheering]

RR: Wow … I mean, listen to that, listen to that. World exclusive. That's a world exclusive unseen studio session by my guest, the man himself, the one and only Zach Crystal!

[Cheering]

RR: That was 'From the Start' , which stayed on the cutting-room floor when you wrote your *Damage* album. Zach; can you tell us a little bit about that song?

ZC: Of course, of course. A lot of my songs, they come to me when I'm in the forest, when I'm with nature. You see, nature allows me to look inward and outward; my past, my present and my future. 'From the Start' is all about where we come from and how it shapes where we're going.

RR: I noticed a profound lyric in there: 'We never wanted anything and now that's got us everything.'

ZC: Absolutely. It's about growing up. My sister and I, we were so young when we began performing, and all we wanted back then was to make people happy; that's all we wanted. It was never about money – it never was and never will be. But look what that got us. Look where we are.

RR: You and Naomi, you're still close?

ZC: Oh yes, very close. She has her daughter now – Bonnie – and they now live with me, in Crystal Forest, where they have everything. But most importantly, they have love. We have love, as a family.

RR: Bonnie's father – he's not in the picture?

ZC: Unfortunately not. But that was their choice. That's their situation. I am just focusing on being an uncle.

RR: It's not a famous person, is it? Bonnie's father?

ZC: No, he's someone that Naomi met not long after she'd dated a famous musician.

RR: That's Skexxixx, right?

ZC: That's right. I think that was hard for her, and she just wanted someone normal. She wanted someone who wasn't a celebrity. Unfortunately it didn't work out. But that's her business. Bonnie's father is just a normal guy, but he doesn't want to be involved. He doesn't want to be a dad. That's so sad.

RR: Do the two of you reminisce about the old days, as The Crystal Twins?

ZC: Oh yes, all the time. We have a lot of old footage, and we've been showing Bonnie some of those old concerts. She's been loving seeing her mum and her uncle as youngsters on the stage.

RR: Would you want that life for her?

ZC: I think … I think she should be able to do what she wants. If that's the life she chooses then we are there to help her, to guide her. Naomi and I, we didn't have that. I had Naomi to help me but we were just kids, trying to make sense of that world, that industry. It's a hard place and we can explain that to Bonnie.

RR: Is having your own children something you'd ever consider?

ZC: Oh, I don't know. I'd like to adopt – adopt someone who missed out on having a mother and a father. I'd always liked that idea. But right now, I'm being an uncle. I'm being the best uncle I can be for Bonnie. She's starting her teenage years and those are hard, believe me.

RR: You were twenty when you decided to go solo. You'd been in the music industry as a teenager.

ZC: It was 1994. I'd never really had proper teenage years. It was concerts, rehearsals, practice, interviews. Before I knew it, those years were gone … *poof!*

RR: You've never really talked about that time in your life. I imagine it must have been a tough decision, right, to go it alone?

ZC: Um … not so much. I think … I think it was harder explaining it to Naomi. She'd always been the big sister; she'd always been in charge of everything.

RR: What do you think it was that brought you to that decision?

ZC: I remember wanting something else. I mean, The Crystal Twins, we were sensational, we were talented and people loved us. But I always wanted to push things a bit more, do things a little differently. Naomi was much more sensible. She wanted to keep things as they were, keep things familiar, and I respect that. She respected what I wanted to do too.

RR: There are a lot of rumours that the split wasn't entirely mutual.

ZC: That's just the tabloids, just stories people make up to sell papers, to get clicks. We'd been performing since we were little, and I think that Naomi was glad not to have to do that anymore. It also meant that I could look after her, after all she'd done for me when we were little kids. I could help her in her life.

RR: You certainly have as well. Naomi has moved in to Crystal Forest now and helped take charge of your affairs after the sad passing of James Cryer.

ZC: That's right. She's astounding. She's a mother and she's shrewd, she doesn't miss a thing. She's the boss up there now *[giggles]*. Be afraid!

[Laughter]

RR: It's Naomi who's now spearheading your comeback isn't it? The tour. When you were … away for a year, did Naomi know where you were?

ZC: It's … it's complicated. It's all … What's important now is that we're back together, that we're working together. I'm helping Naomi raise her beautiful daughter and we're a team again. Just like we used to be.

RR: How does it feel to know that Naomi wanted to sell Crystal Forest when the world thought you had vanished?

ZC: I mean, I understand. I would have done the same in her position. She couldn't live there. It would be too painful.

RR: It was Naomi who found the body of James Cryer wasn't it?

ZC: Yes, that's right. James was a beautiful soul, a wonderful human being. It was such a terrible accident. They told us he hadn't suffered. His death was instant. It really affected Naomi, I think. She knew what James meant to me. He meant a lot to her too. You see, James had been a fan of The Crystal Twins. I don't know if you know that? We'd both known him from the start. He lived on the same estate as us when we were growing up, and that's why we trusted him.

RR: James became your right-hand man, didn't he? Your top aide.

ZC: That's right. The day I decided to go solo, James was with me. And stayed with me until he died. That's testament to how close we were. I trusted James above anyone else. He took care of much of my personal and business dealings. He allowed me the time to write and create. James was a loyal person. I saw him as family, more than an employee. He was loyal to the end.

RR: Can you talk about what happened to James?

ZC: Yes. It's good to talk about these things. He'd been missing that morning, which was strange, as he never took a day off, never, not once. So when he was gone, it was strange. I knew something was wrong. Naomi found him not far from the house, in the forest. He'd fallen, hit his head on a rock. The poor guy. It could have happened to anyone. It was a tragic, *tragic* accident and there's not a day that goes by I don't miss him.

RR: I'm so sorry for your loss. For both of you. I hope time will be a healer for you.

ZC: Thank you, Ruby. But that's the past now – it's all in the past. What's important is the future. The tour, the album. That's what matters right now. There's no point dwelling in the past.

RR: Zach, it's not long until the end of the show. This has … this has been such a pleasure. *Such* a pleasure. I still can't believe it's really you sat there in front of me.

ZC: I do have a decoy you know. Maybe it's him!

[Laughter]

RR: A decoy, really? Wow… it's a different world that you live in…

ZC: I need him. Sometimes when things get too crazy, the fans, as much as I adore them, can get too much. He's a very talented guy. He's a fan too. I found him a number of years back. He's the same age, same height. He even looks like me, and he can do my voice. It's spooky.

RR: Zach Crystal, I want to say thank you – thank you so much for spending so much time with us tonight. I'm just feeling so honoured, so blessed. I feel that there are so many questions still to ask, about you, about your life. About the future. It's gone so quick. You're a very busy man.

ZC: That's right. That's true. I never stop – never stop working. I have rehearsals for the tour. I have to do everything. It's relentless.

RR: We're going to cut away for a few moments so Zach can be refreshed, and we're going to watch a promo for the upcoming *Forever* tour. Then we'll be back, for the end of our chat with Zach Crystal.

[Applause]

Episode 5: You Get to Go Home.

—I was, you could say, pretty much their guinea pig. I got pushed into line by the orderlies, waited at the hatch for my meds and was sent to go watch TV. Day after day it was the same. You had to stand there and take your pills, open your mouth so they knew you'd swallowed them.

I was on a mixture of medication. I didn't know what exactly. Lithium was one, I think. Antidepressants. They kept changing them week by week, different combinations, to see what would happen. If the staff were watching me, monitoring anything, I didn't know about it. I have little memory of that time. I remember not having much energy. I remember mainly walls and ceilings, staring at the patterns on them for hours, making connections with the cracks and the smudges of the paintwork. I just … retreated into my imagination, man.

I read a lot of books too. You had two choices there: comic books of bible stories – picture books aimed at really little kids – or the actual bible. I know the Good Book better than most men who call themselves holy. I bet you never expected that.

If that wasn't enough for us, they brought in the 'specialists'. Back then, I actually had hope; I thought they would find out what was wrong with me. That's what I always believed, you see, that there was something wrong with me. That I was ill.

Maybe I was? Maybe I still am? There's plenty who'd agree. I've been psychoanalysed by half the world, haven't I?

I had two specialists assigned to me. There was a man and a woman. Bill and Betty, they said they were called. The woman, Betty, was very motherly; I remember that. She always wanted me to play with these dolls she had, these knitted things. I always thought it was a bit too little-kid for me, but she told me it was OK, that it was just me and her. Betty always wanted us to do 'playing' – I always had to pretend to 'be' someone or something for her. I remember she wanted me to pretend to be an animal. I was always a pig. Betty would always ask what I was going to 'do' with the doll. I never knew, so usually I pretended to eat it. That made her laugh. It was goofy but I liked it. Then we had to be people. I was always a pirate. She liked that. She asked me my name, let me make up this huge back story. One of my favourite books in school was about Blackbeard. It was old – a hardback with a tattered front cover. No pictures. I loved it. I told Betty that I would put gunpowder in my beard, that everyone was scared of me. I even started growing my hair long, that's how much I fucking loved creating this character.

Betty always encouraged me, she always spurred me on to be more bloodthirsty, more horrible, describe how I liked to kill people. Sometimes she would write things in a big notepad. I remember once asking her why, and she told me it was so we wouldn't forget our stories. Betty once asked me if I had a whip. I said I did. She used to ask me to pretend to hit people with it.

Bill was different. Bill always wanted to talk about real things. Bill always called me 'little man' and 'young gent'. He wore a suit and always took his tie off before we talked. I never understood why. Bill liked to do all this man-to-man posturing. He always said I was a 'big guy around here'.

The contrast between the two was … confusing.

Bill used to get me to tell him stories about my dad. He meant memories, but he called them stories. I only had one or two. I don't remember much of him. One of those stories was about a time we found a dead cat near the railway bridge, back in Aigburth. Bill used to get me to tell that story over and over again. He used to say that I remember it because it had 'emotional impact'. He explained what that meant, and it kind of made sense. I can still see that cat now. Just a moggy, someone's pet. It must have been hit by a car and hid under the bushes to die. Or else someone put it there. It was night. I remember that. I remember being scared as well. I remember crying. I remember my dad hugging me. I remember his smell. Tobacco and damp. His big, black donkey jacket. I remember how my face felt on those plastic bits that go over the shoulders.

One day Bill asked me if I was sure that wasn't the only cat we found. He said it and he raised his eyebrows. I remember because he was bald and his skin crumpled up all the way to the top of his head. I said I was sure and he asked again. Was I sure?

Bill told me that sometimes our brains make good memories out of bad ones. He said it wasn't my fault. He said I wasn't lying. He said that's just how brains work. I remember insisting: that was my only memory of a cat.

He kept asking me if I was sure, if I was really sure that was the only dead cat. He just kept saying that over and over again, until I thought maybe there was another cat. I tried to remember walking down Mersey Road with my dad, looking for cats.

Bill asked why we were looking for cats, and I didn't know. Bill said that was my brain again, making a nice memory out of a bad one. Then I thought of Betty and Blackbeard and I said we were looking for cats to kill them.

I remember Bill telling me I was very brave and a 'super lad'. He gave me a Marathon bar.

Next week I told him about more cats we found. Cats, dogs, birds. I got another Marathon bar and I got to leave early. A few weeks later I was telling Bill how we chopped them up with a curved dagger. How my dad made me drink their blood and swear my soul over to the devil.

I was eight years old.

Welcome to Six Stories.

I'm Scott King.

The voice you've just heard will be familiar to some of you who've joined me before. To others, this American Deep South drawl with its distinctive Merseyside twang may provoke fear or admiration. There's very little between.

For those of you who don't know, we have a returning interviewee on this episode of Six Stories. *The first time I spoke to the man who formerly went by the moniker Skexxixx, he was being blamed for the 2014 Macleod Massacre, in which twenty-one-year-old Arla Macleod killed her family with a claw hammer. After pretty much disappearing from the world in 2017, it's good to see that age hasn't changed him too much. His hair, still long and black, is tied up in a bun. Tattoos snake over his arms and hands, and a silver ring catches the light of the recording studio where we sit.*

—Music. Computer games. They're the easiest to blame – the first scapegoats when anything goes wrong, aren't they? I mean, we had a narcissistic maniac running a country, inciting racial hatred from his Twitter feed, but woe betide some kid who wants to sit in his bedroom playing *Fortnite* with his buddies and listening to Drill, right? Look back in history and see what hasn't changed. 2019, AM and Skengdo go to actual prison in the UK for performing a song. Nothing's really changed has it? No one wants to look at why, fundamentally, people do bad things, not really. No society wants to look in a mirror and see something they don't like.

Skexxixx is no longer the shock-rock musician of the early noughties, the dervish in fishnet and makeup who filled arenas across the US and Europe, his vast armies of fans screaming along with him to 'Embrace Your Nothing'. These days, he has a quieter life. He's aged gracefully, like the whisky he no longer drinks. He grins at me from behind vast sunglasses, his teeth no longer caked in the Ohaguro-style blackener than had been his trademark.

Skexxixx knows all about what it's like to be a giant in music. He knows how it is to be suddenly responsible for the well-being of a million young people, despite never asking for it.

—It's easy to go crazy, having that much responsibility. I never asked for it and I certainly never thought that I'd become the devil because I wrote some songs.

I never thought it would be me that was the evil one, not in a society that values money and possessions over love, a society that tells its children they have to be rich and popular and if they're not, they're no one. Amazing what some lyrics and a guitar can do, huh?

This is, as I say, the second time I've talked to Skexxixx. The first time, I was considerably more nervous. I'd read a lot about the singer's reputation and his unpredictable nature. Like you, I was all too aware of the famous DEPRAV *interview, in which Skexxixx decided he would lead a documentary team on a tour of the swamps of his Louisiana property and then sit there in silence, allowing their boat to be surrounded by alligators. He sat back, watching them squirm from behind his sunglasses.*

The same ones he's wearing now, he tells me, and laughs, his voice still rough with the echoes of old debaucheries.

—I'm still involved in music. It's something that was always a release for me, a way of getting out whatever … demons took up residence inside me. But my time as the face of a furious generation? That ship has sailed long ago. Sometimes I miss it. Most often, I don't.

Today, we talk in Skexxixx's recording studio in the Marylebone area of London. It's suitably dark inside, the walls peppered with oddly angled spines of foam. Skexxixx talks to me from behind a vast pair of mirrored sunglasses, sat in front of a mixing desk that looks like something from Star Wars. *The death of Skexxixx's son, Olli, was the beginning of the end of his celebrity, and brief notoriety. After having bottles thrown at him by a hostile crowd at the Reading Festival in 2007 and subsequently walking offstage, his career never really recovered.*

—I decided to bow out gracefully. The Macleod thing happened in 2014. That was the final straw for me, you know? I let the new album rot. Pissed off a lot of record-label people, paid back a bunch of money. You know how it goes. There's better people coming through now, kids with the same anger, the same struggle. There always will be. I'm in a place now where I can help them make that struggle into music. It's always the way. I'm no longer relevant. It's time for the next angry voice to come through.

Skexxixx actually received a flurry of attention after my series a few years back. Remastered versions of his most critically acclaimed albums – 2004's Embrace Your Emptiness *and 2007's* Through the Mocking Glass *were recently re-released.* Through the Mocking Glass *was a flop in terms of sales at the time, but seems to have drawn retrospective appeal.* DEPRAV *ran a rather interesting article recently about Skexxixx's legacy: 'The Spooky Kid We Forgot We Loved'. They even mention the swamp incident.*

Skexxixx goes so far as to thank me, but he assures me that it's not because of this that he's speaking to me today.

—I don't pretend you ever became a fan of mine, Scott, but I have to say, I became rather a fan of yours. Your podcast, at least. When I heard you were taking on the story of Zach Crystal I wondered if you'd lost your mind.

—*Why?*

—I mean … with respect, you're not exactly a big podcast gun, are you – like Marc Maron or Joe Rogan? Not that either of them could get anywhere near Zach Crystal either. What chance do you have?

—*I don't believe I have any chance whatsoever, if I'm honest. Especially now he's gone. But with all the new allegations against him, I just wanted to see what I could find, I suppose.*

—And that's what brought you here? The last resort?

Skexxixx gives a smoky chuckle and sits back in his chair.

—You know I didn't date his sister for very long. Certainly not long enough to become his friend … again. Zach Crystal's not capable of friendship. He never was. He never will be. To him people either have their uses or they don't.

This time, I had no trouble getting to interview Skexxixx – no back and forth for weeks with a publicist, no awkward meeting in a hotel. No restrictions. This time, the man, whose real name is Leonard Myers, was happy to pick up a call from me and arrange this interview. It was almost as if we were old friends … almost.

I got back in touch with Skexxixx after drawing a bit of a blank. There's still so much that I don't know about Zach Crystal, that's been hidden, covered up, smoothed over and, I guess, burned. After talking face to face with Marie Owen, I feel like at least, for her, I have to keep going. There's something absolutely not right with what happened to her daughter, Kirsty, and the lavish house that Crystal had bought them. It seemed to me, as it did to Marie, that Crystal was paying them off, buying their silence.

I'm not sure what I want right here, with Skexxixx, but my tenuous link with him and his rather brief link to Naomi Crystal might take us somewhere unexpected. When I got in touch and Skexxixx's reply was 'I thought you'd never ask', I knew there was something to be heard here.

—Zach Crystal wasn't a musical genius. That was well known within the industry, I can tell you that.

Skexxixx cackles again.

—Maybe he's me and I'm him? That would be a nice little twist in the tail of this series, wouldn't it?

To be fair, I'd already thought of that, but I'm not telling Skexxixx. So what is it that Skexxixx could possibly tell me about Zach Crystal? He's already hit me with this revelatory statement about Crystal, right off the bat. I wonder if, during the time he and Naomi Crystal dated in 2005, he was able to get any other insights into the man.

—I mean, you can believe me or not. I imagine many won't, but contrary to what I just said; he and I were actually friends … well, as much as someone like Zach Crystal is capable of having friends.

—Really? You became friends when you dated Naomi? It's an odd pairing.

But is it, really? Skexxixx, the 'God of Nothing' in his black-toothed glory, and Zach Crystal, the eccentric recluse with his bizarre, haunted forest, his capes, veils, masks and makeup.

—The only real difference between us was that when I got home, underneath the makeup and the music, I was Leonard Myers again. Behind the masks, Zach Crystal was never anyone else. Unfortunately he would always be Zach Crystal, and for him, that just wasn't enough.

—It sounds like you knew him rather well.

—I don't think anyone knew him well. But yes, I think I came close briefly. But it was long before I dated Naomi Crystal. I met Zach Crystal long before then.

This is something of a revelation. I had no idea that the two had ever even met, let alone been friends. Like everything to do with Crystal, it was kept quiet. Crystal, who rarely did interviews, has never mentioned it. Skexxixx tells me that's because it would have ruined both their images back then.

—Your peak, shall we say, was 2004–05, around the same time as Zach Crystal's.

—You may be surprised to know, I existed before then. Back in ninety-four, when I was about eighteen, I was front man of my old band, Chüd. We were a struggling experimental-industrial outfit, playing shitty bars up and down the country to a gaggle of uninspired metalheads. They didn't like us because we were too weird, and the experimental noise scene didn't really like us either – too poppy for that scene … Well it wasn't really a scene, unless you count six people stood in a basement bar while a guy in a horse mask plays terrorcore drum loops over the modulated sound of a screaming baby on a laptop for forty-five minutes.

—It sounds the polar opposite of Zach Crystal's rise to fame and fortune, if I'm perfectly honest.

—It was. But here's something you may not know. Zach Crystal did a lot of his early solo gigs under a different name. Just after he kicked his sister to the kerb and The Crystal Twins were no more, Zach also did a lot of gigs in shitty basement bars to crowds of people who didn't give a fuck. That's where we met. On a cold night in his home town, Barlheath, in 1994. He was only a kid too – twenty years old.

Another revelation. As far-fetched as it sounds, I have no suspicion that Skexxixx is lying. I can't figure out why he would. The music industry is a funny place. There's an element of pantomime about it sometimes – goodies and baddies. Skexxixx certainly falls into the latter category, but he tells me that, the young Zach Crystal he encountered was rather confused about his own identity.

—They'd been kids, hadn't they – he and Naomi, when they were The Crystal Twins? Cutesy, wholesome shit. Sing-a-longs for drunk people in bars. They got signed early as well, when they were only children. Fifteen, sixteen, whatever.

—*Zach was writing his own songs by then, wasn't he?*

—Correction: Naomi was writing the songs, not Zach.

Skexxixx raises one hand and stares at me. At least I think that's what he's doing from behind his glasses. Despite being much older, there's nothing less intimidating about the man who was once called the scourge of the Christian West. He leans back in his chair and runs his hands through his hair, shaking his head at me. His tattoos peer from under the sleeves of his shirt. Eventually he sighs, long and loud.

—I'm going to tell you some things, Scott, that you don't know, that no one knows. I'm telling them to you, because – well, I know how you do things. You'll tell it like I say it. You won't twist my words. I have a certain *reputation* with the rest of the media. Imagine if I decided to make a statement to the press, now. I'd be 'washed-up rock star trying to stay relevant', or I'd be 'rabble-rousing Satanist trying to smear the memory of a great musician'. So let's talk. Let's clean out the closet shall we?

—*How exactly did you and Zach Crystal meet?*

—It was at one of our last shows in 1994. The rest of the band and I, we were barely speaking. I was already planning on doing something else. Going solo, perhaps. We've just played this little festival, a clusterfuck in some bar in Barlheath, to about ten people. The dressing rooms are filled with bottles and food, everything's a mess, there's people all over the place, equipment everywhere.

I just want to get the fuck out and go home, when these two guys walk in. Not much older than me. One's done up in a suit and the other's … well, he's some local celebrity. Everyone looks up, starts laughing. Who the fuck are these guys, you know? A pair of fucking straight dorks. The guy in the suit walks over and says his friend's name is John Smith and he wants to meet whoever was singing 'You've Lost That Loving Feeling'.

—*The Righteous Brothers song?*

—Correct. We always closed with it; turned it into a beautiful mess of noise. People either loved it or they fucking despised it. I loved singing that one.

—*Did you recognise Zach Crystal when you met him?*

—No. I'd never heard of the guy. 'John Smith', really? But it was him alright. The guy in the suit? He became his right-hand man, his partner in crime.

—*James Cryer?*

—That's the one.

—*What a bizarre coincidence.*

—It was. What I also found odd was that James Cryer seemed to worship the very ground 'John Smith' walked on. I mean, he was just some ten-a-penny pop singer. What was he even doing at my show? Crystal was all in trendy sports gear and a baseball cap. Cryer looked like he'd borrowed his suit off his dad. I nearly told them to go fuck themselves.

—*Why didn't you?*

—To be honest, I was too surprised. That they had just walked in like that, just walked backstage. Crystal shakes my hand and he says to me in this quiet, little whispery voice, he says, 'We cover that song too, "You've Lost That Loving Feeling". It's a song about pain. I like that.'

There was just something about him. I don't know what it was. According to Cryer, they'd been walking about after a gig, overheard us playing, and Crystal had stopped. He'd wanted to come in and listen. They'd stood at the back and watched our show.

—*Why were they just wandering around the street after a gig?*

—They'd fallen out.

—*With each other?*

—No. Zach and James had fallen out with Naomi for some reason. They were tired of her. He wanted to go solo. When they told me they already had an agreement with Orpine records in place, they had my interest.

—*So what was it he wanted – to meet you?*

—More than that. To work with me. James Cryer gave me a business card. It looked homemade. He said that the record label were onboard but they had to keep it secret. He told me to give him a call and then off they went.

It was, Skexxixx says, a bizarre circumstance. Here he was, faced with no band, no income and little hope, and this guy with a record deal walks into his life. At first he thought it was an elaborate joke. He nearly threw away the card, but the next day, just to see what would happen, he decided to give James Cryer a call.

—He tells me all about his friend, this 'John Smith', who's actually Zach Crystal, and that he's some prodigy, that he and his sister were already famous, that he was about to go solo and conquer the world. I asked him what he needed me for. Who was I? Just some kid from Aigburth, sat here in some ripped up fishnet tights and makeup I robbed from Bodycare in Bootle. Why not get in touch with Trent Reznor or Nivek Ogre, the big US industrial producers at the time, if this kid wanted to change his image? Fly the kid to LA. Make the money that they clearly wanted. How could I help?

I remember his words. I've never forgotten them:

'I don't know what to tell you, dude. Zach digs you and … he gets what he wants.'

I have to taper this rather long and extraordinary story. A cynic might accuse Skexxixx of using this as free publicity, another attempt to resurrect his career, but I'm sat here before him and I don't believe that.

Zach Crystal and Skexxixx formed an unlikely friendship, meeting together occasionally at a recording studio in Birmingham. All of it kept secret, especially from Naomi Crystal.

—*Why you specifically? Did you ever ask him yourself?*

—He told me that it felt 'right'; that was all he ever said on the matter.

—*What was it you two were doing, exactly?*

—The thing about Zach Crystal was that the guy could sing. His vocal range was beyond anything I've ever heard before, and his performance ideas were so new, so fresh. He seemed ahead of the curve on a lot of things. But his song writing … sucked.

—*Really?*

—'Burning Eyes' – that was mine. Orpine Records purchased it from me for a sum that I'm not going to tell you. I didn't get a writing credit on the record, but let me tell you something: it's made me a lot of money, that song has.

I'm almost speechless. I have no way of proving any of this. Skexxixx doesn't get excited. He tells me all this in his slow drawl, quite matter-of-fact.

—*What about … the others, the other songs?*

—Mostly we cowrote. Zach had a concept and lyrics, and I helped him realise them. I helped bring it out of him. We just … clicked.

—*But why wasn't this known? Surely you wanted credit. You wanted to share some of his fame. The guy was a global megastar. I can't believe that you didn't want some of that.*

Skexxixx is quiet. Another sigh. He looks around at his array of recording equipment. There are golden discs and awards in glass cases.

—I have everything I need.

—*I just don't believe that a younger you would be happy to sit back, let him take all the credit. Why?*

Skexxixx grins at me.

—You ever heard of *Euderus set?* Named, quite correctly, after the Egyptian god of war, chaos and storms?

—*What?*

—It's a bug. Otherwise known as the crypt-keeper wasp. You see, our little crypt-keeper lays its eggs in the niches carved out in the sides of trees by another wasp species. Once *Euderus set's* little ones hatch, they eat their way into the wasp in the hole and take control of its mind. The wasp, under control of the larvae, starts trying to tunnel out of the tree, providing a safe passage to freedom for the larvae, are you with me? It gets better. The tunnel ends up just too small for the wasp to escape, allowing the mini crypt-keepers to eat their way to freedom, emerging from the head, out into the big, wide world.

—So … if I'm right in thinking, you wrote songs for Zach Crystal to what? Get them out into the world?

—I knew he was going places. So he was the vessel for the songs I wrote – that we wrote together. I, like him, had an image I had to curate, and these songs just didn't fit. We talked as well as making music. I learned a great deal about Zach Crystal in those years. I learned what sort of a person he was. I learned about what he wanted, the way he saw the world. And let me tell you, people think *I'm* fucked up.

—What did you learn?

—The songs, at least, I was paid for. I still am being paid for. The other stuff … not so much.

—Other stuff?

—I learned from Zach Crystal that we both had … unconventional upbringings, shall we say? I know his squeaky-clean rags-to-riches story. From an estate in Barlheath to stardom – only possible with the love of his family and a cheap Casio keyboard. Please, spare me.

—It wasn't true?

—Some of it was. The place, the people. But Zach Crystal's home life was far from happy. His tyrannical parents forcing him to play keyboards and sing for them, making the poor kid practise and practise so they could get the adulation they wanted in their church group. When he started being asked to play at religious concerts and festivals, they took whatever money he made for themselves. Then they got Naomi involved too. They made this image – this squeaky-clean, good Christian image. Naomi told me all about it – the therapy she'd had to go through after. When Zach decided to go solo, she was finally released. She'd never been so happy. They broke their son and they very nearly broke her too and, like me, music was their only way out.

—I had no idea…

—I don't think anyone did. The Crystals have been masters of curating their own image. He learned how to do that from the very start. Their whole life has been secrets and cover-ups. A happy smile painted over an open wound. That was Zach and Naomi Crystal's childhood. He saved her from that, believe me. It was them, their parents, who unleashed Zach Crystal on the world. So in a lot of ways, he and I were more similar than we knew.

I don't know a great deal about Skexxixx's early life. What I do know comes from a Kerrang *magazine feature on him in 2004, entitled 'Emptiness's Sweet Embrace' and an unofficial biography entitled* Black Eyes and Mocking Glass *from 2008. When Skexxixx was Leonard Myers, child of Marvin and Greta Myers, both of whom were drug addicts, he was taken into care and raised in a children's home on Merseyside. His father took custody of him for a few years when he was six, but by eight he was back in the care system. Skexxixx tells me these early experiences shaped him, made him what he eventually became.*

—The drugs didn't help either. I'm not talking recreational here, I'm talking about the ones they fed me in the home. You see, my parents were also addicts of something much more dangerous, much more poisonous than heroin – and that was Christianity.

Young Leonard Myers was placed into Saint Nicholas Residential Home in Aigburth, a suburb of Liverpool. Saint Nicholas was a privately owned care home, funded by churches and private donations. Outside of local authority control, it sounds like it also medicated its residents – with unregulated drugs. The home is now long gone, the site flattened and replaced by an estate.

—They'd sucked my parents in when my mother was pregnant. They'd seen how vulnerable she was and, like good Christians, pounced. I have vague recollections of a preschool at the home, in its garden. There were rabbits, fluffy white rabbits, and wooden toys. A Noah's ark with a pair of wooden sheep. I liked them the most. I remember the sunshine. But I remember being taken home afterwards. Back to hell.

Things get more sinister when Skexxixx tells me the story you heard at the top of the episode – about the 'specialists' the home brought in once he was living there. He admits that his memories are distorted, messy, and the accuracy might be off, but those meetings with Bill and Betty, the things they would discuss, have stayed with him.

—Always, with Bill, it was about what I would get if I told him what he wanted to hear. I would be allowed to leave early, I would be allowed a sweet, an extra hour of television. A good report from him to the home. Bill was obsessed with this idea of 'turning a bad memory into something good', and, it seemed, the worst I made them, the better I did. 'Just tell me the truth and you get to go home' … Easy!

Pretty soon, I just began to make things up. The stories grew more and more elaborate. At first, Bill would ask me about the real memories I had of my mother and my father, and then he'd twist it.

'Are you sure that was right, Lenny?' he would say. 'Are you sure it happened that way? Or is your brain just trying to make something nice out of something horrible? Is your brain replacing things for you?'

I began to work out what were the right and the wrong answers. I began to understand what he wanted me to say and I'd say it.

By the end of our sessions, my mother and father were full-blown Satanic priests in charge of a coven that sacrificed animals, ate babies … the whole shebang.

—*And none of it was true?*

—Not a word of it. For a long time, I believed what they wanted me to believe. Up until my parents' death. It was only after that I came to realise what these people were. They talked about demons and devils and evil with no self-awareness.

It never crossed their minds that they were the real monsters – the evil they were telling me to be scared of.

Skexxixx's career, and the type of music and image he portrays make a great deal of sense in this context. He once told a magazine that the purpose of his music was 'all-out war against Christianity and the blind sheep that follow it'.

It's a tragic and terrible tale of coercion and manipulation, of religious zealots taking advantage of a child. The similarities he shared with Zach Crystal are much more obvious now.

—Did the two of you share stories about your upbringing?

—We did, sometimes. We both harboured a hatred for what we'd been brought up to believe, to become. We just went about that in different ways. Whereas I wanted to scream about it through a mic, he wanted to do things another way…

Skexxixx sits back again in his chair. He lifts a couple of bottles of cold sparkling water from a mini-fridge and offers me one. We both drink. Refreshed, Skexxixx continues.

—Zach and Naomi Crystal, The Crystal Twins, were an unmitigated success, mostly because of their wholesome image and Naomi's flourishes with the song writing. Without her, Zach was insipid – as uninspiring as his songs. A single Jonas Brother if you like. I mean, that reference is probably too old now, right? He was looking for something to undo all of that, to become something else.

I'm going to tell you some more things now. Things that I've not told anyone yet. I wish there was some way I could negate the publicity that will follow this. You know what people are going to say about me.

Last time we spoke, you asked me a question about an album of mine. You asked me about the themes of some of my songs.

Instead of a recap, I'm going to play the audio from that particular episode. For context: the case I was covering was that of twenty-one-year-old Arla Macleod, who bludgeoned her family to death with a hammer in 2014. Arla was suffering from a very specific delusion – that she was being pursued by 'black-eyed kids' or BEKs, as they're known; paranormal creatures of urban myth in the form of pale children with black eyes. Arla Macleod was also an avid fan of Skexxixx, perhaps because she was able to identify with a particular song of his from the Through the Mocking Glass *album, 'Dead-Eyed March', which contains the lyrics:*

A thousand black-eyed girls
A thousand black-eyed boys

Marching to a distant drum
Looking for a place called home.

Last time I spoke to Skexxixx I was starstruck and flustered. I'm not proud of how I breathlessly asked the following;

—*Can I ask you something about* Through the Mocking Glass?

—Sure, go ahead.

—*Who are the blacked-eyed boys and girls in 'Dead-Eyed March'?*

—I think you're asking the wrong kind of questions...

I remember that long silence back when I interviewed Skexxixx the first time, when Six Stories *covered the case of Arla Macleod. I remember sitting there in front of him, wondering about the people I talk to about their demons and struggles. My interpretation was that this song was about that. I see now that the song is about blindly following something like religion.*

—You were right about the album. It was clever marketing on my part – all the stuff about the black-eyed kids, the rumour that I started about how I'd gone into their world and come back again … Do you see any similarities with someone else here yet?

—*I'd never even thought of that.*

—No. No one else did either. Zach Crystal and I, we're similar people, we have similar damage. Crystal though … the hatred in him, the darkness inside him. People call me a monster, you know. I used to get the blame for a great many things: violence, terrorism, the corruption of the youth. All I ever talked about was black-eyed fucking kids, man. That guy, fucking Crystal, he was truly terrifying. Something evil lived inside that man. Something cold.

The not-quite-friendship and coproductions between Skexxixx and Zach Crystal ended more or less the following year, in 1995, when Zach Crystal released his first solo album, Yearn, *to huge critical acclaim. The majority of the songs on that album, Skexxixx tells me, were the results of their song-writing sessions.*

—Then he dropped me. Just like that. Bye-bye. I had served my purpose and wasn't needed anymore. That's how he's been brought up to see people, man. James Cryer made sure I got my money, and I didn't speak publicly about it. Fine with me. I was rich. I didn't have to do anything if I didn't want to. But I went back to work, used the money to buy a studio, equipment, start writing again. I used that money to begin cooking up Skexxixx. Planning my own world domination.

The two didn't cross paths much after that. Skexxixx sat back and watched Crystal's star rise, the percentages from Yearn *dropping regularly into his bank account.*

—You describe Zach Crystal as 'terrifying'. I'm interested in what you meant.

—People refer to Zach Crystal as a genius. I think perhaps he was, man. But in the same way that someone might call Stalin, Hitler or Trump a genius. His genius had nothing to do with his music, man. I'll make that very clear. Zach Crystal's genius lay in how he was able to get what he wanted. Power … and more…

—Go on…

—Because what he wanted wasn't just sex, drugs and rock 'n' roll. Zach Crystal had grown up performing, he wanted … he *needed* … a harem of young women around him, worshipping him, believing he was their everything. I found out years later why he'd been walking past that bar in Barlheath; why he and James had fallen out with Naomi.

—Can you tell me?

—He'd sent James Cryer out to find girls for him. He felt he was entitled to girls, and James was only too willing to do what he was told. He'd been getting girls for Zach Crystal long before that too. When Naomi found out, she lost her shit. As she rightly should.

—How has none of this come to light?

—Amazing isn't it, man? Imagine if that had been me, cavorting around with teenage girls? Imagine if it had been you? But it was OK for him to do it because of what he was to everyone, what he was to you and people like you.

Just like I became the world's devil for a time, Zach Crystal became the opposite.

—*Quite.*

—But how did he do it? How did he get to such an elevated position? How was he always seen with underage girls and there was no outcry until after he was safely scorched to a crisp in his mansion?

—*That's one of the many questions about Zach Crystal that has been bothering me all this time. I spoke to someone whose daughter was a regular at Crystal Forest. Now, out of context, it just seems insane that anyone would let their children anywhere near him.*

—His light is diminishing, man. The mask has aged; it's melted, slipped, corroded. What we're starting to see now is what was behind it. We're starting to see who the great and terrible Oz truly is. Now he's gone, we can sit back and look at his long game.

—*How do you mean?*

—Let me guess one thing before you go on man: did this girl whose mother you talked to have a troubled past? Maybe from a home or her family had problems? Did she go to Crystal Forest and was told she was 'special' in some way?

—*Yes. Her mother had only just got custody of her again.*

—Do you remember a small part of you, when you were younger, that wanted to have a problem, that desperately wanted there to be some kind of strife in your life, just so that a Zach Crystal could come and fix it for you? That's what he was known for, wasn't it? The help he gave. He came down from on high to help the needy. We all wanted it to be us, we all wanted to be chosen.

We all wanted to be one of Zach Crystal's 'special girls'.

Skexxixx's words seem to wriggle their way inside me and find an old, vulnerable place. A soft place. I think back to myself at the age Kirsty was when she encountered Zach Crystal. Twelve, thirteen. You think you know so much at that age. It's the same as being sixteen or twenty one – you think you've learned it all, you're indestructible. This is the first time that I'm glad I only found out about my past a few years ago. If I knew who I was back at that age, I could have been vulnerable too – vulnerable to someone like Zach Crystal … It's amazing how little you know when you're young. The world seems to pull itself open for you, just a crack, and you're at the edge, desperate to push further. I remember the feeling Skexxixx is talking about; I remember seeing the promotional photos in magazines, the music videos, the press releases, Zach Crystal surrounded, sometimes hand-in-hand with young girls, girls the same age as me. I remember now that the feeling I had was jealousy. Why hadn't I been picked?

Skexxixx watches me for a while as if he waits for this feeling to land. He nods, slowly.

—Who would question it? Who was there to tell them to stop, to examine credentials, to scrutinise what exactly was going on. This was Zach Crystal, after all. When you come up against a titan, a deity, you want to be approved, you want to be a part of it, you want to follow, to be picked. You're not going to get that by asking awkward questions, am I right?

—*But how do you know this?*

—I'm not saying I know anything for sure. What I can tell you is that all his life, Zach Crystal was looking for a path to divinity and it had nothing to do with God. Or did it have everything to do with God? The god that Zach Crystal became?

Look at his MO. As soon as he could, he vanished into an exclusive realm. A realm of angry sprits. He wouldn't do interviews. He graced the world with his presence only when he chose to. He was allowed to choose his victims. Remind you of anyone? Some imaginary bearded dude in the sky?

Don't get me wrong. None of us are saints. We are put on a pedestal by fans whether we want that or not. But show me an up-and-coming star, an emerging Zach Crystal – nineteen, twenty – who says they *don't* want that, and I'll show you a liar. It's about what we do with that power that matters. That's how we'll be remembered, in the end.

—*How will Zach Crystal be remembered?*

Another silence before Skexxixx's face cracks into a wide smile.

—Now you're asking the right questions.

—*You talked about the goings-on at Crystal Forest, and you used a term I've heard before: 'special girls'. What do you know about that?*

—Right. Now you're on the right lines. You see, after I split up with Naomi, there were a lot of people, former fans, who wanted to talk to me about him.

—*Why was that?*

—Maybe they thought he and I were friends, I don't know. But I heard some things that I didn't know about him. They were things I wasn't surprised about though.

Skexxixx stops grinning, his demeanour changes. It's subtle, but I can feel it. I don't feel like he's manipulated me here. I feel like we've both worked toward this point and now we understand each other. What he's about to say will carry significant weight.

—I talked to one or two young women – women who weren't so young anymore. Women who had been through … things. Messed up women; women who were broken inside, with no idea who they were anymore. I spoke to women who carried trauma inside them, who had deep healing to do. They were former Zach Crystal fans – former 'special girls'.

I know man, it's hard to believe, isn't it? That these people came to me for solace. I'm no angel. I've never claimed to be, but what I'm not is a predator. I wish I could prove the things I've heard about him. The problem is the problem there's always been with him: who is going to believe the devil over God?

Certain things are starting to make sense to me now. It's like uncovering something old, smoothing away the dirt and finding something grotesque beneath.

—I imagine there were many more. The women I spoke to carried deep shame about what they allowed to happen to them, about how they let not only themselves, but their families, be seduced, chewed up and spat out by that monster. And look what's happened to their names? Look how our media reports on his victims. Look at the rhetoric. 'Accusers' they're called. Man, if I punched you in the face right at this moment and you called the cops, you'd be 'the victim of an assault by Skexxixx'; you wouldn't be 'Scott King, the Skexxixx accuser'.

This is true. There are numerous tabloid stories concerning the five victims of Zach Crystal who've spoken out: Sammy Williams, Mary Wooton, Gabrielle Martinez, Zofia Kowalski and Jennifer Rossi. All these stories describe them as 'accusers', speculate on whether they should be believed, ask questions about their motives. Their trauma is treated with suspicion.

—Did anyone ever think that now he's dead, these women might simply not be so scared anymore? Believe me, the women I spoke to were scared.

—*Were any of them…*

—…Any of those five? Maybe. It's not my place to tell you that. What I can tell you is that all of them had been fed the same bullshit by Crystal. They were all lost young girls who were offered the chance at touching divinity, of purification. They were all lied to. They were all coerced. These poor, confused young women would say yes to anything. They would tell Crystal what he wanted to hear, they would have their memories twisted and manipulated until they believed that they weren't just saved by Zach Crystal, but that they needed him and always had done. They would say terrible things about their pasts, about the people who cared for them if it meant that they'd be seen by Zach Crystal, that they could spend time in that tree house in the forest. It wasn't just that they said these things. It was that they were made to *believe* them.

—*Zach Crystal's 'special girls'?*

—These were girls who'd never been special to anyone before, not even their own parents. Now you've got a star leading them into the woods late at night.

—*Why though? That's something I just don't get. What was the purpose of taking them into the forest?*

—I wish I could tell you for sure. For me, it felt like the final stage of the brainwashing, the last part of giving your mind over. If you saw whatever he believed was there – you became his and you validated him. They were made to believe they saw ghosts in that forest. They were made to believe that their lives had been plagued with omens, that their tragedy could have been foreseen. All for one thing. His gratification.

—*Jesus Christ.*

—To coin a phrase: 'not quite'.

It is almost like the pieces of this puzzle have slotted together in a hideous way. The magic of Zach Crystal and more importantly, the power of Zach Crystal overrode any sense of reason.

—He was clever. Never went so far that it was unbelievable. Those former 'special girls' said that they still had nightmares, that they were still confused and conflicted about what had happened to them. Some of them, man … he had them fully believing that they were being pursued by demons. Real, actual demons. Others he was more subtle with, made them believe that they were only capable of happiness when they were with him. Whatever it was, I recognised it from my own days back in that home in Aigburth. I remembered how they'd messed with me; I remembered how I'd believed for a long time that my real parents were true evil. All to suit an agenda. If what these women told me is true, it was the same with him.

—*Why, though? Why did he do it? Was it not enough to simply have fans?*

—That's the thing about power, isn't it? It corrupts, it consumes. Zach Crystal didn't just want fans. He'd had fans since he was a little kid.

When I dated Naomi, she told me a bit about what it was like for them. Zach was the star and she had to look after him the whole time or face the wrath of her parents. Zach was used to getting what he wanted, when he wanted it. And what he wanted was teenage girls. He wanted them in his thrall and when he was done with them, he got rid of them. That's the difference though, man. The difference between Zach Crystal and the rest of us. Like I said to you, I'm no angel. I've seen things backstage at shows that … let's just say weren't exactly great. All of it though was driven by *want.*

He was driven by *need.* And he made people *need* him. He couldn't just be a person who wrote songs, he had to be more than that. All his life he'd been more than just that. He *needed* to be needed. To be worshipped.

—*Did Naomi know this about her brother?*

—I think she did, but we didn't date for long, and it was a long way back. She certainly never knew about what I'd done for him. I didn't tell her. I was as good as my word. I will tell you something though, she once asked me if I would help.

—Help?

—She asked me if I would talk to him. This was 2004, 2005? He was the biggest thing in the fucking world, man, and she felt like she had no control whatsoever.

—Did you try?

—I did. We met one time and … well, let's just say he wasn't the kid I met back in the nineties anymore. That kid who loved music, he was long gone.

—Where did that young boy go?

—Music's a funny thing, man. You start off as an angry kid, writing lyrics in the back of your school books, practising guitar in your bedroom on your own, jamming with other kids in a shitty church hall. Then suddenly you're allowed to choose your rider, you stay in the presidential suites in hotels all over the world. You have legions of people who will wait up all night just to see your face. Whatever you want, you can pretty much have. You just have to pick up that instrument you spent so long practising in that bedroom. You have to scream out those words that mean nothing to you now but so much to those fans. All you have to do is what you love, and people, they turn you into something you're not. They turn you into an idol. It's hard to stay humble; it's hard to remember where you came from.

I don't think there was much humility in Zach Crystal. I'm not sure that was all his fault either. Look where he came from, and look what he became. Imagine when you were nineteen, twenty years old, being able to have anything you wanted, having an army of people who would say yes to your every whim, however crazy. If Zach Crystal wanted to alter his appearance, he had no one telling him it was a bad idea. There was no one to challenge him. So he ended up as this total enigma – in a mask or a veil. By the end, no one was sure what he even looked like.

—What do you think? Why did he become what he became?

—I think he lost himself entirely. I think by the time I met him, he was already half gone. Was that his fault? I don't know, man. Maybe it was age? Maybe he couldn't handle getting old? Maybe he was always like that. Maybe he'd always been ill.

Zach Crystal's world was a crazy one. And no one ever curtailed that craziness. The world, instead, bent to his will. Imagine being in that position?

And the scariest thing is how many were willing to follow him into that world. Kids and adults were ready to believe in him. Whatever he did and whatever he said. Predators like Zach Crystal, with the power of Zach Crystal, don't hide in the shadows and reach out to snatch people. They stand there, brazen and bold in the open, and invite you in. They open their hands and lead you into their fucked-up worlds. A few years ago you asked me who the black-eyed boys and girls are from my song. All of them looking for a place to call home. I told you that you weren't asking the right sort of questions. But now you are.

—When was the last time you spoke to Zach Crystal, face to face? Do you recall?

Skexxixx thinks for a few moments as we sip water together. He shakes his head.

—Actually not long ago. Not long at all. The Lazy Dayz music festival.

—Really? You were there?

—I was there but I wasn't playing. I'd produced Matthew Godfrey from Horaldo's Head's solo album and had come to watch, from backstage of course. My name still carried some clout with the young ones…

A quick reminder: this was the spring 2018 charity musical event in Hyde Park at which Zach Crystal was set to perform 'World in Our Hands' – his charity song written with Ed Sheeran. Zach vanished not long after.

—I didn't think he'd give me time of day, really. To be fair to him, he was very pleasant.

Skexxixx was allowed into Zach Crystal's backstage dressing room, which was twice the size of everyone else's. He found Crystal in a vast, empty space with sofas, food, all the luxury anyone could want. But no one else was there. At least that's what he thought at first.

—We kicked back. Talked about the old days.

—*How did he seem?*

—Odd … distant, distracted. I wondered if he was on something. I didn't ask. Then things got a bit … intense…

—*What happened?*

—From out of nowhere steps this … *kid* … all dressed up all like him, with the leaves and the antlers and all the makeup. Some kind of forest nymph. She sits down beside us. I say beside us, she *drapes* herself over him, and I think, no fucking way, I want no part of this. I'm about to leave when he says, 'This is Bonnie, my niece. She's a special kinda girl.' The kid looked older, but man, she was a fucking *child.*

As if that made it OK, as if that didn't make it any more weird, he tells me she's performing with him onstage, dancing or whatever, and I'm nodding and smiling like it's fine.

—*Did you say anything to him?*

—I knew there'd be no point. I knew you shouldn't question Zach fucking Crystal man, but fuck that, I pulled him aside and I said, 'Dude, are you sure that's a good idea?' I fully expected to be thrown out of there but he looks at me, with those fucked-up eyes of his, and for a moment, for a second, I feel like he's heard me. He nods and I can see he's thinking about it. All those allegations coming out, and he's about to get onstage with his niece done up like a fucking elf hooker or some shit. But then he starts humming and mumbling to himself, his usual bullshit, wanders off across the room. I was gonna leave but … I just looked at her and I just couldn't do it…

—*So what did you do?*

—I spoke to her. I walked right over and I said, 'You shouldn't do this, you know. You should run, as far and as fast as you can.' I just fucking said it. Her answer just fucked me up, man. I didn't know what to do.

—*What did she say?*

—She looks at me, man, and she's got eyes like his, all big and blue, and she just nods, like she knows, and I think, yes, at least she gets it, you know? At least she understands. But that was so far from the truth, man.

—How so?

—I'll never forget what she said next. 'I saw it too,' she said. 'Last night. Seeing it means something terrible's going to happen.'

Then she looks at me and I see, I dunno man, I see pure fucking madness in her eyes. I see whatever's in him is in her too. Whatever the fuck they were talking about, they weren't listening to me. I thought, to hell with you both. Then Naomi comes in and starts going crazy. She wants me out of there, she wants the kid, Bonnie out of those clothes, and I think, at least they'll listen to her. At least there's someone there to keep that madness in check.

Just a few hours after this meeting, there was an explosion in the lighting rig over the main stage and two of the technicians, Peter Williamson and Gavin Jermaine, fell to their deaths. Crystal's performance never went ahead.

—That was a fucking tragedy; a horrible accident. He vanished after that didn't he? Zach Crystal. Disappeared for a whole year.

There's no way of proving these claims, no way at all. However, I'm finding it hard right now to disbelieve what I'm being told. For me, there's no reason why Skexxixx would lie.

—Did you ever feel a sense of responsibility? I mean, there were songs you had written together? Songs that gave Zach Crystal his power.

—I wish that it was as simple as that. I wish I had acted quicker. Perhaps if I'd come out and spoken about it, something could have changed. I'm guessing you're wondering why I didn't. Why did I wait? Why did I sit on all of this for all this time? Why haven't I joined the chorus of voices against him?

To be honest, I've always felt like I'd do more harm than good. Trust me, you don't want Skexxixx to be on your side. I'm King Satan aren't I? I'm the antichrist. The other reason is that I was never a victim of Zach Crystal. We wrote some songs together. I sold those songs to him. Everything was legit, above board. He was careful to keep it that way too. That was another thing about him, I suppose, man. He was meticulous, he was smart. He made sure he wouldn't get caught out. Can you imagine what the media would have thought of someone like me speaking out against the great Zach Crystal? I worried about what would have happened to me and my career. I worry about you, Scott, when this goes out. Dead, he might be, but man, the guy has a fucking *army* of seething, dedicated, maniacal fans. They would have torn me to shreds. Zach Crystal didn't just seduce those few young women, man, Zach Crystal seduced the fucking *world.* But now he's gone. Now he's finally fucking dead, we can start poking through the remains, we can start…

—…*Raking up old graves…*

—Right.

There's something deeply unpleasant, almost frightening about all of this, and it leads me on to what is, however much we don't want to see it, the esoteric angle to this case.

—I've talked to many other people involved with Zach Crystal, and there are consistent, disturbing elements that I cannot explain. The most powerful of these are the strange sightings of some being. The women involved with Crystal saw it, Crystal himself claims to have seen it. His own security have seen it. Now you say his niece mentioned it. What do you make of that?

Skexxixx contemplates this for a long time.

—Man, I've asked myself this many, many times. What I can tell you is that Zach Crystal had some strange beliefs. He's always said that there's been something after him, all his life.

—*What about the video – the one from the forest, the one with the two girls?*

—If that video is real, I'd suggest that it came from Crystal himself, and was made by his people.

—*Why, though? Why do that?*

—Maybe in some fucked-up way he wanted to be caught. Or maybe it was part of his need to control the narrative. If people are gonna believe in that beast, that phantom, he has to be the one to make them do it, perhaps…

—*Is that what you think?*

—His world's a crazy one … we just live in it.

It was easy for us to sling mud at Skexxixx in his heyday, accuse him of corrupting young people and encouraging them to do terrible things. Yet there was Zach Crystal, centre stage, actually doing just that.

It's slightly impertinent to quiz a musician about his lyrics, but when I discussed Skexxixx a few years back, many of my interviewees focused on the lyrical content of his 2007 album Through the Mocking Glass *– which thematically focuses on escaping to a place where mistakes and failure are embraced. Skexxixx has regrets, and I wonder if some of them involve not speaking out against Zach Crystal. But, like he says, who would have listened?*

We finish our interview on this heavy note and I wonder where I can go next. What we've heard this episode is insights into the making of, not just a musical icon, but a god. When someone's desires are untamed, unlimited and never questioned, they lose all sense of humility and reason.

If what Skexxixx tells me is true, it seems that Zach Crystal was not happy with simply being universally adored, he wanted to be needed and was willing to use whatever methods necessary to achieve that. Zach's most obsessive fans were willing to sacrifice everything for him, and through coercion and manipulation he gained unlimited access to the most intimate parts of their lives.

There were those who enabled him in this endeavour, who, by saying yes when they should have been telling him no, in my opinion, were jointly responsible for the terrible things Zach Crystal did.

I sometimes wonder if it's simply a good thing that Zach Crystal is dead. No one else can be hurt by him. However, it means he's never had to be answerable to his accusers and that irks me. Was his death an act of cowardice? Did Zach Crystal bow out of the world before a storm descended on him? Were these sightings by Crystal and his associates merely, like Skexxixx suggests, some kind of guilt. Was the video put out by the Crystal camp? Were they trying to condemn the man? Was this the result of someone thinking enough was enough? Those closest to Crystal knew that if they were to expose him, it would have to be in a way that matched his style so they could avoid being sued. Or else was it some final attempt by Crystal to manipulate the world around him?

I've tried numerous times to get in touch with Naomi Crystal, all to no avail. After this last revelation, I feel that to speak to her, or else someone who knows her and more significantly, Bonnie Crystal, would be to find some kind of resolution to this deeply troubling case. I know Naomi has made huge efforts to keep her daughter out of the limelight, and both women have pretty much vanished from public view.

Maybe it's time to be bold, like Skexxixx was, backstage at the Lazy Dayz festival, when things were not right. Maybe it's time to take that step forward and speak out of turn.

Maybe it's what we need to start doing more.

Before we depart, I'd like to leave you with some lyrics from the final track on Through the Mocking Glass *by Skexxixx, which I feel are pertinent to this moment.*

…and in the end what have we done?
What have we become?
Let fall our final curtain call
And bowed out, let it all fall.
…and in the end what have we brought home?
Just scars on our skin
and memories
black like wings.

This has been Six Stories.
And I have been Scott King.
Until next time…

RUBY
Episode 246: Zach Crystal

Legendary Presenter Ruby Rendall's exclusive interview with pop megastar Zach Crystal. ***More >***

---

1 hr 45 • 9pm 20th Nov 2019 • Available for 28 days

RR: Wow! Welcome back everyone, live with me, Ruby Rendall and Zach Crystal. Remember, this is live TV, so we must apologise again for the technical mishaps we've had, but as they say, the show must go on.

[Applause]

RR: And the show must go on for you, Zach Crystal, isn't that right? What we just saw was a promo for the upcoming *Forever* tour, and tickets go live next week, is that right?

ZC: That's right, Ruby, all the details will be on ZachCrystal.com in the coming days.

[Cheering]

RR: Zach, we're coming to the end of the show. It's been … I mean it's just been a blast, but it's gone by so *quickly.*

ZC: I know, I know. It's been such a pleasure.

RR: How does it feel doing your longest, most in-depth ever television interview, after all these years? Finally getting to talk to your audience on such a personal, emotional level, after all this time. It must feel liberating.

ZC: You know … it's been … Well, I wonder what I was scared of.

[Laughter]

RR: Was that it though, Zach? Was it fear that kept you hidden for so long?

ZC: Always, always fear. I've always been so scared of the world, ever since I was a little kid.

RR: You had your sister to look out for you then, didn't you, before you went solo? Is that when things got scary, do you think?

ZC: I think so. Naomi has always been my protector. She still is. She always protected me from … things … at home and when we used to play in those sleazy bars when we were kids. Even though we're the same age, she's always been the strong one.

I've been so frightened of what people think of me. That's why it hurts so much when people make up such horrible things about me. All these accusations. That's where I've been, you know, getting my courage together, finding my courage to speak out.

RR: What is it you want to say to the world? You have the world in the palm of your hand right now. We expect this to be the largest audience we've ever had for anything on the BBC. What does Zach Crystal want to tell the world after forty-five years?

[Cheering and chanting begins from the audience and from outside.]

RR: What is that, they're saying?

[For the first time, Crystal looks flustered. He mouths along with the chanting for a moment, his lips seeming to form the word 'Frith'. He shakes his head and continues.]

ZC: Fri … I guess I just want to say … to say thank you. First and foremost. The fans, the people who believe in me, have made me who I am. It is through you, the people, the fans, that I've been allowed to find my true voice. They're the ones who protect me now. I'm able to come out and do an interview because of the people that have my back.

There's been some disgusting, horrible things said against me in the press. There are terrible, ruthless people out there who want things from me. It's these people that make me want to vanish, to disappear. So for every one of them out there, for every naysayer, I am so glad to see two Zach Crystal fans ready to stand up for the truth.

RR: What is the truth, Zach? I have to ask. I have to ask you about the things people are saying about you. What would you say to the people who don't believe you?

ZC: I would tell them that the first place to look is inside themselves. Sadness, pain – those things fester inside us, those things can hurt us, can make us angry, make us want to lash out. When we do bad things, when we allow bad things to happen, those things leave a shadow behind. They leave pain. People don't want to hold on to pain, so they lash out, they wield it. Pain is hereditary, hurt breeds hurt. It fills us up and drips down to those below us. I believe I have the capacity to heal that pain. People might think I'm crazy, but it's true. And if I'm wrong, at least I tried.

[Cheering and chanting]

RR: And that's what you do, isn't it, Zach? That's what you've always done – tried to help people with their pain.

ZC: I'll keep doing it as well. They can say what they like about me – the press can print whatever they want, but I'll keep going.

RR: So what does the future hold for Zach Crystal? There's the next album, the tour…

ZC: I want to go out there, Ruby, and do more work for those who are less fortunate, those who haven't been able to have a good life. I want to help those whose parents have been abusive or absent. I want those people to believe they still have a place in this world. I want them to know that if no one else loves them, I do.

[Cheering]

ZC: I do, I *do*! I love you. You don't have to be scared. You're not alone.

RR: That's admirable, Zach, I—

ZC: But also, Ruby, I have to say that something terrible is coming. I wish I could say what, but I can't.

RR: Are you talking globally? Climate change? War, that sort of thing?

ZC: I wish I could say, Ruby. I wish I could tell you. Maybe it's about the world, but most probably, it's about me.

[The studio lights flicker on and off, the picture becomes pixelated and the audio is distorted by a hissing sound.]

ZC: *[inaudible]*

RR: *[inaudible]* … technical issues again. I do apologise, Zach, I don't know what's going on.

ZC: It's OK…

RR: You say something terrible? I'm surprised. Your future right now seems so hopeful, the world has opened up and you've stepped back into it.

ZC: I know, Ruby, I know. Sometimes though, you can't help knowing when great tragedy is afoot.

RR: And you're sure of this.

ZC: It's as real as me, right here, right now. It's as real as I am.

[There is a sudden crashing sound and the studio lights go off.]

RR: Oh not again. I'm so sorry … I—

[The picture goes completely blank before cutting back to Zach Crystal in closeup.]

ZC: It's as real as me…

[The picture dissolves into a mess of pixels and the audio's pitch drops]

ZC: …right here, right now. It's as real as I am.

[The picture cuts to a brief scene from the studio. Zach Crystal, standing, pointing at something in the distance, behind the camera. There is a scream from the audience and cheering from the fans outside. The BBC One logo appears on the screen for a few seconds.]

Programme information – technical difficulties
We are currently experiencing some technical problems with our live broadcast. We are looking into these and hope to have the issues resolved soon.

RR: Ooh, I'm sorry, I do apologise, we're back, we're back and … listen. Listen, can you hear them?

[Chanting from the fans outside]

RR: Amazing, almost … er … well. I suppose we draw to a close on good news, and that's that those members of our wonderful audience who were having some issues earlier in the show, seem to have made a full recovery. That's so great to hear, right?

ZC: Of course. They're all wonderful. All of them.

RR: Zach, I don't want to end this on a downward note. I want to thank you. I want to say thank you from the fans, from everyone who has followed your music and your career. It's safe to say you've been an inspiration to so many. I hope that you continue to inspire others for many years to come.

ZC: That's all we have isn't it, Ruby? Hope. That's one thing we can hang on to in this journey of life. Always, there is hope.

RR: This has been me, Ruby Rendall, and this has been Zach Crystal. It's been an absolute pleasure to speak to Zach and here's to hope.

ZC: To hope…

Episode 6: Being Nobody

—1988. I was thirteen. I remember because it was my birthday. We were too poor to have presents, really. I'd got some new clothes, a dress that my mum had got from a charity shop and done some work on. It was beautiful, but even then I remember thinking *where on earth will I wear that?* Then realising where I *would* have to wear it and my heart sinking.

It was sunny as well, a beautiful day. There was one park in Barlheath; probably the only nice thing there, to be honest, and even then it wasn't that great. There was a summerhouse, which had mostly fallen down and smelled of piss, but there was also a few paths that converged in a little cenotaph right in the middle, with a stone statue of a soldier in a tin hat waving goodbye to his family. I don't know why but I loved that statue. It never got vandalised and there were always those little balsa-wood crucifixes with poppies sellotaped to them lying all over the base, where the soldier's boots were. There were roses planted underneath in two neat little boxes.

It was always peaceful there. Sometimes there'd be a pensioner or two sat on the benches, but usually no one else. Everyone stayed in the kids' play area over the other side of the park. I used to sit at the soldier statue and read for an hour after school. It was a wonderful place.

That day, my birthday, I had homework. I had to write a war poem. We'd been doing Wilfred Owen and Siegfried Sassoon, and I remember I was just full of inspiration that day. The cenotaph was a little suntrap, and I remember pulling out my exercise book and sitting, the sun on my face, staring at that soldier, trying to conjure up some words. Who was he? Where had he come from? What were his fears, his hopes? Did he believe he was ever going to return? I just sat there, waiting for it to come, the inspiration. I was basking in just being a normal kid in school. That was what brought me peace.

I must have drifted off, because when I opened my eyes, there was someone sitting next to me. This boy. About my age, maybe a bit older. He had my exercise book in his hands.

I don't know what it was about him, but I just got a bad vibe, almost immediately. That sounds nasty, doesn't it? I couldn't help it. I was polite though. He told me I'd dropped my book, so I said thank you and pretended I needed to leave. I sat there, packing up my bag. He asked my name, and I didn't know what to say so I just told him. He told me his and asked if I fancied a walk through the park. I said I had to get home. He asked where I lived.

Right now, today, there'll be all sorts of alarm bells going off, but back then I just thought he was being kind. I said that I lived on the Hopesprings and he made this face, like, *oh man!* He said that it was a dangerous place, that estate, and wasn't I scared? I told him I'd lived there my whole life and no, I wasn't scared.

He was sat really close to me – far too close, really invading my personal space. He was inching closer and closer, and I could smell mints on his breath, and aftershave, like my dad wore, but he was blatantly too young to shave. It was like he'd prepared himself for this. Now, I wonder how many times he'd seen me there, after school, reading books my parents wouldn't let me read – the Judy Blumes, *Sheila the Great*, *Superfudge* and, of course, *Are You There, God? It's Me Margaret*.

Honestly, I felt a tiny bit flattered at first, but the … the *intensity* of him disturbed me; so close to me. I stood up. I was trying to be nice, trying to smile. I was giving him the smile I gave Dad when he was in a rage, when everything was my fault, as usual. I said I had better get going as I had homework to do, and he said he'll walk me home. To the Hopesprings Estate. I told him it was fine, I didn't need him to, but he told me he was going to come anyway, so I was safe. The way he said it – he didn't ask, he *told* me.

I felt all tight inside, scared, and I thought I was going to cry. He then said that he knew who I was, that he'd seen me perform. His dad had taken him to The Sow and watched me sing. I didn't know what on earth to say back. I just mumbled thanks and began to walk, but he followed me. I couldn't speak, I decided I wouldn't go home straight away, so we just walked, and he was chatting away. He kept asking if he could carry my bag, and when I said no, he tried to hold my hand.

I remember him asking me where I was going – we were walking in the opposite direction to the Hopesprings; we were beside the indoor market where you can smell the butcher's, thick and meaty. I said that I'd just remembered I had to meet someone, and he asked who. I told him my dad was a policeman. I'd heard about someone doing that, in a book maybe; that was what you were supposed to do if you meet a stranger. But strangers were old men in cagoules, asking you if you want to come see their puppies, not a kid, not someone my age.

It worked, because he balked. He said he had to be somewhere too, actually, and asked for my phone number. I didn't know what else to do so I gave it to him, but at the last moment I changed the last digit. This was before the days of someone drop-calling you immediately on a mobile. He said he would call and we could hang out sometime. He told me again, that's what we could do.

I hung around the market for hours and spent the last of my dinner money on a bus home. I was terrified, looking out of the window all the way, wondering if I'd see him.

I didn't go to the park after that. I just went straight home after school. After about a week or so, I forgot all about it.

Then, one morning, my dad called me into the kitchen. I was terrified. When Dad called you into the kitchen, it meant you'd done something wrong – something 'against God', usually.

I walked downstairs, the walk of shame. It was always me who was in trouble. It was never me who got to listen to records on a Sunday afternoon; it was always me who had to practise harder, to rehearse longer.

He was sat there, at the table, with a letter in his hand. The envelope was torn open and I could see photocopied handwriting. Dad's face was unreadable. He handed it to me without saying anything. To this day, I remember what it said.

Dear fellow resident of the Hopesprings Estate, Barlheath,

I met someone the other day, beside Barlheath Cenotaph. She was beautiful and talented. We chatted about everything and when we parted she gave me her phone number. Unfortunately that number has either been disconnected or she made a mistake.

All I know is that she sings with the voice of an angel and lives somewhere on the Hopesprings Estate. Can you help me find my lost love?

It was the creepiest, weirdest thing I'd ever seen. And when I realised that he lived on the estate too, that made it even worse. He'd acted like he was just some passer-by, when really he'd been this close to me all along. He'd been utterly convincing, and that's what made me scared of him. There was a phone number. I remember that twisted fear inside me. I told Dad it had nothing to do with me, that he wouldn't leave me alone, that I didn't even want to talk to him. But Dad wasn't angry. Not at all. In fact, he laughed. He told me that this was 'romantic', it was 'sweet'. I know he didn't approve of me having a boyfriend, that was out of the question. But he told me that this was The Crystal Twins' first 'proper fan'. He thought it was brilliant.

So I called him. I called that number. I spoke to that boy. I don't even remember our conversation, but I recall that Dad said I should tell him to invite all his friends to our next show.

It went from there.

That was how James Cryer ended up in our lives.

Welcome to Six Stories

I'm Scott King.

For the last five weeks, we've been sifting through the remains of the enigma that was Zach Crystal – his bizarre life, his suspicious death and the allegations of abuse. This has been, so far, the most trying case I've ever covered. Six stories – six people's views on such a famous person – are not nearly enough for someone like Crystal. There's a multitude of other voices that we could have aired instead, hundreds more angles I could have taken to present what I have presented so far.

But here we are.

It is almost impossible to say you grew up without the music of Zach

Crystal playing some part in your life. He was all over the radio, the television, and as the internet became a stalwart of the family home, he was there too. Zach Crystal, for many of you, played a significant part in your lives. If he didn't, I'm going to guess you know someone for whom he did.

For many, Zach Crystal was a hero – a philanthropic genius who could do no wrong. His odd appearance and behaviour, his strange beliefs, made him who he was; they made him stand out from the crowd. To this day, I still catch myself humming or singing his songs. Since the allegations of abuse came to light, I have found myself at an impasse – should I still listen to his music, or not? It's the same for so many people.

I wish that one of the voices in this series came from one of Crystal's five high-profile victims: Sammy Williams, Mary Wooton, Gabrielle Martinez, Zofia Kowalski or Jennifer Rossi. For legal reasons, they have chosen to keep their silence, for now. What I have established, however, is that there were many more victims of Zach Crystal than just these five women. I want all their voices to ring true where they matter – in court, where I hope they will receive justice for what was done to them.

There are those who want to cast Crystal's victims as money-grabbers, as opportunists looking to make a quick buck from a man who can no longer defend himself. But I don't doubt their stories. Not anymore. Not since I recorded this last episode.

I know that when this goes out, there'll be a horde of detractors. I know that there are many who'll accuse me of opportunism and character assassination. But ultimately, I hope that the time and money I've invested into investigating the myth that is Zach Crystal will go some way to help repair the damage he's done.

While driving to the town of Barlheath in the English Midlands, to meet Naomi Crystal, Zach's sister, I am overcome with just how surreal the entire situation is. Thanks to Skexxixx, who passed her details to me, I was able to get in touch with her. I was surprised at how calm she seemed when I told her who I was and what I was doing. Naomi seemed more annoyed that Skexxixx gave me her details than anything else.

So now, for our final episode, here we are, back in Naomi and her brother's home town. The place where it all began.

Barlheath is not a picturesque town. Like much of the Midlands its industrial past is long over; vacant factories now just crumbling wasteland. Barlheath is not an affluent place either. It is merely functional: houses, shops, a cinema. Naomi Crystal has not lived here, nor visited, for a great number of years, yet it is here, where she and her brother grew up, where she wants us to meet.

We meet in a bar on the edge of a sprawling housing estate, an estate that has a plaque and a statue commemorating its favourite son. There have been petitions recently asking for the statue of Zach Crystal to be removed, and the plinth on which it stands has been vandalised with red paint.

MONSTER it reads.

Initially I was utterly flummoxed by the idea of meeting Naomi here, at The Sow, the site of The Crystal Twins' first ever live concert. Surely this would create pandemonium, with fans and press in attendance. She tells me to trust her. She also says I have no choice on the matter. We meet here or not at all.

The Sow is quiet though. It's certainly changed from those early days of The Crystal Twins, beautifully reconstructed in faux weathered wood and glass. A kitchen serves à la carte Sunday lunches, and local craft ales are behind the bar. The Sow has its own plaque, pride of place on one wall, beside a huge frame that contains a stained section of wooden tiles from its original dancefloor.

'Site of The Crystal Twins' first-ever gig' it reads underneath. 'Zach and Naomi Crystal'.

Naomi is waiting for me when I arrive. She's wearing her vast, trademark sunglasses. There are a few others in the pub. I'm expecting a barrage – phones held aloft, a media circus. But not one person looks around at us.

—A group of lads came in earlier. One of them looked at me and nodded to the others. 'Look,' he says, 'fat Naomi Crystal.' Just loud enough for me to hear. And they all fell about laughing.

—*What? Do they think you're a fan?*

—You'd be surprised how often that happens. But it means I can hide in plain sight, I suppose. I'm not even that fat, am I?

It's surreal. Super-surreal, being sat here, opposite Naomi Crystal, just chatting away like everything is normal. Naomi has a very dry sense of humour, and her presence is hugely intimidating, I have to admit. There are a few Crystal fans in – young and old; but mainly people from overseas. A few have looked over, but no one gives us a second glance. Naomi tells me that since her brother's death, since the attention in the press about the allegations, people don't want to be seen as Zach Crystal fans anymore. I ask her how she feels about that.

—It's almost … almost a relief, in a way. It's been relentless, since we were very young. You don't get a break from it. The fame. This time has helped me think, to be honest, helped me reflect on our life. On him. On us. On all of it.

—*There's so much I want to discuss, I don't really know where to begin. I think the thing that I am wondering about the most is why you agreed to talk, at last? To me?*

—I wish I could say because you're very special and I'm a huge fan … but that's not it. Sorry. I will tell you why – I'll tell you all about my reasons – but at the end. I'll explain at the end of the interview, if that's OK?

—*Of course.*

—I mean, you don't have a choice, to be honest. I'm just being polite. I'm in control of this, not you.

—*So where's good for you to start? At the beginning? What was it like, growing up here, in Barlheath? There's been so much written, so much said. I'd be interested to get your take.*

—Barlheath isn't a nice place. The only thing going for it now really, for me, is the fact that it was once home. I had a walk up to our old house before I came here. I was expecting some wash of memory, some profound feeling, but there was nothing. It just made me sad.

—*Why was that?*

—Just old memories, old pain.

—*I'm so sorry.*

—Don't be. There's a great many children in the world with parents like ours. And worse.

—*They were religious, weren't they?*

—Yes, but it wasn't that, you know? Religion was just the stick they beat us with. They were ambitious, they wanted much more than what they had in their life, and they used Zach and me to get it. Religion was their method of control. Zach and I were commodities – we were their ticket out of the gutter.

—Is that why the music started?

—I think that it started, with Zach at least, for purely innocent reasons, for the love of it. Zach and Dad listening to records – that old story that everyone loves. I think that's the only really true part of that story. They listened to Dad's old jazz records together and they enjoyed it.

—And there's a different story after that?

—There is. Zach says that he had this natural gift, that he learned to play by touch, by ear. Don't get me wrong, he was talented, he had musical ability, but he didn't have a choice in the matter, any more than I did. As soon as Dad realised Zach could play and sing, and that he was good at it, it then became a 'gift'. That was the story Mum and Dad wrote. They called it a gift from God, of course – it was never Zach's, it was never because *he* was good, it was because Zach had this gift bestowed upon him. Zach was nothing. Zach was their ticket out of mediocrity.

—And what about you? What was your part in this story?

—Me? I spent most of my childhood trying and failing to get the approval and love of my parents. It was only when I started singing with Zach that I got something back. So I kept doing it, no matter how much I hated it, no matter how much I felt demeaned, used, like a piece of meat. I did it because it made them happy, it got us noticed, we became somebodies.

—But behind that facade, things weren't as rosy?

—They were really good at creating a believable story, especially in front of others. Especially the people at church. We had nothing in the way of money, so for them, it was about making us seem better than everyone else in other ways. We were the holiest, Zach and I, the best-behaved children, that sort of thing.

—So would you accuse your parents of being abusive in any way?

—That's a hard one, because I think in their heads they genuinely believed they were doing good. I think their behaviour came from a good place, and a place of anxiety, perhaps. A place of fear. And to quell that fear, they had to have total control. I feel sad for them now. But I didn't then.

—*It sounds like Zach was the favourite.*

—It felt like that for me. I never understood why. I could never understand what it was that I had done wrong. I tried, God knows I tried. I tried to do everything right, I tried to be what they wanted and I always fell by the wayside. A lot of the time, I think they thought they'd failed with me.

—*I wonder why neither of you have ever spoken about this, in all these years?*

—I guess that's their legacy. Their shadow still falls long and dark over both of us. Zach and I were used to having the perfect image. We knew how to maintain it and we just … did I guess. That's partly the reason why I'm talking to you right now, I suppose. It's something we should have spoken about a long time ago. But now Zach's gone and they're gone…

Naomi tells me about growing up under the control of Maureen and Frank Crystal – the early-morning trips to church, the endless practising in their living room.

—We weren't allowed to watch telly or anything, so what else were we going to do? For Zach it was always books. He was obsessed with reading – the scarier, the more forbidden, the better. He had this one he used to keep under the floorboards, *Highland Folktales.* He'd bought it from a charity shop and it was full of stories about selkies and kelpies, and that sort of thing. He used to read the tales to me at night, scared the shit out of me. But I loved it. Forbidden fruit. If Mum or Dad had caught him with it, there would have been hell to pay.

Could it have been here, all those years ago, reading a forbidden book of Scottish folktales where the story of the Frithghast first awoke in the mind of a young Zach Crystal? I put this to Naomi and she gives a sharp intake of breath at the word.

—Possibly. I don't remember all the stories. I just remember being scared, lying there under the sheets while he whispered. Where Mum and Dad had the bible, Zach had his stories. They became almost religious to him; he knew them all off by heart. I used to close my eyes and believe I was there, up in those forests, those magical places. I think we both did. For us, those stories were our escape after having to practise those songs all afternoon, over and over again.

—Did the music give you any pleasure?

—For me, making up songs, singing, they were my way of pleasing our parents. I sang and danced and led the show, and it made them smile.

—You and Zach began to get quite famous in the late eighties and early nineties, as a duo. You were in your mid-teens – fifteen, sixteen – when you really started making a name for yourselves. That must have been tough.

—Zach always said we never got to be teenagers, and he was right. What is it that teenagers do? They explore who they are, they take risks, they do stupid things, have relationships. It's all about growing up, learning about life. We learned how to be stars. That was our teenage-hood, learning to be what people wanted. Learning to be perfect.

—It seems like that affected Zach quite significantly.

—It affected us in different ways. I grew up quick, became independent. I did things for myself. I wasn't going to be waited on. Zach was the exact opposite. I blame myself in a way – I did everything for both of us. I looked after him. I protected him from our parents and I tried to protect him from the attention we were getting.

—Deserved attention though, am I right? I mean the two of you were an act.

—It was Mum and Dad's ideals rather than any sort of God-given talent we had. You work hard enough at something, and yeah, you're going to do OK. We were popular because we were young. We played songs to drunk men in bars, got them all singing along. I was the eye candy and Zach was the talent. That's how it worked.

—*That sounds rather unpleasant.*

—It was. For all of Dad's piousness, all his God-bothering, he didn't mind dressing up his twelve-year-old daughter to look like a woman and have her singing and dancing in front of a load of lecherous blokes. I had to grow up very quickly, so I had to find strength from somewhere. I had to learn to stand up for myself and stand up for Zach.

—*Zach was the weaker of the pair?*

—Always. He had night terrors as a kid, woke the whole house up with his screaming. Mum and Dad always used prayers to calm him down. They used to say the devil had a hold of him. Zach didn't make friends easily. He never did. He was an easy target in school, so I had to look after him. And he was easily influenced, too – he was naive, infuriatingly so. All it took was one person to try and convince him of something and he'd be sold. That was what I was protecting him from. But as time went on and we got older, the only people who could never convince him of anything were Mum and Dad. They'd say black and he'd say white.

—*Why was that, do you think?*

—He'd watched me grow up being utterly in their thrall, under their control completely, and I think he just decided that he wouldn't let them do that. Anyone else could but not them.

Then he met James. And everything changed.

James Cryer. His name has come up all the way through this podcast – it's bound to Zach Crystal's. Yet, aside from being a long-term friend of Zach's, eventually becoming his top aide, there is little known about James Cryer, save for his death in 2018.

—Zach always told everyone James was his friend. I don't think that was true. Not really. James started out as a fan. Our biggest fan. Well, mine, really.

Naomi tells me the story you heard at the top of the episode, about how she and James Cryer first met. It's a sinister and unpleasant tale, as is the reaction of Naomi's father – allowing James into their lives.

—James Cryer was obsessed with me from the start. He didn't give two shits about Zach. It began right here, those first few gigs in Barlheath. His dad brought him into the bar, I think, to watch us play. After that he never left me alone. It always troubled me that even at that age, so young, he was able to create a character – this chivalrous young man who would walk me through an estate he seemed to consider rough and beneath him, when he lived there too.

Naomi explains that James Cryer soon became a constant in her and Zach's lives. Either shifting equipment, microphone stands and Zach's keyboard, or else drumming up huge enthusiasm for the pair wherever they went. James Cryer had become The Crystal Twins' personal cheerleader. What I want to know now is how he got there. How did a creepy experience in a park lead to him being a permanent fixture?

—He'd created this wholesome, helpful image; he was a fan and just wanted to help out. Our dad fell for it hook, line and sinker. James knew how to play to his audience. He was good at it too; he was convincing. I don't know how many times he managed to get onto local radio or into the papers, always championing us, The Crystal Twins, always telling everyone how great we were. It seemed that being close to us, close to *me*, was his repayment. I was a commodity. Dad dangled me like a carrot in front of James Cryer, to get us the publicity, the attention. He knew what he was doing. No one ever paid James until Zach went solo. I was enough before then.

This is hard to hear and it's only now that I see how insidious the influence of James Cryer was for the Crystals. He was always there, Naomi tells me, a constant presence, allowed to hang about backstage, so long as he helped out setting up and selling tickets for the show.

—He had this really quiet, breathy little voice, and he would tell me just how great we were, just what a wonderful voice I had. He was forever trying to get me on my own, and I just … I just refused to let it happen. I would never be overt about it. Dad would lose his shit if I'd done that.

As the years went by, James Cryer would bring cards, flowers, cuddly toys to give to Naomi. It became, she says, acutely embarrassing.

—There wasn't anything *wrong* with him as such. It was just … it was just too much when I was so young, like that.

—*What sort of things would he do?*

—He used to stand right at the front of every gig. I used to spend entire concerts trying to avoid his eyes. Ugh, the way he used to look at me, at my body. I was so self-conscious at that age, and the way James looked at me used to creep me out.

When we stayed over in hotels, he used to share a room with Zach, but in the middle of the night he used to call my room, always asking if I wanted to go for a walk with him the next day. I used to spend the car journeys coming up with all these different excuses – dentists, doctors, rehearsals, that sort of thing.

—*Your father, though, I can't imagine he was very happy with this. Did you ever express to him how uncomfortable you were?*

—I never told him because I knew what his response would be. I knew he wouldn't listen. I actually think he enabled James. Yeah. There, I've said it. I know you shouldn't speak ill of the dead but it's true. If he didn't enable him, he did absolutely nothing to stop him, and for me, that's just as bad.

These are poignant words. I think it's important we remember that doing nothing, that standing by in silence is just as bad as the abuse itself. While I have this opportunity to talk to Naomi Crystal, I want to pick apart her thoughts on the accusations of abuse against her brother – to find out if she might have had any role in that abuse.

If she gets up and walks, then so be it. But I'm not going to sit by and not ask the questions. But I'll build up to that. I will get there.

—*James Cryer ended up working for Zach. The two became close. But were they friends? Do you think this was solely to get to you?*

—I mean … the whole reason he became friends with Zach was to get close to me. That was his mission. It wasn't long before he was backstage at every gig, always helping Zach out. He was always getting things for him, treating him like a little prince. Dad thought he'd be great company for Zach, another boy like that. I remember an incident where I was getting changed, and Zach and James 'accidentally' walked in on me.

—*Do you think Zach helped that sort of thing to happen?*

—The thing was, Zach had never really had friends before. He was open to any sort of manipulation. I'd protected him for all this time, then James Cryer got in his head. I think James thought if he could get to Zach, then he could get to me.

As the years went by and we got more independent, that's when it started getting worse.

As The Crystal Twins' star began to rise, Zach, Naomi and James began travelling without their father. This was around 1993, 1994, when Zach and Naomi were leaving their teenage years behind.

—They went by in a blur, those years. Never-ending tours – buses, trains, lugging equipment about. By then we had people doing it for us. Don't get me wrong, we weren't massive but we were living off the gigs. It was still hard work but we were starting to do well.

—*What sort of gigs were you playing?*

—Back then it was all very strange. We'd play in a dreadful working men's club in the middle of some estate in God knows where, but then we had some wholesome kinds of gigs – Christian music festivals mainly, Praisefest, Greenbelt, those sorts of things. We were going down well but we both knew we had to branch out, start getting away from the church stuff. I didn't mind it, but Zach was having none of it anymore.

—*Why was that?*

—I think, by twenty years old, Zach, with the help of James, was starting to want more. He was always arguing for a higher place on the bills, for better facilities backstage, that sort of thing. James would act as his PA, sometimes his manager, always in a suit, demanding things, playing the charmer while Zach was the spoiled brat. The act worked.

—*And James was still crushing on you?*

—Always. He never stopped. Ever. It was exhausting, and he

was so close to Zach by then, I could never do anything about it, I could never *fire* him. I just put up with it, until one night, when I just … snapped.

Naomi says she doesn't know what brought it on. There was no big incident. Another bunch of flowers, another handwritten poem, perhaps? Whatever it was, it was the straw that broke the camel's back.

—I made it clear to James that it was never going to happen for us. Not ever. I told him straight. I thought that would make him leave us alone, leave Zach alone too. Unfortunately, it didn't work. In fact, it was probably the worst decision I made.

The story took a darker turn after this incident. James Cryer, having been shunned by Naomi, began using his charm to bring girls backstage to meet Zach. And by default, him too.

—It was like he was doing it on purpose to piss me off, to make me uncomfortable. I saw him and Zach in compromising situations far too many times than was healthy. Far too many. It was awful. I think that was on purpose too.

It all culminated at a gig back in Barlheath. Zach and James were just gone. I was doing everything, all the prep for the show, laying out the clothes, everything, and they were out.

—Did you know what they were doing?

—I knew. I always knew. It was easier just to let Zach do what he wanted – let the baby have his bottle. It was when they came back that I lost my rag. I got really cross.

We heard some of this story last episode. From Naomi's perspective, it's a lot darker. Zach and James came back to the gig with four young girls in tow. Teenagers. Naomi was shocked. They looked really young, more like children.

—James was giving them booze. They were all screeching and laughing, they were all over Zach. It was … I was just so uncomfortable with it all. I told them to stop. I kicked them all out of the dressing room. I told Zach that this wouldn't be happening, not again. No way. I told him to go and take them back home to their parents. I thought James was going to protest, but he didn't. He didn't dare. Zach came crawling back … eventually. He said sorry. He asked if we could never speak of it again, and I gave him the benefit of the doubt. When James wasn't there, he was my brother, he was Zach again.

—Did you ever ask Zach why on earth he'd brought such young girls backstage?

—I did. I told him to be straight with me. I told him I wouldn't be mad. And of course, he said it wasn't him. No way. It was all James. I actually believed him as well.

According to Zach, it was always James who wanted to bring girls backstage. Naomi told Zach she thought James was using him and would help him get rid of James if he wanted. She notes that then, she saw something in her brother, a struggle.

—The thing was Zach had never been told 'no'. About anything. He was our parents' favourite. If anything went wrong, it was my fault. If Zach wanted anything, he knew how to get it from them. Maybe he was just better at reading them. That's what I tell myself anyway. Maybe he'd watched me fail with them and worked out how to get what he wanted.

—Did the two of you ever discuss what must have felt so unfair to you when it came to your parents?

—I wish we could have. I really do. We didn't have that kind of relationship. People thought we were close, but really, we weren't. It was … professional I suppose. There was always someone else there, someone interfering.

—Like James Cryer?

—Right. James was the nail in the coffin, the final wedge between Zach and I. That night, after the gig, Zach told me he was going solo. I knew James had a hand in it somewhere, and I was relieved. I was so sick of being in the spotlight, being scrutinised and judged everywhere I went. I was sick of fans and long drives in the middle of the night, costumes and stage lights. I wanted rid of it all. I told Zach I was happy for him, and I was. Look what he became.

We all know the rest: Zach Crystal's ascent to mega-stardom via Skexxixx. When I reveal to her what Skexxixx told me about writing the majority of Zach's songs, Naomi tells me she's not surprised. As Skexxixx did, she tells me that she wrote the majority of The Crystal Twins' songs herself, and actually thought Zach had his solo songs written for him by professional songwriters at the label. That was quite common practice. Regardless, she was happy to stand back and watch as her brother became a pop star.

—It's what he always wanted – the fame, the glory. The only thing I was uncomfortable with was James Cryer being there. I knew what he was.

—*And what was he?*

—An opportunist, a leech. I knew why he was with Zach – for his own desires, to be able to live that life without having to do anything. He became Zach's 'sin-eater', surrounding them with yes men and legal sharks. He built a wall around him and Zach that no one could penetrate. And no one ever stopped to ask if that was a good thing. Me included.

Like everyone else, Naomi says she too was seduced by fame and money. Zach bought her a house, and she never had to work again.

—*You didn't seek celebrity though, did you? You never wanted a slice of it?*

—Never. I'd been too close. I saw how rotten it was inside. Money talks in that world, over values, over integrity, over everything. No one cares, so long as they get paid. I just wanted to live a quiet life.

—*You visited Crystal Forest regularly though. That's right isn't it?*

—I did. To see Zach – as much as one could see Zach. He was still my brother, and I loved him. I was worried about him, as were my parents. There was this … distance between us all that had just sort of crept up on us. He'd become this enigma, not just to the fans, to the public, but to us too. That's the thing – people wonder if I have this amazing insight into him, but really, no. He was hard to speak to. It often felt like I had to make an appointment to see him. And always, James Cryer was there, behind it all. A puppet master.

—*Did he really have that much control?*

—As far as I know, yes. Zach's image, his brief, elusive and carefully choreographed interviews, all of it. That was down to James.

—*Why?*

—I think it worked in two ways. Zach was most comfortable being told what to do and James was power mad. Zach Crystal, what he eventually became, was James Cryer's creation. I wish … I just wish the two of them had never met. I blame myself, for being me, for becoming the object of Cryer's affection. Maybe if I'd just said yes, then all this wouldn't have happened.

It's truly horrifying that Naomi Crystal blames herself like this, that it's become easier to blame everyone around the powerful, rather than the powerful themselves. It's soul-destroying how that mentality purveys society. Look at Crystal's victims – being judged for their choices when they were troubled children.

Now seems the right time for us to enter into that really dark place. I have to ask Naomi about what she believes occurred at Crystal Forest and what she actually saw happening. A part of me doesn't want to hear her answers, yet I know we must. The truth hurts sometimes but that pain is essential. Speaking the truth is the cleansing burn of antiseptic on a deep, sometimes unhealed wound.

I tell her this is where we're going and Naomi sighs. It's hard to read her expression behind the sunglasses. Now I think I know why they're there: protection. They act as Naomi's armour. No one can see in. But there's vulnerability behind them, and my heart aches for her.

With a deep breath, Naomi eventually speaks.

—I visited Crystal Forest many times. I said it before, and it's true – I felt like I had to make an appointment to see Zach and it was always through James.

—*First off, Naomi, what was your initial opinion of the place?*

Lots of people think it strange that Zach would move somewhere so remote.

—Not me. He'd been talking about a place like this since we were kids, as if he had seen it in his future or something. He always wanted some kind of vast tree house to live in. It was probably all those books we used to read, under the bedclothes – the Highland folk tales and the Enid Blytons. I always thought that Crystal Forest was like something out of *The Magic Faraway Tree*, the tree house on the top, a sort of Famous Five, Secret Seven Clubhouse.

—Zach invited many young people to come and stay there, didn't he?

—That's true, and I just wish that I had been brave enough to object more than I did. But I'd had a lifetime of being beaten down, of being some sort of accessory to Zach that I just … couldn't. It sounds so pathetic, doesn't it? That's partly the reason why I'm here, with you, right now. If I go on TV and make a statement, it'll be thrown back at me: 'Zach Crystal's sister now angling to get money, destroying her brother now he's dead.' That's how it'll be framed.

But no, I wasn't comfortable with any of it. The place was full of teenage girls running amuck. I was far too scared, even then, to speak out, to say anything. Any dissenting voice, even mine, would have been taken down. There would have been no mercy. James had seen to that. You see, the thing is, it was never Zach I wanted to speak up against. Not at first.

—It was James Cryer, right?

—I was seduced. I never knew it until now, but I was. As much as I resisted it, he'd seduced me. It wasn't the flowers this time, the aftershave, the hair gel. It was the same way he seduced everyone else in the world.

—I don't follow.

—Not him as such, but the money, the fame, the spectacle of it. Because it was all so carefully choreographed. James had learned from my parents how to make Zach into what he was. And it all spilled over to me – money, fame. Zach only ever appeared in a mask or a veil and hardly ever spoke from his heart. That was James's idea. He said it would turn Zach into an 'enigma'. So who was offered ridiculous money to speak to the press? Me. I was his sister after all.

James had made himself untouchable. Without James, there was no Zach Crystal. Without Zach Crystal, I didn't have a beautiful house, a blessed life. Luxury for nothing. That's how I was seduced. Disgusting, isn't it?

But that all changed in 2006 when I had my daughter. They say having kids changes your brain, changes your perspective. It's true. The cliché is real. When Bonnie was born, I began to look at things differently.

Naomi tells me that Bonnie's father was, as I've been told, just a normal guy. No one famous. He's not relevant in our story. Naomi had previously tried living the celebrity lifestyle for a bit, which culminated in her briefly dating Skexxixx.

—He was good to me, Leonard was. He treated me well. I even asked him to see if he could talk to Zach. He had no luck. Ultimately, it just didn't work out for us. I couldn't bear being in the spotlight anymore. I hated being judged for how I looked, what I was wearing. I'd been through that so much when I was young, I couldn't do it again. So I tried to do things normally. A man, a baby. I even considered working for a living. Becoming a songwriter, maybe.

—*What changed in you, when Bonnie was born?*

—It's hard to say, specifically. I looked back at my own childhood, probably for the first time. I'd been running from it for so long. I just didn't want to look back.

—*What started that introspection, do you think?*

—It was funny, really. It was my dad. He told me that I needed to set a date for Bonnie's christening. It was that control again, and it all just suddenly crashed into me, all of the past. Mum was talking about how they were looking forward to looking after her, and I just thought … no. No way are you two going anywhere near her. I had this sudden surge of protection. And the worst thing about it, probably the reason we split up in the end, was that her father told me I was just suffering from postnatal depression.

'What parent doesn't want their kid to see their grandparents?' he said. He knew all about it, everything that had happened when Zach and I were young, and still, it was my fault. Still, it was me who was doing something wrong. I just decided that no one was going to treat her the way they treated me. No one. That was that.

—*What about Zach?*

—I wanted Bonnie to have a relationship with her uncle. I really did. But I didn't want James anywhere near her. That was the battle I had, raging inside me.

—*Did you explain it to Zach?*

—Not overtly. I just told him I wanted to spend time, just the three of us. Me, Bonnie and Zach. I was one hundred percent committed to Bonnie, and I just blocked all the Zach stuff out – all the rumours, the allegations. I just buried my head in the sand. And there was money coming in for Bonnie too. I'm guilty of letting that blind me. And James was clever, he kept things pouring in for her – the best of everything: clothes, shoes, riding lessons. Everything. I wanted to give her everything. I grew up with nothing and James Cryer knew that. He knew how to keep me quiet.

Naomi was happy to let the years go by – leave her brother alone in his mansion in the forest, concentrate on being a mother. However, in 2009, when Bonnie was three years old, something changed yet again.

—Zach had begun dating Zadie Farrow. That confirmed it to me – that he was normal. That's all it took, because that's what I wanted to believe. I began letting Mum and Dad see more of Bonnie too. Only when I was there too – I wouldn't let them see her alone. Then they passed away.

—*How difficult was it for you, at that time?*

—More than I thought it would be. There was a side of me that couldn't forgive myself for not forgiving them, for not patching things up. There was another side of me that was glad they were gone. Those two sides collided and messed me up. I couldn't cope with it.

—*It had a profound effect on Zach too, right?*

—I feel like I lost him utterly. Mum and Dad meant so much to him, you know? He was the apple of their eye. When they passed, he was bereft. He stayed up there, at Crystal Forest. Never coming out. He and Zadie broke up. He'd got these strange ideas in his head. Ghosts in the forest, premonitions.

—What was your take on all that?

—It made me sad. It reminded me of when we were children. Zach used those stories to hide in, to block out reality with. It felt like he was retreating into a childlike state – regressing, that's the word. All this talk of a ghost in the forest. And you know what? James Cryer enabled that too – he actively encouraged it.

—Why was that, do you think?

—I only found out later. It all made sense. I'll come to it in a while.

—I've heard some strange allegations; that Zach had a room dedicated to your mother's things – he called it 'the memorial room'.

—Yeah. I saw it. It *was* weird. I was worried. Zach idolised our parents like they idolised him. I hated that room. It was sinister, cold; like our mother, really. All her belongings were there, like she was still alive.

—Do you think it was his way of coping with the death of your parents?

—I think that's interesting. Death was something Zach couldn't control. I think he wanted to though. I think he'd had James Cryer in his ear, making him think he should or he could have control, even over death.

But again, I was raising my daughter. It was so difficult to see Zach. I took Bonnie to his concerts, they hung out a bit. He used to take her for walks up in Crystal Forest or they'd spend time in that tree house. But he was always so distant, there were always people around, aides and yes men; we never got to spend time, just the three of us.

I feel like Naomi knows as much as anyone else. She has very little insight into her brother. Zach Crystal, the real person, had been lost, hidden behind a veneer of eccentricity, elusiveness. Truly, he had become the enigma he always wanted to be.

Also, I'm aware there's a huge contradiction between what Naomi tells me about her presence and influence at Crystal Forest and the accounts of others who stayed or worked there, who say Naomi brought a semblance of order to the place and had a commanding presence there. I draw Naomi's attention to this.

—I wish that was true. I tried my best over the years, I wanted that control, but Zach and James were always one step ahead of me. I was sensitive at first, always trying to talk to James, get him to back off. I used to argue with him a lot, always out of sight of Zach – usually in the forest.

I imagine it was one of these discussions Marie Owen was witness to when she and Kirsty were asked to leave Crystal Forest.

2017 eventually rolled around and the internet was beginning to become rife with speculation about and allegations against Crystal. Naomi became extremely concerned about her brother.

—I'd spent so many years not getting anywhere with him. But when it began to affect Bonnie, that galvanised me into trying a different approach. People at her school knew who she was, of course, and she was beginning to get bullied. People were saying her uncle was a paedophile, that sort of thing. I wasn't going to stand for it anymore.

—*What did you think about those accusations?*

—I didn't know. I really didn't know. But I also didn't believe these women were after money. I was reminded of how I felt at thirteen, when I was onstage, when I was being objectified, when I had James Cryer following me around.

Bonnie was becoming withdrawn. She didn't want to go to school, she didn't want to join me visiting Zach at Crystal Forest anymore.

—*Was there any particular reason she gave for not wanting to go?*

—She said … It sounds crazy, as crazy as, well … She said the forest scared her. She said that she'd seen things in there. That had never been the case before. She said there was something terrible in there, some presence, watching her. She never went as far as to say she saw something in there, but she always kept her blinds closed when we were there. She didn't want to go with Zach on his walks into the forest anymore. She wanted to stay with me the whole time. And at home she regressed a little bit. It was a really hard time. For both of us. She had nightmares every night and would climb into my bed. I just thought, *no way*. I needed to get this all sorted with Zach. So I went to Crystal Forest. I wanted to find out what the hell was going on.

When we spoke to Craig Kerr in episode three, he told us about the effect that Naomi had on Crystal Forest.

—I thought if I try and stop everything, work against him, Zach would push me away. So instead, I worked *with* James Cryer and the rest of his team. It was fire-fighting on a larger scale than I could have possibly imagined.

—How do you mean?

—I looked through all the books, all the finances, everything. I wasn't going to take no for an answer. This was my brother. There were things I found that opened my eyes.

Naomi says she called a meeting with Zach and James to discuss her discoveries. Huge payments to families, to the bank accounts of teenage girls. Sometimes there had even been bank accounts set up in their names. There were properties, elaborate gifts. Whether it was innocent or not, it looked bad, Naomi says. It looked terrible.

—I had to make them see sense. I had to tell them that this wasn't just me poking my nose in and stopping their fun, like I did back all those years ago. This was serious. Remember, Zach hadn't had an album out since 2007. I could see the press starting to turn on him. I had to make that clear. So I said things had to change. We had to work on Zach's public image. We had to make him look less weird, less sinister and he had to get some new music out there.

—Did you face resistance?

—They were like a couple of surly schoolboys who'd been caught. James wasn't stupid though; he knew I was right. I said I'd help, and to be honest, I think they both welcomed it. I also saw how bad Zach had become.

—*In what way?*

—It was the degree of his paranoia. He was paying out ridiculous money for security, PIs, everything. After those poor girls died in 2007, it had only escalated. I never knew the extent of it all. All those things had affected Zach badly, and no one was helping him; there was no one to steer him right. He had security patrols all over the woods at all hours. He was convinced something was out there. That's what got into Bonnie's head – all that paranoia. It was so bad for her, for him, for all of us. And no one tried to stop it; no one told him no. That was where the problem lay.

Naomi tells me that it appeared, at first, that things were getting better. Her influence at Crystal Forest looked to be positive. Zach seemed more at ease. They were talking more. Zach was spending time with Bonnie. Bonnie, however, seemed to be getting worse. She was withdrawn, quiet, clinging to Naomi for much of the time, even though she was thirteen years old at this point.

There were, Naomi says, still a few girls and families left staying at Crystal Forest. She thought it would be good for Bonnie to be able to meet other girls her age, but she wouldn't. She spent a lot of her time alone in her room. Naomi thought of trying a different approach.

—I actually had a few discussions with James, one to one, about stopping the visits, the girls everywhere. I wanted it to just be me, Zach and Bonnie. A family unit. Maybe that would help her. Maybe that would help Zach.

—*How did James Cryer take that?*

—Oh, he became very defensive, told me I was meddling. He basically said that it would look worse if we stopped the girls visiting. That's where we clashed. I told him Zach had a teenage niece who was in crisis and she should come first. Things came to a bit of an impasse. So I decided I *would* start meddling, I *would* start sticking my nose in where it didn't belong.

Naomi began watching James Cryer, just as James Cryer had watched her for years. She began turning up when he wasn't expecting it, asking to look at files and plans. Cryer attempted to act the innocent, but Naomi tells me it was yet another performance, another character.

—I was getting to him. I knew that. He was pretending to be open with me, telling me I could look on his laptop, his phone, if I wanted to. Calling my bluff. I did it and I found something – something he'd tried to hide. It made no sense at first.

Searching through Cryer's computer, Naomi found a file that had been concealed in a maze of dull, administration documents.

—It was called 'SG plans' and it was some kind of … design, for something in the forest – a technical document. It made no sense to me so I typed 'SG' into Cryer's email.

—*You got into his email?*

—It was easy. His password was a version of my name wasn't it? N40Mi.

—*When I typed in 'SG' I found an email to a light-and-sound company about something they were building in the forest, not far from the house.*

Could SG possibly stand for 'special girls'? Naomi doesn't know for sure, and says she only became aware of Zach's 'special girls' after he was dead. Unfortunately, Cryer wasn't stupid and had managed to hide a great deal of his emails, Naomi believed he'd done so in case he was caught.

—I hung around outside doors, I 'accidentally' walked in on him when he was on the phone. Nothing. It was making no sense. I knew there was something going on in the forest. So I started to put my foot down about certain things. Like the teenage girls. They had to go. I insisted.

Naomi tells me that she did get her way in the end. The girls were all sent away. James Cryer, however, was not happy.

—After that the atmosphere at Crystal Forest became … charged. I just don't think James was used to facing any opposition. I didn't care. Until I got my way, I was intent on making his life a living hell. For Zach and for Bonnie.

—Did things get any better for her?

—She was scared a lot of the time, which wasn't like her at all. She began to have … accidents in her bed at night. It was night terrors. She was becoming more and more withdrawn at school as well as at home. The things she said, her dreams, her fears … they began to get to me too.

—I'm so sorry that happened to her. What was scaring her so badly?

—Here, now, in the light of day, it sounds like kids' stuff, but then, in the dark of the night, when you wake suddenly and you have your daughter sat beside you, bolt upright, or else standing next to the window, half asleep, her eyes pale in the dark … it's frightening.

Her fear was always the forest. She would point out movements, shadows. We'd sit up for hours, listening to the wind in the trees. She called it 'the whispering', and she'd tell me the words that she could make out. They were telling her to *eat, eat, eat* she said. It was horrible, chilling. Then … then I started to hear them too; I started to see things as well.

—What sorts of things?

—Shadows, the glow of eyes. I thought it was all in my head. It had to be, right? I thought I was going insane, maybe we both were. I was worried. Really worried. Bonnie was starting to say she'd seen something in the forest – a creature with red eyes looking at her. I didn't know what to do. I thought she might need psychiatric help. She just wasn't the same girl anymore.

—How is Bonnie doing now? Is she any better? What about yourself?

It's an innocuous question but Naomi stiffens. She pushes her sunglasses up her nose, and I sense a degree of tension between us. I wonder what to say, whether I should apologise. It is clear that Naomi does not want to discuss Bonnie's current life.

There is something else dawning on me too. I can't quite believe how candid Naomi is being with me. The silence that has enveloped Zach

Crystal for all these years is being discussed in a bar, for a podcast … with me, and by Naomi Crystal, sister of the star. That in itself is starting to dawn on me, and I can't help wonder what is coming. This can't be all of it. We can't just pack up and go our separate ways, can we? Naomi looks at her phone and goes on. I notice she's speaking more quickly now.

—OK. So I need to explain what happened next. Just after New Year, 2018, I went to see James to tell him to stay away from Crystal Forest for a while. I was now convinced his presence there was toxic, it was only making things worse for us all. He lived there, had for years, and I was going to tell him how important it was that we had time just the three of us. For Bonnie. I had everything planned out, what I was going to say. It was evening. James always worked late in the office in the evenings, doing admin. Bonnie was staying up in the tree house with Zach, so I thought this was a good time.

James wasn't in his office though, when I went in. I noticed his computer was on, and I walked over to it. I'd already looked once but I couldn't pass up the opportunity to look again. Something told me he had to be up to no good. Maybe it was because he sent all those letters years ago. He was in his early teens and he'd sent a letter to everyone on the Hopesprings Estate, trying to find me. I never forgot that, the scale of it, the creepiness of it.

—*What was on his computer? Anything new?*

—Nothing. Nothing incriminating whatsoever. Just the same as last time: tax, finances et cetera. I was about to go and find him when there was a buzz from his desk drawer. I nearly jumped out of my skin. I opened it and there's a phone. The screen's locked of course, but I pick it up and wonder if I should try, just try something … and I put in my own birthday. It worked for the computer, didn't it, putting my name in as a password? What do you know – the phone unlocks.

I start poking about, and bring up the photo gallery.

My blood runs cold.

The content of the pictures Naomi saw, she says she can never forget.

Teenage girls in Crystal Forest. Sometimes James himself was in the pictures.

—I put the phone in my pocket and went to get Bonnie. We were getting out of there. All the rumours, all the vile things people were saying about Zach – it was him, it was all James. James used Zach as a lure to do these things to girls. All here, in Crystal Forest. I'm sure he had these pictures as some kind of sick trophies or some kind of reminder of his own power, what he was capable of doing, what he could get away with. I went to tell Zach. But then I remembered something: the email, 'SG'. Suddenly, things started to make sense.

Rightly or wrongly, Naomi decided that she would confront James first, before she told the police, before she told Zach. She says that there was a terrible question burning inside her that overrode her pragmatism.

Bonnie.

Bonnie was thirteen years old and she'd stayed at Crystal Forest. Naomi had no doubt in her mind that her brother was innocent, that Bonnie was safe with him, but she'd had doubts about James since they were young. She needed to know if he'd attacked Bonnie.

—I told James I needed to speak to him, out in the forest. He refused at first, tried to fob me off. He said it was too dark, that we could do it tomorrow, during the day. I couldn't give him time to think, to plan, to plot, to cover his tracks, so I told him I'd had someone from a lighting company on the phone, something about 'SG'. That's when I saw him falter, just for a split second, and I knew I had him. We walked out into the forest. It was January – pitch-dark and freezing cold. Horrible. He was getting mud all over his shoes and was in a terrible mood about it. At one point he tells me to stop, we've gone too far. So I get him to press on. He's babbling, trying everything to get me to stop, but I won't. He tells me he's going back, and that's when I pull the phone from my pocket. It takes him a few moments to realise, and finally, we keep going. We're far away from the cameras and the perimeter fence, deep in the forest. It's muddy, uneven, uphill. Then I see something and my blood runs cold.

Lights. Red lights. And there's something between the trees, some shape. It's not human. I can feel myself starting to get faint, and I turn to James. He's staring, just staring into the trees, staring past me.

—*That must have been terrifying.*

—It was. But you know what, I thought of Bonnie, all her sleepless nights, all her terror and I thought, *Fuck this*. I start walking toward the lights. James is screaming 'no' at me, to run, to come back, but I just start climbing the hill, getting closer to the lights. About halfway up, there's a clearing, and that's when I saw it.

—*What was it?*

—Lights. A rig of lights in the trees. They were winking on and off all over. Red. In little pairs, like eyes. I think not just of Bonnie, but of all the girls they brought into the forest, all his 'special girls'. I wondered then if Zach knew about any of this. Had Zach been fooled too?

I turn round and there he is. James. He's seen what I've seen and his face changes. I can see this fury on it. He bares his teeth and runs at me. I start running too, higher up that hill, deeper into the forest. It's so thick, dark, muddy, but I'm filled with this adrenaline, spurring me on.

I don't know if it was that … or something else … It's a dense forest, of course there's wildlife in there. But I feel like … I feel like something's running alongside me, in the undergrowth. The branches were grabbing at my hair, and from the corner of my eye, I swear I see movement, as if a large beast is staggering through the trees. I keep seeing flashes of something pale, hear this snorting breath. Maybe it's James behind me – he's panting, gasping like an animal. He knows if he starts screaming that security will get involved. He can't have that. We break out of the undergrowth and reach a rocky ridge, where the ground just falls away. I climb up; the rocks are all slippery with leaf mulch and moss. I can see all these weird marks on the stones, like carvings, and the moon is shining down. Like a spotlight. James is at the bottom of the ridge, panting, gasping, nearly on his knees. I'm filled with revulsion, disgust. I think of him sat next to me on that bench all those years ago; the smell of him. His face.

I stand on the edge of that ridge, in the moonlight, holding out that phone. I tell him I'll get rid of it if he answers my question. He says he'll pay me, he'll do anything. I ask him if he ever touched Bonnie. He's looking at me, and I notice something, something behind him, in the trees. It's like breath. Like someone's breath in the night – clouds of condensation. And eyes. Red, glowing eyes. I'm frozen, totally frozen with horror. There's something just out of sight in the dark behind James, something pale. He's not seen it yet and I ask him again, did he ever touch her?

'Not me, I swear,' he says.

Then he looks around.

He sees it too and he screams; he starts climbing up towards me and the thing follows…

—*What was it?*

—Maybe there were other things in the forest, more than just lights? I don't know. It was a … deer shape, but pale, bones showing through, its skin all black. Horns, a mess of them, like thorns on its head. A skull. A cloud passed over the moon, and it was gone. Just two red lights fading away.

James is screaming, gibbering, climbing up the ridge to where I am. He's shouting that it's true, it's true and he's reaching for me and—

Naomi breaks off. She's pale, pulling herself out of the memory, back from that frozen night into the warmth of the bar. Ketchup and vinegar on the table between us, the smell of oil from the kitchen.

When she continues, her voice is faint.

—I don't really remember exactly … It was all a blur. He slipped and as he fell past me, I smelled him. I smelled that same aftershave from when we were thirteen. Maybe that was a hallucination too, some sensory anomaly. There was silence for a moment and then a thud. He'd fallen down the other side of the ridge. His head had cracked open like a crab shell when a gull drops it on rocks. All this stuff was leaking out and his legs and arms were twitching. I still see that, sometimes, when I can't sleep. Along with those photos. The way he twitched. It was an accident. That's all.

Accident or not, James Cryer was dead. Naomi Crystal pocketed the phone and let security know that she'd found James's body. The rest, as we know is history.

As for the phone, the pictures, Naomi kept them. She says she should have passed them on to the police, she knows that.

—But I just wanted to wait. For things to calm down. This was going to be so bad for Zach's career if it all came out. I know what the media would have said about him. Rightly or wrongly, I kept it. I didn't tell anyone.

For Naomi, this was the opportunity to build a family, the family she and her brother had never had, the family she wanted for her daughter.

—Zach was distraught, obviously. He found James's death hard to cope with.

—*Did you ever tell him what you'd found?*

—I always meant to. I planned to, but later, when he was better, when we were … I don't know, more solid. He needed to get his career back on track first, for all of us.

Naomi orchestrated the resurrection of Zach Crystal. She called on Ed Sheeran, who recorded 'World in Our Hands' with Zach at Crystal Forest, and organised the appearance at the upcoming Lazy Dayz festival in Hyde Park.

—It was getting better. Much better. Zach was starting to turn things around, but the allegations kept coming. The #metoo stuff was happening then. I needed to tell the world that it wasn't Zach, that it was James who had done it, who had done everything.

—*And why didn't you?*

—There was the accident, at Lazy Dayz, those two technicians.

Zach told me he'd foreseen it, that there was something in Crystal Forest, some spectre, some death omen. For the first time, I listened to him.

—Did you tell him what you'd seen? The lights?

—Maybe I should have done, but I just couldn't. He already believed it fully, anyway. And I was so busy working out how to go public with the James Cryer stuff – police, newspapers. It had to be a planned strategy. Zach could not be implicated. This would either save his career or destroy it utterly.

This was March 2018, not long after the scheduled appearance by Zach at Lazy Dayz. Naomi said she was working flat out, 24/7, on Zach's career, on his finances, hiding what she had to hide, trying to right all the wrongs of James Cryer. She had to do this for her family. Plans were under way for Zach Crystal's triumphant return; the Forever *tour and the new album. At the peak of all this, when the world was back on side, Naomi would spill the beans about James Cryer.*

Bonnie, at this point, was spending more and more time with her uncle. Yet she seemed to be getting worse rather than better. She was becoming more withdrawn and argumentative. Her fear of the forest was becoming pathological.

—Zach was encouraging it. He said he was seeing it too. It was all getting too much. I was stuck. If I told her it was all fake, I would have to tell him too, and everything would all come out. And to be honest, after what I saw in that forest, I was having trouble convincing myself it *wasn't* real. What we needed was to get away from Colliecrith; sell up, go live somewhere else. Put it all behind us. I couldn't live with it anymore, the guilt of it.

It was now late-March 2018. There was a skeleton staff at Crystal Forest, and Naomi was viewing a number of potential properties that the three could move into, as well as seeking some help for Bonnie. She went up to the tree house. Bonnie had gone up there to watch a horror movie with her uncle.

—It was just so normal … just a normal day. I went up there and it's dark and all the fairy lights are on, as usual. Zach's bedroom is *huge*; there's this projector screen on one wall and I expected to find them snuggled up watching, I don't know, something horrible. But I walked in and Bonnie's sat, curled into a little ball on the bed. Just her eyes peeping out. The look in them sent a chill through me: she was just staring, straight forward, at the screen, but not at the screen. She didn't even look up when I walked in.

'Where's Zach?' I say. But I can see that there's something wrong. The light from the screen is flickering like a strobe and some monster's screaming, roaring … and then I smell something. That's what all it was at first. Blood. I smelled blood. I start feeling my breath coming fast, and I turn on the light.

Zach's laid there on the bed; blood everywhere.

And Bonnie's just sat beside him, her back to him, rocking back and forth.

She was still holding the knife.

I had to pull her fingers off the handle, one by one.

Almost eighteen months before Crystal Forest burned down, Zach Crystal was dead.

Bonnie Crystal, his thirteen-year-old niece had stabbed him several times in the throat and in the belly. She sat beside him as he bled to death. She wasn't going to take it anymore. As Naomi tells me this, her voice is steady. It feels like there's a rushing sound, like we're in a bubble. All I see is my own face reflected in those vast sunglasses.

—*You're serious?*

—She told me it had been going on for the last year. She told me she was scared to tell because he'd told her she'd end up like all the others – the world would go after her, everyone would hate her. Most powerfully though, he told her no one would believe her. She told me she couldn't take it anymore. She couldn't see him go on tour again and this happen to any more girls. She said she was sorry.

Naomi's voice trembles, nearly breaks, but she holds it together.

—It was him and James, all along. I realised that I'd been duped as much as everyone else. Zach and James had been doing this to teenage girls for years.

—So this surely was the perfect time to tell the police, let the public know? Surely.

—I'm going to tell you something. I'm going to explain now why I agreed to come and do this with you.

I've been someone all of my life. I've been Naomi Crystal for forty-six years. I've been Zach Crystal's sister. Everything I do or say, now, is watched, is reported on, is commented on. It's even worse now Zach is gone. Ever since I sat in that park, beside the cenotaph in Barlheath, I've just wanted to be no one. I've wanted to be like everyone else, one of the herd, just living my life. But that'll never happen. There's no way.

Bonnie, though, she has a chance. I don't want her to have to live her life in the spotlight. Zach chose that for himself, but she never got to choose. So I helped her.

We hid Zach's body in the forest and we planned her escape. Zach had the legacy of a god, a deity. He had enough riches to be someone. Those riches now meant Bonnie could be no one.

—But the fire, the interview with Ruby Rendall?

—Zach had never done a full-length interview before. Thanks to James Cryer's great idea to make him an enigma, no one really knew what Zach looked and sounded like exactly. So we called in Zach's decoy. We drew up the papers and left him a lot of Zach's fortune. He has the rights to all of Zach's music, the estate. I took what I needed for Bonnie to disappear. Then we spent our year making her vanish.

Zach Crystal's year-long disappearance was Naomi's plan to protect her daughter. Everyone across the world was searching, but not for the right person. Bonnie Crystal vanished in plain sight as the world looked for her uncle.

Crystal's reappearance, the announcement of a new album, a tour, the Ruby interview, then the fire at Crystal Forest in September 2019 and the discovery of the charred remains of Zach Crystal, were also carefully orchestrated, in true Crystal style, creating media mayhem, keeping the public's focus, while Bonnie escaped.

—What about Ian Julius. Was he lying? Who was it he caught, if he caught anyone?

—I think Sasha Stewart was right about him – he'd do anything for money. Even my money. I don't know who he was chatting to. And I certainly didn't meet anyone at Inverness airport, like he says. But you see, I couldn't let Zach get away with what he'd done. He would not end up as a martyr. So I decided to let Ian Julius go public with his fabricated story. Suing him was just a way to make the story as big as possible. The accusations came thick and fast after that, so making Zach's death look like suicide made absolute sense. And we had the benefit of showing Zach for what he was. Not a god, but someone who was too scared to face what was coming to him. I know how the media are, I know how the fans are. I wanted that question out there just when a tour and the album were most anticipated, just when everyone thought the great Zach Crystal was back, defying his accusers. I did it for his victims. I wanted Crystal-mania to be at its height, so they would be heard. If there's enough voices out there, they can unite. Now people will listen to them, when they may not have done before.

And after hearing this, they will. They can and they will.

—And me. Why me? Why this podcast right now?

Naomi passes me something. A phone. It lies on the table between us. I don't even want to touch it.

—I'm passing on the story, Scott. The story of Zach Crystal can stop with you. All the questions, the focus, the spotlight – you can share some of it now. You can use what's on this phone to validate everyone who has been brave enough to speak up against my brother. You can be the hero of this story, Scott. This is James Cryer's phone, the one I found in his desk drawer. It also contains the 'SG' plans, the lights in the forest. Zach's Frithghast.

I don't want to ask if the pictures are on it. I don't want to know. But I have to know. We all do. Naomi's right. I came here looking for answers, and now I have them. However awful they are, I have the answers I've been looking for.

I am the one now to denounce a god.

—*Why though? Why not keep it? Why not let the world believe the lie? If what you're saying is true, the authorities will come for Bonnie, surely.*

—All bases are covered, Scott. I'm sure they'll come after me. They might even find me. They won't find Bonnie though. She's had ample time to escape, to become nobody. That was the whole point, all this time – give her time to become an entirely new person. Then wait for the best opportunity to drop this bomb. And then you fell into my lap. The perfect platform for the truth.

—*What about Zach's decoy? What will become of him?*

—What's he done wrong? Except do his job and be paid well for it?

—*There's a couple of questions I need to ask, Naomi, before we finish. It's about the video, the one with Lulu Copeland and Jessica Morton. In Crystal Forest.*

—What about it?

—*Is it real? And if it is, were those two really trying to get* in *to Crystal Forest … or were they trying to escape?*

Naomi lets her shoulders rise and fall. I wish she would take off her sunglasses.

—The thing with someone like Zach, eventually it becomes very difficult to distinguish between what is real and what isn't. I wish I could tell you.

—*Why can't you?*

—The monster in the woods, it's just another story isn't it? All stories have a purpose. Like the story I've told you. I can't tell you if the video is real or not because I don't know. What I can tell you is what I suspect: and that is that maybe, *maybe*, it was created by James, or Zach, or both of them together. Why? Because they were ready to do anything to get people to believe their stories about monsters in the forest. It became another part of their brainwashing. That's what I suspect. They've always wanted to control the narrative, and if two young girls die so that narrative – and all their victims – can be controlled, what of it? That would've been their thinking.

I can leave you with something I *do* know, however. That's that there *were* girls who tried to escape Crystal Forest. Quite a few of them. Why do you think the security was so tight? And I know that the belief in that Frithghast among the girls was unshakable, thanks to Zach and James. So if that horrific story *is* true – that one ended up eating the other's flesh – that's down to them. To what they made those girls believe. Mark my words though, Scott, this story – the story of my brother – is a poisoned chalice. You might be the hero when you put the facts out there, but they'll come for you too. The fans, the followers, the believers, those who think they love him still. To them, it doesn't matter what is real and what isn't. He is all that matters to them, and soon you'll see just how much.

Goodbye.

And with that, Naomi Crystal leaves. A few heads turn her way, but the tourists, some wearing 'Zach Crystal is Innocent' T-shirts, turn back to their drinks and their food.

I don't know what to say. What to do. I could call the police, but then what? Ian Julius, Sasha Stewart, Craig Kerr, Skexxixx and Naomi Crystal – they've all played a part in the construction of the story of the world's most famous pop star. But that's all it is – a story.

Maybe Naomi's lying. Maybe she's not really Naomi Crystal. Is Zach Crystal guilty or innocent? Right now, I have only stories. It is not me who now needs to be listened to.

I sit for a long time by myself, with all of these stories whizzing through my head, and gradually, a shadow builds at the back of my mind, it sprouts horns and a pair of glowing, red eyes. It snorts through its skull-like face, twin breaths of steam.

It is a conscience.

The right decision lies with me. I take the phone and without looking at it, place it in my bag.

You see, it's now up to me to destroy Zach Crystal – just as Naomi intends me to, the final stage in a plan she hatched in March 2018. With the pictures on this phone, I can wipe away the happy memories and defining moments Zach Crystal's music was part of, for many. I wonder how many people's first dance was a Zach Crystal song, how many people leaned into those lyrics when times were hard. How many children delighted in singing along? How many young girls sat and yearned for a man like this to take them away?

If Naomi Crystal's telling the truth, the pictures on this phone will shatter it all.

The pale bone and glowing red eyes of my conscience push me forward, out of my seat and through the doors of The Sow.

I walk through Barlheath for a while, breathing in the fresh air. I walk past Zach Crystal's childhood home. The place where he dreamed of something beyond an ordinary life. I wonder if these terrible impulses were already there then. How much of it was learned and how much of it was innate? Was a monster swimming below the surface, out of sight, biding its time?

What we want is an end, everything tied up and placed neatly into little boxes. Zach Crystal should be exposed for what he was – a predator, an abuser. Those who excused him or validated his behaviour should be condemned too. Blame should be laid at the feet of James Cryer, who coerced and manipulated, preyed upon the vulnerable and led them, like some kind of pied piper into the lion's jaws. Then took his share of the spoils.

I want justice for the victims of Zach Crystal; for Kirsty Owen, for her mother, for Bonnie Crystal. But I also want justice for everyone who had a Zach Crystal poster on their wall, for everyone who dressed up like their idol and sang those words, feeling like they'd been created for them and them alone. Anyone who found solace in the words of Zach Crystal, who felt that the world was against them – I want justice for all of you.

It feels like we were all deceived.

Zach Crystal went from being powerless, a nobody, a poor kid from the Hopesprings Estate in Barlheath, to an untouchable deity. Through the power of his music, he became a god. Whether his songs were written by Skexxixx or by his sister, Naomi, it doesn't even matter anymore. What we know is that Crystal was the vessel that carried these songs, that made them into what they were. Weaponised them.

All the talent, the music, the lyrics, the stage shows, all of these things have been betrayed, turned into weapons by someone who was so used to getting exactly what they wanted, they never stopped to think whether what they wanted was right or wrong. And those who enabled and those who stood by and did nothing to stop him, betrayed the music too.

I turn away from the house, the shrine to fame in the midst of a bleak council estate in the English Midlands, a beacon to those who have no hope. I am going to take what I know to the police in Barlheath and in doing so, will extinguish that hope forever.

Because it's the right thing to do.

Like Naomi says, I know what's coming now. I know that by the time this final episode airs, my name will be mud. The community of fans who believe in Zach Crystal, who adore him, will see no words said against their idol. Just like Frank and Maureen Crystal, just like the staff in that Christian children's home who once coerced a young boy named Leonard Myers into believing that the evil in this world came with cloven hooves, a pitchfork and a promise.

It is possible to believe in Crystal's genius and to believe he was a monster too. It is also possible to reject the bad and keep the good, close your eyes and ears to the pain of others and believe what you like, cherry-pick what brings you happiness and gives you peace. I believe that Zach Crystal was haunted, but not by any ancient spirit. Going up and hiding in the wilds of the Highlands didn't stop him from being followed everywhere by the terrible knowledge of what he was doing and how it was wrong. He just believed he didn't have to be accountable, and placed enough people around him to assure him he was right.

For me, I am decided. An old part of me still wants to sing along with Zach Crystal's music, remembers the spine-tingling magic that even the mention of his name would invoke. But the side of me that has heard six stories about Zach Crystal now feels very differently, and whatever joy Zach Crystal brought to the world now has to turn to disgust.

I am going to act. Regardless of what that will bring to me. I am going to ensure that there is a degree of justice for the victims of Zach Crystal, even if that justice is simply to be believed.

Because it's the right thing to do. Because to say nothing is to be complicit.

I've proudly been Scott King.

I've proudly told stories. For Lulu Copeland, for Jessica Morton, for Bonnie and Naomi Crystal.

This has been our sixth.

ACKNOWLEDGEMENTS

I wrote the majority of *Deity* during the first coronavirus lockdown in the UK, which began in March 2020. I could pontificate for ages about how hard it was to write a book during that time, but really, sitting in an attic, making up a story was one of the easier ways to get through the existential horror that descended upon us all. The people who really helped write this book were the supermarket workers, the cleaners, the care-home staff, the NHS workers; the nurses, doctors and dentists; the educators, lecturers and bin collectors; the delivery drivers, the postal workers, the carers, the chefs. The people who kept our spirits up: the comedians, musicians and entertainers, the writers, editors, proofreaders. You all helped write this book. Those who worked tirelessly and gave everything they had to keep us going – you helped write this book.

Anyone who wore a mask, who stayed at home, who had to endure the ache of loneliness, not seeing family, friends and loved ones. You helped write this book too.

For me, writing was an escape from all the horror. It was one of the things that kept me going through that first lockdown, and without the following people, *Deity* would never have been possible:

Karen Sullivan and the Orenda team – there's a reason you're CWA Crime & Mystery Publisher of the Year 2020. Cole Sullivan and West Camel, Team Orenda is not Team Orenda without you, and Mark Swan, you designed the best cover you've ever created.

Huge thanks to my phenomenal agent, Sandra Sawicka, whose belief in me never wavers. She's always there with a good idea up her sleeve and a spookiness in her heart.

The book bloggers: your reviews, your kindness, your love for books is truly astounding, and I am forever in your thrall. Just know I read and appreciate every single review and kind word.

Fellow authors: your books help shape my own, you provide solace in the bleakness and I hope we'll be able to meet in person again soon.

My family and the Zoom-quiz Tuesday-night taskmasters: Ben and Claire, Richard and Sally, Jimmy and Sassy, Bryn and Lesley: you mean the world to me, even more so now, and I can't wait to hug you all.

My emotional-support animal, Sarah Farmer, for being predictably brilliant through everything. You're a beautiful creature who deserves extra kudos for having to spend the entirety of lockdown in my company.

My son Harry who, during lockdown, understood that I had to spend a couple of hours a day writing: you showed such strength by being such a good lad, doing your home-school work, playing, laughing, drawing and being the best company anyone could ever want in a dark time. We got through it together, mate, and you showed such unbelievable endurance and strength. I'm so immensely proud of you.

And of course you, lovely reader. Here we are, blinking in the light at the end of another little journey in the darkness. Please make sure you have all your valuables and personal possessions with you. I hope we'll see each other again soon.